TO KILL A KETTLE WITCH

A NOVEL OF THE MIST-TORN WITCHES

BARB HENDEE

A ROC BOOK

ROC

Published by New American Library,
an imprint of Penguin Random House LLC
375 Hudson Street, New York, New York 10014

This book is an original publication of New American Library.

First Printing, May 2016

For more information about Penguin Random House, visit penguin.com.

ISBN 978-0-451-47134-5

Printed in the United States of America
10 9 8 7 6 5 4 3 2 1

Again, for Jaclyn,
who convinced me to make a pitch for the series

PROLOGUE

I hadn't used the sight in over five years, having given all that up when I left my old life behind. I'd almost forgotten the scratching feeling at the back of my head when something called to me, something that needed to be seen.

With so much time having passed, I ignored it when it first began again, the scratching, scratching, scratching at the base of my neck, begging for my attention.

"Go away," I said aloud, over and over, until the other servants in the castle glanced at me with more trepidation than usual.

It didn't go away.

That night, I couldn't sleep at all. Finally, I heaved myself out of bed, my knees creaking, and I sighed in resignation over what I had to do. I didn't want to, but once the *nag, nag, nag* started, it wouldn't stop.

Though I'd tried to deny it, that much I did remember. With some effort, I lowered myself to the cold floor and folded my aged legs beneath me. Then I reached up for the oil lantern beside my bed, set it on the floor, and turned up the light so that I could see the flickering orange light.

I focused on the flame, shutting out the walls of my small bedroom, shutting out the world around me.

Without speaking I repeated an old, trite litany in my thoughts over and over until everything but the single flame faded.

> *Blessed fire in the night*
> *Show me what is in the sight*
> *Show me what brings fight or flight*
> *Blessed fire in the night*

The room vanished, and mists of white and gray surrounded me. When they cleared, I found myself standing in a meadow at dusk. I knew the meadow well, for I'd spent countless summers here earlier in my life. Horses, chickens, and the wagons of year-round travelers surrounded me, each wagon looking like a small home on wheels.

I remembered this as a lovely place, with green grass and fields of apple trees and long rows of berry bushes stretching endlessly on the south and east sides.

Right away, I knew something was wrong.

The grass was brown, the apple blossoms were dead on the trees, the strawberry plants were shriveled in dried dirt, and the raspberry vines had withered.

"You were seen!" a deep voice shouted. "What were you doing out there?"

The vision sharpened, and I looked ahead past a few wagons to see a shirtless young man with his hands up over his head and tied around the branch of a tree. Blood flowed from his nose and his left eye. There were burn marks on his arms and chest.

"I wasn't there, my lord," he whispered, exposing bloodstained teeth. "I never went into the orchard."

Three guards in chain armor and orange tabards stood near him, but I focused on the angry man standing about six paces in front of him.

He was tall and broad-shouldered with short silver hair, wearing a leather hauberk. Though he must be at least fifty, his face was handsome with few lines and high cheekbones. His expression twisted into dark, cold rage as he turned from the suffering young man and toward a crowd of people all watching helplessly.

"Prince Malcolm," an aging woman pleaded. "Gallius has done nothing. The apples were still blossoms, not yet ready for harvest, and so he was with the rest of us picking strawberries before . . . before."

"He was seen!" the prince shouted back. Then he pointed to the dying apple trees. "One of you has done this, and no one leaves this place until you tell me who it was and how to stop it. I don't care if you all stay here and starve into next winter. There's no drought this season, and no natural blight would kill every crop on the same day. Someone has cursed the land and the crops."

His hand moved from pointing at the trees to pointing at the bound young man. "He was seen in that field with his arms in the air." His voice softened. "I hate this as much as any of you. But if Gallius has cursed the harvest, you only need tell me."

A middle-aged man with dark hair stepped forward from the crowd. "It wasn't Gallius, my lord. It was none of us. You search for blame in the wrong place."

The prince's expression shifted to anger again, and he motioned to a guard with a shaved head and a white scar running from the center of his forehead to his right temple.

"Ayden," the prince said.

This guard wore a metal gauntlet on his right hand. He stepped to Gallius and swung hard, striking him across the face.

Without hesitating, he swung back the other direction, and this time, the blow was accompanied by a popping sound.

After Gallius's head snapped to one side, it dropped forward at an odd angle. The guard stopped. Reaching out with his other hand, he touched the side of Gallius's neck. "I'm sorry, my lord. He's dead."

The tall prince drew in a long breath. Then he turned and began striding away.

"No one leaves!" he called over his shoulder. "No one."

He mounted his horse.

The faces of the onlookers were stricken, and more guards in orange tabards fanned out all around at the edges of the meadow.

The people inside were prisoners.

CHAPTER ONE

As a healer and an apothecary, Céline Fawe had sat through death vigils before, but none had affected her more than the one that she and her sister, Amelie, faced now.

Céline, Amelie, and Lieutenant Kirell Jaromir all sat around the edges of the bed in Jaromir's private apartments. A great wolfhound lay in the center of the bed taking shallow breaths.

"It's all right, Lizzie," Jaromir whispered, stroking her head.

The wolfhound's muzzle was mottled with white. She'd lived fourteen years, which from what Céline understood was old for a dog of her breed. But Lizzie had been with Jaromir longer than anyone else in his life.

Earlier this evening, he'd sent for the sisters down at their apothecary's shop down in the village, and they had come quickly.

Lizzie had fallen and could no longer rise.

Jaromir carried her in here. Since then, Céline had been doing whatever she could to keep the dog comfortable and to ensure that Jaromir didn't have to go through this alone.

She looked across the bed at him. He was the military commander of Castle Sèone and personal bodyguard to Prince Anton of the house of Pählen.

In his early thirties, Jaromir was more striking than handsome. He wore a small goatee around his mouth and kept his light brown hair tied back at the nape of his neck. From his weathered face to the scars on his hands, most elements of his appearance marked him as a professional soldier. He was tall and strong and comfortable inside his own skin. He wore the tan tabard of Sèone over chain armor. At times, he was too fond of being in control, and he would do anything—*anything*—he deemed necessary to protect Prince Anton.

But right now he was just a man suffering at the prospect of losing a beloved companion.

"Do you think she's in pain?" he asked.

"No," Céline answered. "I've given her a little poppy syrup, only enough to help her rest."

Poor Amelie sat beside Jaromir with a sad expression. Her relationship to Jaromir was more complicated than Céline's. Although Amelie would insist that she and Jaromir had no relationship at all, Céline knew better than to believe that.

She knew Amelie cared for Jaromir and felt his pain now.

"You don't have to stay," he said quietly.

"We're not leaving," Amelie answered.

Céline felt a rush of love for her sister. The two of them were close but had little in common and shared few physical traits.

At the age of nearly twenty-two, Céline was small and slender. Her overly abundant mass of dark blond hair hung in waves to the small of her back, and both she and her sister had inherited their mother's lavender eyes. Tonight, Céline wore a wool gown of the same lavender shade.

Amelie was three years younger and even shorter than Céline. But where Céline was slight, Amelie's build showed a hint of strength and muscle. She despised dresses and always wore breeches, a man's shirt, a canvas jacket, and boots. She'd inherited their father's straight black hair, which she'd cropped into a bob that hung to her shoulders. She nearly always wore a sheathed dagger on her left hip—which she knew how to use.

Until the previous spring, one year ago, Céline and Amelie had been living in a grubby little village, running a small apothecary shop, often taking skinny chickens and turnips as payment. But fate and mixed fortune had landed them in the prosperous village of Sèone, living in a fine shop, with the protection and patronage of Prince Anton.

"How long does she have?" Jaromir asked.

"I don't know," Céline answered. "Have you eaten? Should I send for some food?"

He shook his head. "Not for me."

A soft knock sounded on the door, and before anyone could speak, it opened. Prince Anton himself
stood in the doorway.

"My lord," Jaromir said, rising quickly.

Anton put up one hand. "Sit. I just wanted to come
and check. I know what Lizzie means to you."

Coming from Anton, this was quite an emotional
speech. The two men were good friends, but they were
both guarded in different ways. Jaromir often hid
behind a joke, and Anton was a reserved person who
held himself apart from everyone.

It was good of him to come tonight.

Céline met his eyes.

Anton was a young leader, in his mid-twenties. He
was of medium height with a slender build, but with
a definition of tight muscles that showed through the
sleeves of his shirt. His face was pale with narrow,
even features, and he kept his straight brown hair
tucked behind his ears.

"Is there anything I can do?" he asked.

"No, my lord," Jaromir answered. "But I do thank
you."

After a nod, Anton stepped out and quietly closed
the door.

Céline wished she could offer Jaromir some comfort. It would be a long night.

As the first light of dawn washed through the window,
Amelie opened her eyes. It took her a moment to
remember where she was: Jaromir's bedroom.

Sitting up, she found herself lying across the foot
of the bed. Céline was asleep in a chair. Jaromir knelt

on the floor with his face down on the bed and his arms stretched out over Lizzie's body.

The dog was still.

At Amelie's movement, Jaromir raised his head. "She's gone."

"Oh." Amelie was suddenly guilt-ridden for having fallen asleep, and she longed to say the right thing to comfort him. She was no good with words. She never had been. Instead, she crawled over and grasped the back of his hand.

Instantly, he put his other hand over the top of hers.

"I'm sorry," she said simply, and she was.

Lizzie had spent the past year living mainly in the dining hall by the hearth, where Jaromir had torn her meat into small bites, but the solider and dog had traveled and fought and hunted side by side from the time Jaromir was a young man.

"I know you are," he answered.

Céline stirred and opened her eyes. Looking at the scene before her, she wouldn't need to ask any questions.

Again, Amelie wanted to do something to help.

Still gripping Jaromir's hand, she said, "Why don't we take her down to the shop, to the herb garden? We can bury her between the rosebushes and the beech tree. I think she would like that, and we can look after her grave there."

Jaromir looked at her, and she imagined for a moment that his eyes were wet. Perhaps not.

He nodded. "Yes."

Standing, he wrapped Lizzie's body in a blanket so that she was fully covered and lifted her off the bed.

Céline gathered her medicinal supplies, and they left the room, heading for the stairs and down to the main floor. As they emerged from the stairwell, a familiar face came toward them from the direction of the dining hall.

Helga.

Normally quick on her feet, she was at least seventy, with thick white hair up in a bun that was partially covered by an orange kerchief—nearly always askew. Her wrinkled face had a dusky tone, and she wore a faded homespun dress that might have once been purple.

Though she was officially a servant here in the castle, Amelie had long suspected she was more. For one, everyone else treated Jaromir with deference and respect—even fear on occasion—but Helga often referred to him sarcastically as "His Lord Majesty lieutenant" and had a tendency to boss him around, and for some reason, he let her.

Even more, Helga had been responsible for helping Céline and Amelie understand at least the roots of who they were and where their mother had come from: the Móndyalítko or "the world's little children," who traveled in wagons and viewed the world as their home.

Before arriving in Sèone, Céline and Amelie had known little of their origins.

Their father had been a village hunter for Shetâna, and one year, he'd been off on a long-distance hunt, traveling for days. He'd come back with their mother and married her. Then the couple had built an apothecary shop in Shetâna and started a small family. Once Céline and Amelie were old enough, their mother taught them to read. She taught Céline herb lore and the ways of healing—while saying nothing of her own past.

Neither of the sisters had ever heard the term "Mist-Torn" before they came here and Helga explained to them that not only were they born of a Móndyalítko mother, but they were of a special line called the Mist-Torn who each possessed a natural power. As sisters, Céline and Amelie were two sides of the same coin, one able to read the future and one able to read the past.

The full comprehension of this knowledge had changed their lives, as now they not only served Sèone as healers, but as Anton's seers.

Taking a closer look at Helga, Amelie thought the old woman's step was less spritely than usual, and her normal, caustic expression was subdued.

Reaching out, Helga touched the blanket in Jaromir's arms. "It's over."

He didn't answer, but her words had not sounded like a question.

"Where will you take her?" she asked.

"To the herb garden, to bury her," Amelie answered.

Helga nodded. "I'll come."

An hour later, Céline stood beside a fresh grave as Jaromir used a shovel to pat down the last of the dirt.

She was glad for Amelie's suggestion that they bury Lizzie here in the herb garden out in back of the apothecary shop, the Betony and Beech. There was no place up at the castle for a proper burial, and Céline found this garden the loveliest spot in all of Sèone. The shop itself was a solid one-story wooden building, stained a rich brown with yellow-painted shutters. It was her and Amelie's place of business as well as their home.

The herb garden was divided into eight large separate beds filled with medicinal plants: cumin, colewort fennel, mint, lavender, lovage, sage, rue, savory, foxglove, pennyroyal, and rosemary. Red poppies lined the back fence. One portion of the garden nearest the shop had been designated as a "kitchen garden" for lettuce, carrots, onions, potatoes, peas, and strawberries. An apple tree graced one corner, and a beech tree the other. Roses grew along the sides of the fence.

Lizzie's grave was between the beech tree and a rosebush with white blooms.

"I'll make a marker later today," Céline said to Jaromir. "You can come and visit any time you wish."

He nodded, but she didn't know how often he would come. He'd loved Lizzie, but he was a man of duty and responsibility.

"Thank you," he said, looking at Amelie.

Helga hadn't spoken since leaving the castle, and although she'd been fond of the dog, Céline was beginning to wonder if something else might be wrong. Had the four of them been engaged in any other task, the dynamics between them all would have been quite different, with Jaromir teasing Amelie mercilessly, Amelie taking the bait, and Helga bossing everyone else around.

They were a sad little company this morning, and Céline decided to take charge in Helga's stead.

"This is all we can do here," she said. "Amelie and I have bread, butter, and strawberry jam inside. Everyone, come along, and I'll put together some breakfast and spiced tea. Jaromir, you need to eat something."

He didn't argue and let her lead him through the back door. This rear section provided their living quarters, and all four members of the funeral party passed down a short hallway, through a set of swinging doors, and into the front half of the shop, where the work and transactions took place.

Céline took pride in knowing that all this belonged to her and Amelie.

There was the sturdy counter running half the length of the large front room, and the walls were lined with shelves of clay pots and jars. The wooden table was covered in a variety of accoutrements such as a pestle and mortar, brass scales, small wooden bowls, and an open box of tinder and flint. A hearth comprised the center of the south wall.

Céline's enormous orange cat, Oliver, sat on the counter licking his paws. He kept the place free of mice.

"I'll slice the bread," Amelie said. "Céline, can you get the water started for tea?"

"Yes, I'll be quick."

As Céline headed for the hearth, again she glanced back at Helga, who would normally have taken full charge by now, insisting upon slicing the bread herself and throwing a few insults at Jaromir. She often told him that he "needed to be taken down a peg or two," and he never disagreed. Anyone else who dared speak to him in such a manner would have been given reason to regret it.

In spite of his state of sorrow, Jaromir himself finally noticed Helga's uncharacteristic silence and walked toward her. "What ails you? Try not to be too pained over Lizzie. I keep telling myself she had a good life and a peaceful end, and that's more than most of us can hope for."

Helga started slightly and looked up him. He towered over her.

"Oh, it's not . . . yes, I'm sad about your Lizzie, but . . ."

"But what?"

Helga's gaze moved from him to Amelie to Céline.

Kneeling by the hearth, Céline asked, "Helga, what is wrong?" Forgetting the tea, she stood, hurried over, and led the older woman to a chair. "Please talk to us."

As Helga sat, her expression was deeply troubled. "What do any of you know of Prince Malcolm of Yegor?"

Amelie blinked, and Céline had no idea what to say. The sisters knew little to nothing of politics outside the house of Pählen.

Jaromir shook his head. "Prince Malcolm? Not much. I know he's had the title only about five years, after inheriting from a brother who died with no heir. He holds a good deal of the southeast province, and his house earns most of their profits from agriculture. He's also shown no interest adding his name to the upcoming royal election."

Droevinka had no hereditary king. Instead, it was a land of many princes, each one heading his own noble house and overseeing multiple fiefdoms. But they all served a single grand prince, and a new grand prince was elected every nine years by the gathered heads of the noble houses. At present, Prince Rodêk of the house of Äntes was in rule.

In one year's time, next spring, a new grand prince would be elected, and Anton was hoping for the opportunity not only to put himself up for election but to gain enough support to win.

Helga studied Jaromir's face. "Agriculture?" she repeated. "Does that mean crops?"

"Yes. Why?"

"I've been looking for a way to get the three of you alone since yesterday. I need your help." She looked to Céline. "To save some of your mother's people."

"Our mother's people?" Amelie echoed.

"There's a meadow about half a league from Castle Yegor," Helga went on. "The lands all around it are covered in apple orchards and berry fields. Years ago, when I was just a girl, the prince in power found he didn't have enough serfs to handle the harvest, so he let it be known that if any of the traveling Móndyalítko were willing to work to bring in the crops, they were welcome to camp in the meadow all through late spring and summer."

Céline knelt down at her feet. "You traveled with the Móndyalítko?"

"Course I did. Fourteen to sixteen caravans came to that meadow every spring. We picked strawberries first, and then raspberries, then blueberries, and then apples in the early autumn. We were asked to pay nothing in rent for our stay, and we were allowed to keep a portion of the berries and apples we picked—and also to fish in any of the streams and set snares for rabbits. It was a haven." She paused. "The next prince and the next made the same offer. They needed the help."

"And something caused Prince Malcolm to stop allowing this?" Amelie asked.

"No," Helga answered. "The caravans still roll into that meadow every spring."

"But what happened with you?" Céline asked. "Where is your own family, and how did you come to be here?"

Helga's expression closed up. "Don't ever ask me that again. I told you your mother's people need help, and they do. This year, someone has cursed the land of Yegor, and Prince Malcolm blames the Móndyalítko in the meadow. Whatever has happened, it's no blight or disease. There's no drought and yet everything has withered and died, from the grass to the apple blossoms to the strawberries. The prince is facing ruin if he can't turn this around, and he's started torturing people to find the culprit. At least one has died. The others are all being held as prisoners."

"What?" Céline gasped, trying to get her head about this. "Helga, how do you know this? Has someone written to you?"

Again, Helga's expression closed up. "I can't tell you, but you know I'd never say such things unless they were true. I need help. We have to go there. You and Amelie have to use your powers to find the truth."

"Yegor?" Jaromir said, sounding incredulous. "It would take a week just to travel there, maybe more, depending on the state of the roads."

No one answered him, and the room fell silent except for the sound of Oliver licking his paws.

"You say our mother's people are in this meadow?" Amelie asked finally.

"It's been some years since I did a harvest," Helga answered, "but a small caravan from the line of Fawe always rolled in back then, and I can't see why that would change."

"Céline, we have to go," Amelie said flatly.

This was more complicated than Amelie seemed to realize. They'd never met anyone related to their mother. Were they simply to arrive and introduce themselves? How would either they or their offer of help be received? She knew so little of the situation. And what if one of the Móndyalítko had cursed the crops?

But Helga watched her with fearful hope, and Céline realized they couldn't refuse.

Reaching out, she touched Helga's hand. "Of course we'll go." She turned to Jaromir. "We'll need protection for the journey. Do you think Prince Anton will give you leave?"

Jaromir still appeared stunned at the idea of any of them going all the way to the southeast province, but she didn't think he would refuse, either.

And of course Anton would give them leave.

The sisters had served him well in the past year. They'd used their abilities to help him catch murderers and to shore up his legacy as a strong leader. He had given them this shop in gratitude, but they hadn't asked for it. They'd never asked him for anything. He would certainly grant this one request.

Jaromir locked eyes with Amelie for a long moment. On such a long journey, he'd want to be at her side.

"I'll go and speak with the prince," he said.

Helga closed her eyes in relief.

CHAPTER TWO

Even though Jaromir had been up all night and he still ached over the loss of Lizzie, he left the shop with his thoughts dwelling on Helga's request.

Midmorning had arrived.

The village that spread out all around Castle Sèone was almost like a bustling town. Two walls with heavily guarded gates surrounded the village. Jaromir believed in strong security measures.

He continued moving onward and upward through the people and the shops and the dwellings until he reached a small bridge. This led across a gap to a huge wooden doorway at the front of the castle. A pulley system on the other side would allow the bridge to be raised, cutting off access to the castle if necessary.

He crossed the bridge and entered the walled courtyard of the castle. A number of his men, all in chain armor and tan tabards, milled about the courtyard. They came to attention and nodded at the sight of him.

"Sir."

He nodded back and kept walking, trying to formulate what he would say to Prince Anton.

He didn't want to fail. Every time he closed his eyes, he saw Amelie and Céline sitting on the edge of the bed near Lizzie. Throughout his life, he'd only known a few people he considered true friends, those who would stand by him in both the light and the dark hours. Anton was one.

So were Amelie and Céline.

He'd wanted to be more than friends with Amelie from almost the moment he met her, but she was prickly and held him at arm's length. He knew if he tried, he could charm his way past her reservations, but after that, he wasn't sure how much he could give of himself, and she deserved a great deal. Much of the time, he felt so married to his job there was room for little else. The problem was that he loved his job.

After striding through the courtyard, he entered the castle, walked to the west tower, and made his way up to Prince Anton's private apartments.

Jaromir rarely came up here, but Anton tended to use the midmorning hours for correspondence or to work on financial accounts. In most areas, he was a "hands on" type of leader as opposed to a delegator.

Reaching the door, Jaromir knocked. "My lord?"

"Come in."

Entering his prince's private apartments, Jaromir glanced around.

The decor was somewhat austere. There were tapestries on the walls and a large hearth. The furnishings consisted of a messy writing desk, a few heavy wooden chairs, and rows of bookshelves along the walls. It looked more like the chambers of a scholar than a prince.

A closed door that stood on the same wall as the hearth led to the sleeping chambers.

Anton himself sat at the desk with a pen poised in one hand. He was dressed in black pants and a dark blue tunic.

"What's wrong?" he asked. Then comprehension seemed to dawn, and he stood. "Is it Lizzie?"

Jaromir nearly flinched. The question caught him off guard. "She's gone, my lord, in the night. We buried her in the herb garden of the shop."

"I do understand your loss. I've known dogs I liked better than most people."

Jaromir didn't doubt that.

"Thank you, my lord," he said. "But that isn't why I came. Forgive the intrusion. I . . ." He trailed off, wanting to make certain he worded this correctly. "Céline and Amelie have made a request."

Anton raised one eyebrow, sat back down, and motioned to a chair. "A request?"

Sitting down and bracing himself, Jaromir launched into retelling Helga's story as best he could. He left out nothing involving the situation she had described.

Anton listened politely and then seemed puzzled at the end. "What does this have to do with a request from Céline and Amelie?"

"They wish to go there, my lord, and use their abilities to find whoever has done this and free the Móndy-alítko being held in the meadow. I'd need to accompany them, along with a few men, of course."

For a moment, Anton's expression went blank, as if he hadn't heard correctly. "Go there? To Castle Yegor in the southeast province?" His voice dropped lower, as it did when he was not pleased. "How does Helga even know of Prince Malcolm's difficulties?"

Jaromir shifted uncomfortably in his chair. This was not going as he'd hoped. "I don't know, my lord. She won't tell me. I assume someone wrote to her. But she's not given to fancies or exaggerations. If she says this is the case, then it is."

"And when did you begin taking advisement from the castle maids?" Anton paused and closed his eyes briefly. "Forgive me. I didn't mean that. But the journey to Castle Yegor alone would take a week. There's no telling how long it would take the sisters to solve this crisis, if indeed there is a crisis, and then a week to return. You could be gone a month or longer. This has nothing to do with the safety or security of Castle Sèone, and frankly, I'm surprised you'd even ask such a thing."

Embarrassed, Jaromir stood up, on the verge of dropping the entire subject. Then he remembered how Amelie had grasped the back of his hand over Lizzie's body that morning.

"Such assistance to Prince Malcolm could be well received," he pressed. "Helga said that he'd be ruined if this isn't solved soon. It seems he has no intention of putting his name in for the election, and it could be a good thing to have him in your debt."

If anything, Anton's expression darkened. "I'll not buy votes via favors." He picked up his pen, signaling the conversation was at an end. "I need you, Céline, and Amelie here to serve Sèone. I am sorry for both Prince Malcolm and for the Móndyalítko he is holding, but it is not our concern." He looked back to the letter he'd been writing. "I don't wish to hear of this matter again, do you understand?"

"Yes, my lord."

Quietly, Jaromir left the room and made his way for the stairs. He didn't blame Anton. He wasn't even sure Anton was wrong. He simply didn't want to convey the message to Amelie or Céline . . . or Helga.

After Jaromir left the shop, Céline kept Helga behind for a while so the aging woman could drink some tea and gather herself. Then Helga, too, headed back up to the castle, and Céline promised to come to her as soon as they'd received leave from Anton—so they could make preparations for the journey.

Once the sisters were alone, Amelie shook her head. "I had no idea that Helga actually *knew* our mother's people. Did you?"

Céline struggled not to wonder about a family she'd never met. What would they be like? "I wonder why Mother never told us anything about them."

"Helga won't say much, either, not even about her own family."

Yes, that was troubling, but Helga must care for her family, as she'd come to the sisters to ask for help, and she was prepared to make a long journey as well.

"I hope Jaromir sends word soon," Céline said. "As soon as we know what men and resources Anton is willing to offer, we can make a more solid plan. From what Helga described, the sooner we leave, the better. I'd like to be gone by tomorrow morning if possible."

Amelie nodded. "Agreed."

To pass the time, Céline decided to boil down some marshmallow leaves to make more astringent for insect bites and bee stings. As late spring had arrived, there was already an abundance of insects.

Glad for something to do, Amelie offered to help.

The rest of the morning passed, and the afternoon began crawling by.

The sisters put together a small late lunch of sliced cheese and early peas eaten right out of the pods.

In the midafternoon, they worked in the garden weeding.

As the sun began to set, Céline looked up toward the castle. "I'm going to go see Jaromir."

"Do you want me to come?" Amelie asked.

"No. He and I might miss each other somehow, and he could arrive while I'm gone. You should wait."

Amelie wasn't normally good at waiting, but she nodded.

The truth was that Céline had a feeling something might be wrong, and if so, she preferred to face whatever it was without Amelie. Her sister had a hot temper and a tendency to make unpleasant situations worse.

Still, as she left the shop and headed up to Castle Sèone, she had no idea why Jaromir hadn't come back to speak with them. He'd heard Helga that morning, and he knew they needed to act quickly.

Before long, she arrived at the small bridge and crossed it, entering the courtyard. A number of castle guards came into view, engaged in various tasks, and she spotted a young man with brown, wavy hair to his shoulders: Corporal Rurik. He had accompanied her and Amelie on more than one journey, and she considered him a trusted friend.

"Miss Céline," he said with a smile. Then the smile faded. "I heard about Lizzie."

"Yes, it was a long night for the lieutenant. I'm looking for him now. Do you know where he is?"

"In the barracks, in his office, I think."

Jaromir was in his office? Céline expected him to be readying for the journey. Perhaps he had some last-minute business to complete. After all, they would be gone for some time.

"Thank you," she said to Rurik.

Turning, she walked to the barracks. Much of it was relegated to living quarters for the men, but just inside the main room, she turned down a short hallway and stopped at a solid oak door.

After knocking, she said, "Lieutenant?"

A moment of silence followed and then, "Come in."

Opening the door, she peered in to find him at his desk, but he didn't appear to be reading or writing anything. He was just sitting at the desk near a window in the fading daylight.

Confused, Céline stepped inside. "Why have you not come back to see us? Or sent word? Will we be leaving tomorrow?"

He looked drained both physically and emotionally. She'd never seen him like this, and her feeling that something was wrong grew stronger.

"No," he answered, sounding reluctant to even

speak. "I was going to come to the shop later tonight, after supper. Prince Anton prefers that we remain here in Sèone."

Stepping in closer, she said, "I don't understand."

"He will not give his permission. The situation in Yegor doesn't threaten our security, and he's ordered that we remain here. I tried to convince him, but he's made his decision. We cannot speak of this again."

Céline's mouth fell half-open. "Ordered?"

Jaromir glanced away, and she could see how much he wanted this discussion to end. Suddenly, everything became clear to her. Jaromir had probably spoken to Anton that morning, Anton had refused the request, and Jaromir hadn't wanted to face her or Amelie with the news.

Céline had no wish to pain him further. He'd had no sleep and had just lost Lizzie.

"I see," she said. "Thank you for trying."

At this, he glanced at her in surprise. She was not one to give in easily, and he knew it.

"Try to get some rest," she said. "I'll tell Amelie the news myself. Have you told Helga?"

Misery shone from his face. "No."

"You'll probably see her before I do."

He nodded.

Satisfied that he believed she was dropping the matter, she stepped out and closed the door. Then, with determination, she headed across the courtyard toward the castle.

As was his custom, at the dinner hour, Prince Anton walked into the large dining hall of the castle. He only hosted formal banquets once or twice a month, and other evenings the dining hall served as a gathering place for various factions who either lived or temporarily resided or worked in the castle.

Any of the guards stationed inside were welcome to spell each other and come here to eat. Some of the servants also ate here as opposed to the busy kitchen. These people dished up from a long faded table set near the hearth.

Anton ate at a polished cedar table set at the far end of the hall. This was reserved for himself and any other nobles or guests of importance.

Lieutenant Jaromir also sat at this table—if he took time for dinner. Tonight, he was nowhere in view.

In all honesty, Anton would rather have eaten in the privacy of his apartments, especially since Jaromir wasn't here. Small talk exhausted Anton, but he felt that coming in for dinner was something he ought to *do*.

Looking toward the head table, he was relieved to see only a few people sitting there. Lord Cirren and the Lady Edith lived here at the castle. Cirren was Anton's second cousin and a solid financial adviser. A family of prominent wine merchants from Enêmûsk was also seated, but Anton knew them well, and they disliked small talk as much he did.

Perhaps dinner tonight would not be such a trial.

He had started toward the table when a familiar voice sounded from behind him.

"My lord?"

Turning quickly, he fought to keep his expression still.

Céline stood a few paces behind him, and all

thoughts but her fled from his mind. Her hair was
down, spreading over her shoulders, and she still wore
the same lavender gown from last night. Her presence
affected him in ways he couldn't always control inter-
nally, which was beyond troubling. Though he'd only
known her a year, and she did not know him well, she
knew him better than anyone else in the world, including Jaromir.

He knew the soft feel of her mouth on his, and if
he'd been anyone but a prince of Pählen, he'd have
married her by now—if she'd have him.

However, he couldn't ever remember her coming
to the castle in search of him.

"Céline," he said, for lack of anything else coming
into his head. Then he saw the determined look on her
face, and his pleasure at her arrival faded. Certainly,
she could not be here to discuss that awkward business
Jaromir had mentioned earlier today? Anton had made
it clear that topic was closed, and he was unaccustomed
to being disobeyed.

"May I have a word?" she asked.

He didn't move and pitched his tone to sound cold.
"In what regard?"

His tone had no effect, and she pointed to the open
door of a side room. "Please."

With growing trepidation, he followed her through
the door. The room was small, with a single table, two
chairs, and no window. Several candles glowed from
the table. He often used this chamber for private conferences.

Céline closed the door, and they were alone.

"The lieutenant informs me that you won't give him leave to travel with us to Yegor."

Her blunt manner took him aback. He'd not expected her to simply launch in. Céline was normally a far more tactful, far subtler person.

"I cannot give any of you leave to be away from Sèone for so long," he said, "and I ordered an end to any more discussion in this regard."

Turning, he started to walk past her for the door.

"I'm not one of your soldiers," she said. "Neither is Amelie. Neither is Helga. You can't order us to remain in the village."

He stopped and stared at her in near disbelief.

Céline stood firm by the door with an outwardly brave expression, but on the inside, she wavered.

Anton was a good leader, and by nature, he was fair-minded. She had nothing to fear from him physically, but he was a warlord from a long line of warlords, and he expected to be obeyed. She'd never openly challenged him like this, and she had no idea what he might do.

"My mother's people are being held prisoner," she pressed. "Amelie and I cannot stay here in our safe shop and do nothing."

She could see the battle taking place behind his eyes. It went against his instincts to allow himself to be drawn back into a discussion he'd already closed.

"Your loyalties are to Sèone and to me," he said. "What if I need your skills while you are away? Have you thought on that? What if Sèone needs you? This situation in Yegor doesn't concern us."

"It concerns me. It concerns Amelie, and it concerns Helga." She stepped away from the door, closed the small distance between them, and looked up at him. "And how can you say it doesn't concern you? Do you not hope to be grand prince of this entire nation? Wasn't your mother from the house of Yegor?"

He sucked in a harsh breath, and she worried she'd gone too far. Anton's mother had died when he was only eight years old, but her family was from Yegor.

"You may not be one of my soldiers," he said angrily, "but I gave you my protection and I gave you a liveli-hood when you had nothing."

She flinched as if he'd slapped her. Was that what he thought? That she served him out of some sense of necessary gratitude?

"So because you gave us your protection and the apothecary's shop, our abilities are now to be used *only* in your service? What will you do if we decide to go to Yegor anyway? Will you take the shop from us? Will you order your guards at the gates to detain us? Have we become prisoners here?"

"You asked me for my leave, and I said no!" His voice rose. "There is no need for any of these dramatics. Have I made any threats? Have I threatened to take the shop away or to lock you inside the village? Don't paint me as some blackheart in all this!"

She whirled, taking quick steps toward the door. "Then we'll leave in the morning, even if we have to bor-row the horses and travel alone. I trust you won't begrudge loaning three women a few horses!"

Grabbing the door handle, she'd just begun to pull when his hand passed by her head and pushed the door closed. He stood behind her, holding the door shut, and she turned around to face his chin.

"Céline," he whispered.

Her anger faded, and she wished she understood him better. "Please, Anton. Amelie and I can do something no one else can, and these are our mother's people. Let us go to help them." Leaning forward, she rested her forehead on his chest. "Please."

"And if I don't give Jaromir leave to guard you, you'll go by yourselves? You would do that?"

With her head still pressed against his chest, she nodded. "Yes."

He sighed in what sounded like resignation.

CHAPTER THREE

The following morning, just before midday, Amelie and Céline were in the shop, making preparations to leave.

Amelie was still somewhat uncertain of the events of the previous day. Apparently, Anton had initially refused to give Jaromir leave, and then somehow Céline had changed his mind in the evening. After that, Jaromir and Helga had begun to plan together, and now the sisters were told to wait for further word.

Amelie couldn't help feeling somewhat in the dark.

"I thought we'd leave before now," she said.

"So did I," Céline answered. "I wish I knew what Jaromir and Helga have been up to."

As if by way of answer, a loud knock sounded on the door, followed by Helga shouting, "Hurry up! My arms are full!"

Amelie ran to the front door of the shop and opened it. Helga stood on the other side, carrying a pile of clothing—skirts, blouses, and brightly covered scarves.

"What is all that?" Amelie asked in sudden suspicion.

Every time the sisters had been asked to leave Sèone to use their abilities in Anton's service, Amelie had been forced to play some ridiculous "part" and to dress accordingly. First, she'd had to play a lady of Anton's court and later, she'd had to pretend to be the daughter of a wealthy merchant. In both cases, she'd been forced to wear a variety of silk gowns.

Now what did Helga have in mind?

"You'll be rolling into that meadow as Mist-Torn seers from the line of Fawe," Helga announced, stomping in with her usual energy. "You have to look the parts or you won't be trusted. The Móndyalítko only trust their own."

Rolling in? What did that mean?

Worse, Amelie eyed the garments in Helga's arms. The white peasant blouses looked rather low-cut. "I'm not wearing one of those."

"Yes, you are," Helga responded. "Now get those pants off . . . and that dusty jacket."

Céline had been packing medicinal supplies, but she came over to inspect the clothing. "Helga, it's not that I disagree with you. I know we won't be trusted if we're viewed as outsiders, but won't that become immediately apparent when we ride into camp with the lieutenant and a small contingent of Sèone soldiers?"

"Yup, you would," Helga agreed. "That's why the lieutenant and I came up with something else. He rode out of town early this morning, and he should be back anytime."

"Back from where?" Amelie asked.

"You'll see," Helga answered. "Now come on and

get dressed, girls. I'll need to help with the sashes and jewelry."

"Jewelry?" Amelie repeated.

But by now, she knew it was useless to argue with Helga. No matter how much Amelie had protested in the past, Helga always somehow got her laced into what gown was necessary for the ruse they had to play.

Sighing, Amelie pulled off her canvas jacket. "Lock the front door," she said to Céline.

In a surprisingly short amount of time, Helga had transformed both the sisters.

Céline was dressed in a bright red skirt, a white blouse, and an orange paisley sash tied around her waist. Her ears were pierced, so she wore silver hoops in her ears and a line of loose, dangling bracelets down both wrists.

Amelie wore a bright blue skirt, a white blouse—that was indeed too low-cut—and a yellow sash. As her ears weren't pierced, Helga had to be satisfied by adorning her with a few silver bracelets.

Then Amelie secured her dagger into a sheath inside her right boot.

Though she'd never admit it, this attire was much more comfortable than the silk gowns she'd been laced into on their last venture. At least she could move and breathe.

Oliver, Céline's cat, sat on the counter and watched all of this with interest.

"I have several spare blouses for you both," Helga said.

"What about you?" Amelie challenged. "Don't you need to look a little more . . . Móndyalítko?"

"I am Móndyalítko," Helga answered. "Don't need to worry about looking more like one."

Amelie was about to press this further when Céline said, "I will need to run down to the blacksmith's and ask Erin to take care of Oliver while we're gone. I hate to leave him for so long, though."

When the sisters traveled, Céline's friend Erin came to the shop once a day to put out bowls of milk and water for Oliver. He hunted mice and took care of himself for the most part, but Céline feared he might feel abandoned if no one cared for him.

"Bring him along," Helga said.

"Bring him? How can I possibly do—?"

A sound like rolling wheels could be heard from outside.

"There's the lieutenant," Helga said, starting for the door.

Amelie glanced at Céline, who shook her head in puzzlement as the sisters followed Helga.

Upon leaving the shop, Amelie needed a moment to absorb the scene before her.

Two wagons—that looked like small houses—waited out front, each one drawn by a pair of stout horses. The larger wagon in front was painted white with yellow shutters and a red roof. The smaller one in the back was painted blue with tan shutters and a tan roof.

Jaromir was on the front bench of the larger wagon, driving the horses. He set the brake and jumped down.

Amelie took in the sight of him. Gone were his armor, tabard, and sword. He was now dressed in loose brown pants, a black shirt with an open front, and a canvas vest. She guessed he had knives and daggers hidden up his sleeves and in his boots.

He looked so different, almost rakish, and he flashed her a grin.

"Look at you," he teased, running his eyes from her feet to her shoulders. "This journey might be more enjoyable than I thought."

Oh no, she thought, wondering how Helga would react if she dashed back inside the shop for her pants and jacket.

Céline had barely taken in the sight of the first wagon when she turned her gaze to the second one, and up to the man driving it.

Like Jaromir, he set the brake and jumped down.

"Céline," he said simply.

She found she couldn't answer. The man standing before her was tall and tightly muscled. His coal black hair hung down past his collar, and his black eyes searched her face. She would never have described him as handsome. He was . . . beautiful. There was something almost feral about him, as if he didn't belong inside any four walls.

Marcus Marentõr.

The previous summer, Céline, Amelie, and Jaromir had traveled north to the silver mines of a place called Ryazan. They'd been asked to solve an ugly situation up there for Anton's father. Some of the soldiers who were overseeing the mines had begun turning into mad wolves.

The sisters had uncovered the mystery, but in the

process, they'd come to know a group of Móndyalítko who'd basically become enslaved there, trapped with no horses to pull their wagons and forced to work in the mines.

Marcus was one of them. He and Céline had come to depend upon each other during that crisis, and as the nights passed, they'd found themselves more and more drawn to each other. But Céline allowed nothing to happen between them. Somehow, for some reason she couldn't explain, it would have felt disloyal to Anton.

When the time had come to travel home again, Jaromir arranged for the Móndyalítko group to leave that awful place and come to Sèone. They'd been given an abandoned plot of land well outside the walls of the village. It had a cottage and a small barn. The family now worked the land. Half the crops went to Prince Anton, and they kept half to sell or use for their own purposes.

This must have been a difficult adjustment for a group of natural travelers, but they'd been desperate to escape Ryazan and to make a home, and they'd jumped at the offer.

Céline hadn't seen Marcus since.

"What are you doing here?" she asked.

A flicker of surprise passed across his face. Perhaps he'd expected a different greeting.

"The lieutenant asked me," he answered. "He said you needed a ruse, and that you needed help."

With that, everything became clear to Céline.

After a night of planning with Helga, Jaromir had ridden out that morning and gone to visit the Marentõrs.

He must have explained what was happening in Yegor and asked to borrow the wagons, horses, and, for some reason, Marcus.

Turning to Jaromir, Céline asked, "What about other guards?"

"Helga says this is better," he answered "and I agree. Anyone of quality will ignore us, and bandits don't normally bother with Móndyalítko. Too much trouble for too little reward. But Marcus, Amelie, and I can handle any problems that do arise."

He sounded so certain.

Céline tried to grasp the change of circumstance. So, just the five of them, she, Amelie, Helga, Jaromir, and Marcus, would be traveling in close quarters all the way to Yegor, and then somehow convince the Móndyalítko there that they were a bonded group who had formed their own family. For some reason she couldn't name, she didn't care for the idea of living with Marcus for what might be as long as a month.

As she was about to ask a few more questions, she noticed Helga studying Marcus warily. The aging woman even sniffed the air.

He looked back at her. "Do I know you?"

"How long since you spent a summer in Yegor?" she asked.

He tilted his head. "Four years."

"I haven't been in five," Helga said. "You'd have been young to pay much notice to an old woman like me."

While that might be an unfair assessment of Marcus, it also might be true. Céline guessed him to be about twenty-five.

He motioned to his chest and said, "Marcus of the family Marentõr."

Helga nodded back. "Helga of the family Ayres."

This was the first time Céline had ever heard Helga's family name.

"Yes, I know of your family," Marcus said. "You must know mine. My aunt was the great Moira."

Recognition dawned in Helga's eyes. "I remember her. Jaromir didn't say what family he'd brought back from Ryazan." Still, she continued to study him warily, and Céline wondered what might be wrong.

However, as this did not appear a good time to ask, she didn't.

Hooves clopping on cobble sounded behind her and she turned around to see a small contingent of guards coming toward them. The men were on foot and the horses were loaded with what looked to be food supplies.

Anton walked in the lead.

Céline hadn't expected to see him before leaving, and her mind flashed back to a few things they had shouted at each other the night before. She always felt off-kilter in his presence. A part of her wished he hadn't come, and a part of her wanted to run over to kiss him good-bye.

She remained in place.

He closed the distance and glanced at the first wagon. "Jaromir, have the men load these supplies."

"Yes, my lord."

Anton's eyes moved over Céline's attire. He didn't seem pleased. "What are you wearing?"

She tried to sound light. "Helga says we must look the part."

He had seemed about to respond when he looked beyond her and fell silent. Craning her head, she realized he'd just seen Marcus.

For a long moment, Anton didn't move.

Tension filled the air, and Céline sought to break it. "My lord, this is Marcus Marentōr. He's one of the Móndyalítko we brought back from Ryazan."

Anton glanced down at her. "Is this the man who helped you there?"

"Yes, he was very helpful in our success," she answered carefully.

Marcus looked between her and Anton, but he didn't say anything. Marcus wasn't normally much of a talker.

For a moment, Anton's face hardened to the point that Céline feared he was about to change his mind and rescind his permission. She hoped he would not. This would all be much easier with his grudging support.

Instead, he half turned to watch the guards passing bags of food up to Jaromir and Amelie—who were both now on the roof of the smaller wagon. Marcus noticed this, too, and he moved to help, jumping up to the bench and then swinging to the roof with ease.

"Helga and Jaromir say that we must be trusted by the Móndyalítko being held in the meadow," Céline explained to Anton. "I think they were up half the night formulating this plan. Poor Jaromir has been rather shy on sleep."

"He seems fine today," Anton answered tightly.

She didn't want to leave things like this. "Don't be angry. Don't say good-bye in anger. We only want to do what's right."

"And how do you know what's right?"

"My heart and head tell me at the same time."

He breathed out softly. "I would keep you here if I could, but I won't stop you from going, and I won't let you go unprotected."

"Thank you."

"Don't thank me. You have my hands tied."

The supplies were loaded and secured.

Jaromir climbed down, and Amelie followed him. Marcus climbed to the bench and took up the reins.

"I'll drive the first wagon," Jaromir said to Anton. "The women can ride inside."

"You think this is safe?" Anton asked him. "With no guards, and no men except you and one Móndyalítko?"

"We have Amelie, too," Jaromir returned. "She almost took me down once. We'll be fine, my lord. I'll make good time and bring the sisters back as soon as I can."

Unhappy, but resigned, Anton stepped away. "And yourself, too. Keep yourself safe."

"Yes, my lord."

With that, Jaromir opened the door to the larger wagon. Céline remembered that when the wagons were camped, a small set of steps was always placed behind the door. Now they were missing, and the bottom of the doorway was several feet off the ground. Turning, Jaromir grasped Helga by the waist and lifted her up as if she weighed nothing. Amelie scrambled up and inside on her own.

Céline wanted to grasp Anton's hand but didn't.

"I do thank you," she said to him, "and I promise to return as quickly as possible." Looking back toward the shop, she said, "Oh, wait. I have to get Oliver."

Helga's earlier words made sense now. They would be taking their home with them, so Oliver could ride along. Hurrying back inside, she scooped him off the counter and came out with him in both arms. Anton came over to close the door behind her.

"Can you carry him?" he asked.

Oliver was indeed a large cat. His tail nearly stretched down to her knees. "Yes, I have him."

Walking over, she stood at the back door of the larger wagon and set him on the floor, letting him walk inside to where Amelie and Helga waited.

Anton reached out, grasped Céline by the waist, and lifted her so she could climb inside.

Her hand dropped to grip his fingers for a few seconds and then she let go. He closed the door from the outside.

"Take a seat, girls," Helga said. "I'll make sure everything's been secured."

The wagon lurched forward.

Céline hadn't even told Anton good-bye.

CHAPTER FOUR

Once outside Sèone and on the open road, the wagons headed east.

Amelie, Céline, and Helga had all found someplace to sit, but in regards to the passing scenery, they could see only what was visible through the small windows.

Inside, the covered wagon felt even more like a house. Toward the front were two bunk beds nailed and bracketed into the wall. There were two short benches built into one side wall with a stationary table between them. A large cast-iron pot and teakettle hung from the other wall, but these were secured on hooks so they wouldn't fall. There was a small cabinet nailed to one wall with its cupboards latched shut. Curtains hung from the windows, but Helga had tied them back.

Céline and Helga sat on the benches at the table.

Oliver hopped up to the top bunk.

Amelie took a seat on the lower bunk.

At first she was relieved at the prospect of not riding for days on the back of a horse, but after a few leagues, the motion of the wagon began to affect her, and she felt queasy to the point of worrying her breakfast might come back up.

Helga glanced at her and said, "It'll pass."

Céline seemed immune to the rolling motion, but her expression was troubled. "I think we ought to tell Jaromir about Marcus as soon as possible."

Amelie shook her head her in puzzlement. "Tell him what?"

"Well . . . you know. That Marcus is a shifter."

A rush of embarrassment almost overcame Amelie's nausea. How could she have forgotten Jaromir didn't know about Marcus? Of the Sèone guards, only Rurik knew Marcus's secret, and he'd sworn to keep silent. Amelie chastised herself for not having thought of this the moment Marcus had jumped down from the second wagon.

"Oh, I'm sorry. I'd completely forgotten that—"

She never finished the sentence, as Helga jumped to her feet. "A shifter? I knew it! I thought I could smell it. What does he change into? A panther?"

"A wolf . . . a black wolf," Amelie answered, completely taken aback.

"A wolf? You're sure?" Helga pressed. "That might not be so bad. Why didn't you girls tell me?"

Céline blinked in clear surprise, and Amelie had no idea how to answer. From what she'd been told, any Móndyalítko family with a shifter in the mix was considered quite fortunate. Shifters could bring down deer in harsh winters and feed everyone when little else was available. Also, among the Móndyalítko, shifters were viewed as counterpoints of the Mist-Torn, as gifted or blessed.

Helga's reaction made no sense.

Finally, Amelie managed to say, "It never occurred to us to tell you that the family we brought back had a shifter among them. I'm sorry."

Helga turned on her. "You should be sorry!" She closed her eyes and took a few breaths. "You've never been alone with him? You've been careful not to be alone with him?"

"Yes, I've been alone with him," Céline responded. "Marcus is perfectly safe. Amelie and I wouldn't even be here without him. Up in Ryazan, we were attacked by one of those wolf-beasts in our own tent, and he shifted and fought it off."

Slowly, Helga sank back down on the bench. "The wolves aren't so bad, but shifters only protect you when it suits them. Don't you go trusting him just because he fought off something worse."

Amelie glanced at Céline and shook her head once. Whatever was troubling Helga, more words were not going to solve it.

"You hear me?" Helga asked.

"Yes," Amelie answered, trying to sound assuring. "We hear you."

Céline listened to the soft creak of the rolling wheels for the remainder of the day. In the late afternoon, the wagon stopped.

She stood and stretched, putting her hands to her back. Though riding in the back of the wagon was certainly preferable to spending all day on a horse, sitting on a bench in an enclosed wagon was only marginally better.

As she stepped toward the door, it opened from the

outside. Marcus was there arranging the small set of steps.

Her legs felt shaky, and when he reached out with his hand, she took it and let him help her down. Touching him, gripping his hand was the most natural thing in the world and she was struck again by her reluctance to spend weeks living in close quarters with him.

Everything about him was far too familiar, and she had no explanation.

The first time she met him back in Ryazan, he'd taken off his shirt and let her tend to some deep wounds on his back. In that moment, she'd felt she'd known him for centuries, as if in twenty lifetimes, he'd been a part of each one. In the days and nights that followed, this feeling had only grown stronger, and now here he was, standing in front of her once again.

"How did you all fare?" he asked, reaching back in for Amelie's hand.

To Céline's surprise, Amelie grasped his hand and let him help her down as well. Poor Amelie was looking a bit green.

"Tomorrow, I think I'll walk," she said, putting a hand to her mouth.

Inside, loud clanking could be heard, and then Helga appeared in the doorway carrying the teapot, a bucket, and a tall iron hook.

Marcus hopped up one step and reached out to relieve her of her burdens.

She glared at him. "Get away with you."

Stunned, he jumped down and glanced to Céline as if seeking an explanation. She had none to give him.

Jaromir came striding over, and Céline still wasn't

accustomed to seeing him without his armor, tabard, and sword. He looked so different in that black shirt and open vest.

"We'll make camp here for the night," he said. "There's a stream downhill."

Céline looked at the heavily forested area around them. Jaromir had found a clearing off the road large enough for the wagons. Deeper into the forest, she spotted a slope stretching downward, and she could hear rushing water.

"I'll start a fire," Marcus said quietly, heading away.

Oliver appeared in the top of the open doorway. He yawned and stretched and began walking down the steps.

"You're going to let him out of there?" Jaromir asked.

"He needs to stretch his legs like any of us," Céline answered. "He certainly can't stay in that small space the entire journey."

"He's a cat. Won't he just wander off and get lost?" Jaromir responded. "If he's not inside the wagon in the morning when we're ready to pull out, I'm not waiting to form a search party."

At that, Amelie turned toward Jaromir with her expression darkening. This was another problem with the two of them on lengthy journeys. While in many ways, Jaromir was the best of men, he was so accustomed to giving orders that he often had no idea how arrogant he sometimes sounded. He viewed himself as utterly in charge—which he technically was—and his manner frequently produced a heated response from Amelie.

He might let Helga boss him around and berate him.

But Amelie openly fought with him, and he'd never learned to alter his behavior to stave that off.

"So because he's a cat, you think he's too stupid to look out for himself and stay near the camp?" she challenged.

He turned to face her. "Just make sure he's in the wagon after breakfast."

Amelie's mouth opened again, but Céline cut her off. "We will, Lieutenant. I promise he won't cause any delays."

He nodded tightly with another glance at Amelie.

Helga handed him the bucket. "Make yourself useful and get me some water. I'll start the tea."

With a frown, Jaromir took the bucket and headed toward the slope.

Céline, Amelie, and Helga walked over to where Marcus had started a small fire. The twigs he used were dry, so he must have had them stored somewhere. Crouched there, he focused on the flames and didn't look up.

"All right, girls," Helga said. "You both need to start learning how to be Móndyalítko. All meals are cooked outside over an open fire." She held up the iron hook with a solid and wide base, and then she set it on the ground with the hook positioned over the fire. The base would support even a heavy pot. "We start with tea first, and then bring out that big pot and move on to making dinner. I'll show you what to do."

Somewhat nonplussed, Céline glanced to Amelie, who shrugged. On journeys with Helga, the sisters had played at being ladies of Anton's court who needed to be fed and laced into gowns, but that was all a show.

"Helga . . . ," Céline began. "Amelie and I have been

cooking over a hearth or an open fire all our lives. We would gladly make dinner for you."

The aging woman looked up at her in some puzzlement. Could she be growing senile?

"I'll show you how to cook like a Móndyalítko," Helga insisted.

Marcus lifted his head, and Helga studied him a moment before asking, "You think you could scare us up a rabbit for the pot while I get the potatoes and onions chopped?"

Nodding, he answered, "Of course. I'll be quick." Dropping back on his haunches, he pulled off his boots. Céline knew he preferred to get out of sight before shifting. Then he'd leave his clothes in the forest and get dressed on the way back.

After jumping to his feet, he jogged barefoot into the trees.

"You could be nicer to him," Amelie said.

Helga just grunted. "Where's that water? His Lord Majesty lieutenant is taking his time."

This gave Céline an idea, and she started for the tree line. "I'll go and check on him."

Before either of the other women could call her back, she hurried onward, vanishing into the trees and down the slope. At the bottom of a small ravine, she found Jaromir crouched over a rushing a stream, washing his face.

The bucket was already full.

Realizing she was thirsty, she knelt beside him and made a cup with her hands, drinking a few mouthfuls of water.

"Is Helga yelling for water?" Jaromir asked.

Céline smiled. "I fear so."

He started up.

"Wait," she said nervously, wondering how to word her next sentence. How would he react? "I wanted to tell you . . . There's something about Marcus that you don't know."

Jaromir stood and grasped the handle of the bucket. "You mean that he's a shifter?"

Céline's mouth fell half-open. "You know?"

"Of course I know. Corporal Rurik told me before we left Ryazan."

"He promised to keep silent."

"That was before we'd decided to bring the family home." Jaromir raised one eyebrow. "You don't really think Rurik would have let me bring a shifter back to Sèone without telling me first? And risk having me find out later? He's not that foolhardy."

"Oh." As she thought on this, it made sense. There was no telling what Jaromir would have done to Rurik under those circumstances. "So you don't mind?"

"That Marcus is a shifter? Why should I? He fought on our side. He protected you and Amelie. I'd say he's a useful man. Why do you think I brought him along?"

He started back up the slope, and Céline fell into step beside him. The situation seemed somewhat upside down. She'd expected Helga to be glad upon learning about Marcus, and she'd expected Jaromir to explode. But Helga had been the one to become upset, and Jaromir wasn't even fazed.

To her mild annoyance, he chuckled. "You really thought I didn't know?"

She didn't dignify his question with an answer, and

the two of them came up over the top of the slope, making their way back into the camp.

"There you are," Helga scolded Jaromir. "What did you do, wet down your shirt and use it to wring water into the bucket?"

"Give me some peace tonight, old woman," he growled back, pouring water into the teakettle. "I've had a long day behind the reins."

"Don't you 'old woman' me," she said. "You wanted to play at being a Móndyalítko, and our men fetch the water."

Amelie watched this exchange with some amusement. The large cast-iron cooking pot now sat on the ground near the fire, and Helga was busy chopping onions and potatoes on a flat board. Oliver sat nearby, watching her, occasionally twitching his tail when the knife slammed down on the board.

"Be sure to cut the onions in large chunks so Marcus can pick around them," Céline said. "He likes the flavor they add, but not to eat them."

Amelie looked over and frowned. "When did he tell you that?"

Céline felt herself turning pink. *This* was the problem. She'd never eaten a meal with Marcus, and he'd never told her any such thing. But she knew.

Thankfully, Jaromir didn't notice her discomfort. "I'll go and take care of the horses," he said. Then he looked around. "Where is Marcus?"

As if on cue, Marcus came walking out of the forest. Céline's breath caught, and the sight coming toward them gave even Jaromir pause.

Marcus carried a dead rabbit in one hand and his

shirt in the other. Thankfully, he was wearing his pants, but spots of blood smeared his face and his upper right arm. His black hair was tangled. His bare torso exposed his long, tightly muscled arms and chest.

He stopped a few paces from camp. "What?"

Céline almost pitied him. He was the most . . . natural person she'd ever met. He had no vanity but no modesty, either. Sometimes he seemed more animal than man, even in his human form.

The spell was broken, and everyone but Helga pretended to go back to their duties.

Helga stood up from her cutting board. "Do you have no manners at all?" she asked him. "Traipsing back in here like that? With ladies about? Why didn't you get dressed proper?"

Céline wanted to roll her eyes at the "ladies" comment, but her heart went out to Marcus as he flinched and then looked down at himself in some confusion.

Holding out his shirt, he said, "I didn't want to get blood on it and cause extra laundry."

When those words left his mouth, Helga's face changed. Something happened, and suddenly she was the one who looked chagrined. Stepping forward, she took the rabbit and the shirt. "Of course you didn't. Go down to the stream and wash up. I'll keep your shirt here."

"Thank you for the rabbit, Marcus," Céline added.

Seeming slightly relieved, he headed off.

Helga waited until he was gone and then sighed. "You're right. He is safe."

"I told you," Céline said. "And Amelie is right. You need to be nicer to him."

Helga only grunted again, dropping back to her cutting board. "Come here, girls. Let me show you how to skin a rabbit."

"Oh, for goodness' sake," Amelie exclaimed. "We know how to dress down a rabbit."

"Not like a Móndyalítko. Now, you start here at the neck."

The following day, a change in travel arrangements proved a relief for Amelie.

After breakfast, as they were breaking camp, Céline lifted Oliver to carry him to the wagon. Amelie moved to follow, dreading the prospect of being trapped inside while suffering from the rolling motion.

But Jaromir stopped her. "There's plenty of room on the bench if you want to ride up top with me. I should have thought of this yesterday. I didn't think on what it might be like inside one of these wagons."

Amelie wanted to jump at the chance of sitting in the open air beside Jaromir, taking a turn driving the horses or helping him navigate. But still, she hesitated.

She'd stopped trying to deny the connection, the attraction, between herself and him, but anything beyond their current friendship was impossible. Jaromir would not allow himself to love any woman. He was married to his job.

He also had a long series of women in his past, and he was well-known for having a "type." That type was certainly not Amelie.

His last mistress had been a lovely, haughty, wealthy young woman named Bridgette. Amelie had learned through the other soldiers that Bridgette was never allowed to visit Jaromir's apartments until she was sent for—which was always the arrangement with Jaromir's mistresses. For about six months, Bridgette had slept in his bed whenever he sent for her, and when he got tired of her, he'd cast her aside like baggage and never once looked back.

Amelie was not about to become another one of his obedient mistresses until he got bored with her, and she feared letting down her guard.

As if he could read her face, he turned to walk away. "Suit yourself." Then he stopped. "Oh, just climb up with me. I don't want you losing your breakfast."

Realizing he was right, she followed him.

Marcus had been listening to this as he harnessed the horses to the smaller blue wagon. Upon finishing, he headed for Céline and spoke to her quietly. She smiled at him and nodded.

Moments later, they pulled out of camp with Helga and Oliver in the back of the larger wagon and with Jaromir and Amelie sitting up on the front bench. Marcus and Céline sat together on the front bench of the smaller wagon.

Tilting her head back, Amelie looked up at the sky. It was a fine late-spring day, and she breathed in the morning air.

"This is better," she said.

"I told you so. I thought as much."

Why did he always have to sound so smug? Did he do it on purpose?

After that, though, she forgot to worry about getting too close to Jaromir and began to enjoy the day. The weather was almost warm, and the road was dry. They passed forests and fields and villages along the way.

He did let her drive after a while, and he had a map that he brought out and showed to her.

She liked the idea of learning more about the geography of the nation in which she lived, and Jaromir had a fondness of maps. He had always had a few in his possession when they traveled.

"We'll head straight east for six days," he said, running his tan finger down a line representing a road. "Then we'll turn south here."

She nodded. She also liked knowing the travel plan.

And in this fashion the days began to pass. Sleeping arrangements had been simple to decide. The bunks in the larger wagon were wide enough for two people, so Amelie and Céline slept in the top bunk and Helga took the bottom.

Jaromir and Marcus were allotted the other wagon, but they often slept outside, one on each side of the smoldering campfire. Amelie never asked why, but she assumed Jaromir felt he would be alerted to any trouble more easily that way, and Marcus probably just preferred sleeping outdoors.

With each day, the routine grew more comfortable and familiar, and Amelie found herself filled with a strange contentment she'd never before known.

One evening, as she was dicing up some tomatoes for the soup, she found Helga watching her.

"You're happy out here?" the older woman asked.

Amelie thought on the question for a moment. "I am. I don't know why."

"'Cause it's in your blood. This life is in your blood," Helga said this wistfully, as if she, too, was happy living in a wagon and rolling down a road every day.

To Amelie's relief, Helga appeared to have given up all suspicion of Marcus and did treat him more kindly. But by the time the wagons turned south, those two seemed to huddle in private conferences too often, and Amelie often wondered what they were saying.

When Marcus wasn't hunting or conferring with Helga, he spent every waking moment with Céline. For some reason, this bothered Amelie, but again, she had no idea why.

The weather grew warmer and the forests less dense the farther south they traveled. One evening, when they were about a day from their destination, Jaromir spotted a small open field ahead. Amelie was driving the wagon, and he pointed.

"There," he said. "That's a good spot to camp."

"You think?" she asked. "Won't we be too exposed?"

"No, I was worried up north about camping on private land. There's a lot of mistrust of Móndyalítko up there. That's why we camped so often just off the public road. But your mother's people are more accepted down here. No one will bother us."

"Why is that?"

He shrugged. "It's an easier life down here. A harder life makes for more mistrust of things we don't know or don't understand."

She had no idea what he meant but didn't press further.

By now, the routine for making camp had become second nature, and everyone went about their normal tasks: the campfire, fetching water, caring for the horses, making dinner. Marcus hunted almost every night, but he was quick about it and normally brought back small game like rabbits or pheasants. Once he brought back a large salmon.

Helga did have some things to teach the sisters about Mondyalitko cooking, especially herbs and spices and how to cut any game into very small pieces before cooking it. She said that when cooking for large groups, this would ensure that everyone ended up with at least some meat in their bowl.

Even though their current group wasn't large, this made sense to Amelie, and she stopped questioning Helga's lessons.

After dinner, they normally sat around the campfire and either Céline or Helga would tell stories to entertain the others. Céline told comedies, adventures, or romances. Helga's tales were darker, normally ghost or revenge stories.

Marcus didn't speak much and he was hard to read, but he seemed to enjoy this part of the evening most of all.

Tonight, once the pots and dishes were washed and set aside for breakfast, Helga sat down by the fire and announced, "No stories tonight. We need to make a plan."

"A plan?" Céline asked.

"Yup. We don't have far to go, and as yet, we've no idea what we'll say when we get there."

"To say about what?"

"Who we are, where we've been, how we came together."

Amelie still didn't understand, and Jaromir looked equally puzzled.

Marcus crouched by the fire. "Móndyalítko families are complex. A small group like ours will be viewed as unusual, especially with two Mist-Torn seers. Even having one in the family is considered a blessing, and she will be surrounded by a large extended family." He paused. "And . . . as you know, my family was banished from the Yegor meadow."

Yes, Amelie knew all about this. Two younger members of Marcus's extended family had been caught stealing from other Móndyalítko, and the result was banishment for all the Marentõrs. That was part of the reason they ended up in Ryazan.

"So, what do we say?" Jaromir asked.

Helga poked the fire, and said, "Marcus would be welcome into any family, banishment or no. He's a shifter." She sounded bitter as she said this. "And it's well-known that Eleanor Fawe, the girls' mother, ran off with some outsider and left her own people. No one knows where they went or what happened to them. We can make up a story about Céline and Amelie losing their parents, and afterward, I joined with them. Then Marcus offered us himself as protection."

"What about Jaromir?" Amelie asked.

"He's not Móndyalítko, so he'll need to have married in," Helga answered. "We can say he's your husband."

Amelie was sitting in a crouched position, and she rocked back on her heels. "Say he's my . . . ?" she sputtered.

"Now, don't get all huffy," Helga warned. "Nobody

would believe he's Céline's husband once they've seen him with you."

Amelie stared in near disbelief, and to make matters worse, Jaromir appeared just as uncomfortable at the suggestion.

"You think they'll believe Amelie and I are married?" he asked.

Helga snorted. "I think anyone would believe you're married."

They all fell silent for a while.

Finally, Céline said, "All right, so to be clear, Amelie and I lost our parents, and then Helga joined with us. Marcus was looking to rejoin a Móndyalítko group, came across us and offered himself and his skills as a shifter, and we accepted." She looked over at Helga. "And Amelie and Jaromir are married? That's what we'll say?"

"That's about the size of it. We'll need to fill in a few details, but that should suffice."

Amelie tried to absorb all this while avoiding looking at Jaromir. This was going to be a much more difficult venture than she'd planned for.

In the night, Céline lay in the top bunk bed listening to the sound of Amelie's even breathing.

Helga slept below them, snoring like a badger.

But it was not the snores that kept Céline awake. She'd not slept well since leaving Sèone. In the night, something continued to pull at her, something ancient and familiar. She'd managed to push it away, but sleep remained elusive.

Tonight, the pull was worse.

Finally, she gave in, crawled out of the bed, and landed on the floor as lightly as possible. There she waited, but neither Amelie nor Helga awoke, so she crept to the door and slipped from the wagon.

Outside, Marcus sat by the remnants of the campfire, as she knew he would be. There was a blanket on the ground, and a blanket around his shoulders, and his face was up toward the stars in the sky.

"Where's Jaromir?" she asked quietly.

Marcus lowered his head and looked at her. "In the other wagon. He said that we need not sleep out here tonight, that no one would bother us here."

"What's wrong?"

She could see he was troubled about something.

Opening the right side of the blanket with his arm, he silently invited her to join him. Without thinking, she went to him and settled down, letting him draw her inside the blanket and up against his chest. She wasn't worried or embarrassed. Somewhere, somehow, she'd done this many times before.

He gripped her with both arms. His body was solid and warm.

"I've been happy this week," he whispered. "Happier than I've been in years. I'd forgotten the joy of the open road like this. But by evening tomorrow, we'll be in the Yegor meadow."

"That worries you?"

"I don't want to answer questions. I understand the story Helga wants us to tell, but it sounds as if I've abandoned my own family."

"Do you have to answer? In truth, I don't plan to say anything more than necessary. We've come here to help some of your people. Hopefully, they'll simply accept our help."

He fell silent, and then he lay down, pulling her down onto the blanket on the ground. Again, she wasn't worried. He drew her against himself with her back to his chest and the top of her head nestled in the crook of his neck. He liked to sleep like this. She knew it as clearly as she knew his tastes in food.

"Stay with me," he said.

"What if someone sees us?"

"I don't care, and neither will they."

His warmth and strength enveloped her, and if she'd let herself, she would have drifted off and slept the night away in the comfort of his body. But someone else would care. Someone would care a great deal.

If she closed her eyes, she would see Anton's face looking back.

So she lay by the smoldering fire in Marcus's arms until his breathing grew even and she knew he'd fallen asleep. She waited awhile longer, to be sure. Then she slipped out from under his arm and covered him with the blanket.

As quietly as possible she went back into the wagon and crawled up into the top bunk with Amelie. There, she slept restlessly for the remainder of the night beside her sister.

CHAPTER FIVE

The following morning, Jaromir noticed that everyone was unusually quiet. After breakfast, Céline
announced she would ride inside the larger wagon with
Helga. Marcus glanced at her but said nothing.

As had become the custom, Amelie climbed up beside
Jaromir.

To his shame, he was almost sorry their journey to
Yegor was coming to an end. The past week of sitting
on the bench in the open air, rolling through Droevinka
with few decisions and few responsibilities, had almost
felt like a holiday. His body was lighter without his
chain armor and even though he felt somewhat exposed
without a sword on his hip, he had thick daggers
sheathed up both sleeves and another in his right boot.

Amelie sat close beside him in her blue skirt and
white blouse, tilting her pretty face up to ask him questions about the route or if he wanted her to drive for a
while. He loved to watch her dark hair swing across her
shoulders when she moved her head, and he loved to
see her small but strong hands take the reins. Enveloped in her company, he didn't feel alone.

He knew they would reach their destination today, and then everything would change.

"I've never been in the southeast," she said. "I had no idea what we'd find."

"What do you think?"

"I like it."

So did he, but he'd been here before. In his younger years as a mercenary, he'd traveled all over the country. Though he preferred the rugged lands of the west and the dark, dripping forests of the north, the east had its attractions, too. The weather was warmer here throughout the year, and there were countless open fields of grass or wheat interspersed with uncleared sections of trees.

As Jaromir and Amelie took turns driving throughout the morning, they passed people and dogs herding sheep and cattle as well.

Geese flew overhead and large hawks sailed over the wheat fields in search of mice.

Then, just past midday, the world around them changed. It wasn't gradual.

Suddenly, all the crops around them were dead. The forested areas were still lush and green, but any orchard or vineyard or wheat field was dead and brown. The fruit trees were like dried husks and the wheat, barley, and berry plants were shriveled on the dried ground.

"By the gods," Amelie whispered. "What could cause that?"

"I don't know."

Jaromir held the reins, and he considered stopping but decided to press onward for several more hours.

Nothing changed. The crops and fields were dead, but the forested areas were untouched.

In the midafternoon, he stopped his horses, stood, and waved Marcus to drive up beside him.

Marcus's face was pale and drawn.

"I assume you know where we're going?" Jaromir asked.

Marcus nodded but seemed unable to speak.

"Then you lead."

Wordlessly, Marcus pulled ahead.

A few leagues later, he turned east down a side road, and Jaromir felt a short respite of relief as they traveled through a forested area with wildflowers on the ground and birds in the trees.

But in less than an hour, they rolled out of the trees and approached a large meadow covered in dead brown grass. At least thirty wagons—which was fewer than he'd expected—were parked in two separate rows down the meadow. Looking east, he saw a small castle on a hill. The undeveloped north and west sides of the meadow were still living and green. But the orchards and berry fields to the south and east were dried and shriveled.

The next things Jaromir saw were guards in orange tabards.

"Marcus!" he called. "Stop."

He pulled the larger wagon around in front. He wanted to handle any "greeting" they received here himself.

A guard walked toward them in long strides, but his sword remained in its sheath, and his expression was not threatening.

"Sorry," he said, standing below, near the bench of the wagon. "There's no work for you this season." He motioned toward the orchards. "As you see."

"We haven't come to work the harvest," Jaromir answered. "We have kin here, and we heard they aren't allowed to leave."

"That's the case. Prince Malcolm's orders. He thinks one of your people has done this to the crops. I can let you in, but I'd advise against it. Once you're in, you can't leave."

"That makes no sense," Amelie said. "If we're just arriving now, we couldn't possibly have had anything to do with what's happened here."

"Prince's orders," the man repeated, looking her up and down. "I suggest you turn around now and find somewhere else to spend the summer. That's what most of your kind have decided to do."

So other Móndyalítko groups had been arriving and were then turned away on the threat of imprisonment.

"We'll stay," Jaromir said. "We have people expecting us."

The guard shrugged and stepped aside.

Jaromir clucked to the horses, and they started forward. He could hear Marcus coming behind him.

Dried grass crunched beneath the wheels, and people began emerging from around the sides of wagons to watch the newcomers arriving. Small burned patches encircled by stones showed where campfires had been built. Chickens pecked at the dried earth. Empty cook pots hung on iron hooks with wide stands. Most of the horses were tethered on the west side of the meadow, and some were beginning to look thin.

Jaromir studied the people themselves as his wagon continued through the center of the other wagons. Most had dark hair. Some were pale, and some were dusky. They wore brightly colored clothing, and many wore silver rings in their ears. Their expressions were serious. Most of the faces he saw were pinched, but no one appeared to be starving.

Just over halfway through the meadow, he saw a clear spot, large enough to park both of their wagons in, and he pulled over with the back door of the white wagon facing the inside of the meadow itself.

Marcus pulled in beside him, leaving about a wagon's width of empty space between them, and set the brake.

It was time to climb down.

Amelie's eyes were wide, almost anxious as she looked up at him. This surprised him, as she was rarely afraid of anything.

"These are my mother's people," she said quietly, "and I don't know anything about them."

"It'll be all right," he said, knowing he shouldn't make such a promise.

From the back of the white wagon, Céline had watched what she could of their arrival.

Helga pressed up beside her and began reciting the names of families as they passed.

Some of the wagons were fine with new wheels and fresh paint; some were rickety and decayed.

As they rolled past a set of especially lavish-looking wagons with shingled rooftops, Helga said, "The line of Renéive." At the sight of three shabby wagons, she said, "The line of Klempá." Then she just began providing some of the family names. "Taragoš . . . Kaleja . . . Džugi . . . Ayres . . . Fawe."

"Fawe?" Céline echoed, noting two fine wagons painted deep red with white shutters. She tried not to tremble with anxiety at the prospect of meeting her mother's family. Then she glanced down at Helga. "Ayres? Your own family?"

Helga nodded tightly. Céline longed to ask her what had happened, what had driven her to Castle Sèone, but the older woman still forbade any questions.

The wagon stopped and a moment later, the door opened and Marcus stood outside, setting up the steps.

"It's time," Helga said.

Taking a deep breath, Céline walked to the open door. Marcus reached up for her hand, and instinctively, she took it and allowed him to help her down the steps. She walked slowly, as if his assistance was her due. Helga came out behind her. Jaromir and Amelie joined them only seconds before the first of the Móndyalítko came to greet them.

"Marcus," said a middle-aged man with dark hair.

Letting go of Céline's hand, Marcus offered the man a slight bow. "Rupert, am I welcome?"

Céline remembered his family had been banished from the meadow, but Helga had implied that those rules might not apply to him.

The man called Rupert frowned as if confused. "Of course you're welcome, but you shouldn't have come. You won't be allowed to leave now."

Marcus motioned to Céline and Amelie. "I brought two Mist-Torn seers. They offer assistance."

A small crowd had gathered by now, too many to study at once, but Céline couldn't help taking note of someone standing behind Rupert. She was a stunning girl of about eighteen, small with perfect pale skin and black hair that flowed like silk down her back.

Then many voices began saying "Marcus" or "Helga" in tones of surprise or welcome.

Amelie pulled up close beside Céline as people stared at them in a kind of wonder.

Again, instinctively, Céline knew she had to play a part, a part she had played many times before . . . somewhere. Pitching her voice to a regal tone, she spoke directly to Rupert. "We learned of your plight here and have come to see if we might help."

"To help?" Rupert bowed low as if she were nobility. "You are from the line of Fawe? How . . . how have you . . . ?"

He trailed off as the crowd parted and a woman walked through. She was at least forty, but still lovely with wheat gold hair and light brown eyes. There was something stately about the way she walked with her head high. A large man with a mustache walked close behind her. His hair was dark but peppered with silver.

The woman stopped and stared at Céline in shock. Her breathing seemed to quicken.

Helga stepped forward instantly. "Girls," she said, "this is your aunt, Sinead, your mother's sister." She turned to the woman. "Sinead, these are Eleanor's daughters, Céline and Amelie."

Céline stood frozen. Their mother's sister.

"Eleanor's daughters?" Sinead stumbled back a step, and the large man behind her caught her arm to support her. He looked down upon the top of her head in devotion and protection. Sinead's eyes flew to Céline's face. "Where is Eleanor? Is she with you?"

Céline's stomach tightened. She should have known to expect how difficult this would be.

"I'm sorry," she said. "Our mother has . . . passed from us, some years ago."

Sinead closed her eyes, and the man used both hands to hold her up. Regret and sorrow filled Céline that this exchange had been forced between them in public. She stepped forward, hoping to offer some comfort, but a loud cry rang out.

"Helga!"

A stout woman in a thin faded blue dress came toward them. She looked to be in her mid-sixties, with her gray hair tied back. Her eyes were wild as she came to a stop, taking in the sight of Helga.

Helga put one hand to her mouth. "Alondra."

The woman called Alondra rushed forward, grabbing Helga in her arms and sobbing loudly. The pain in her voice was raw, and her entire body racked with each sob.

Helga clutched the woman back, holding her tightly. "Oh, Alondra, don't. Not here."

Marcus was at their side instantly. "Over here." Using his arms, he ushered them back near the wagon wheel so they could sit on the ground together and lean against it. Alondra continued to clutch Helga.

This arrival in the camp was a good deal more emotional on all levels than Céline could have anticipated.

When she looked back to the crowd, Sinead and her

escort were gone, but another man approached the crowd, and something about him put her on guard. In his early thirties, he was tall and muscular and moved with a swift grace. His hair was dark and cut short. His feet were bare, and he wore loose pants and a loose shirt like Marcus's.

At the sight of her, he stopped cold and for some reason she couldn't explain, she was nervous. His gaze flicked to Marcus and then back to her again.

There were far too many people here for Céline to meet at once, and poor Amelie was watching Helga and Alondra in some alarm. Jaromir hadn't said a word but remained within arm's length of Amelie, keeping his eyes on the crowd as if making sure no one got too close.

For the most part, the gathered crowd had fallen silent, watching Céline and Amelie expectantly, as if waiting for something. Céline didn't think this was the right time to tell everyone why they'd come: to catch whoever had cursed the fields.

Instead, she moved back to the steps of the wagon and walked to the top. There, she let her voice carry.

"I do not know if you have another healer among you now, but my mother taught me her skills, and I have brought a large supply of fresh medicines. If you will bring any sick or wounded, it would be my honor to tend them."

Relief washed over the faces of those watching her, and the small crowd dispersed quickly. She heard some voices calling to each other, such as, "I'll get Tildy. You get Ryen."

Céline looked down at Marcus, standing below her

on the ground. He nodded once and silently mouthed, *Good*.

Jaromir was at a loss.

For the first time, he regretted this ruse. He badly wanted to don his armor, sword, and tabard of Sèone. He wanted to be seen as Prince Anton's lieutenant. Though the Móndyalítko appeared to revere Céline and Amelie, he had no power here and no control.

He had become accustomed to control.

The Yegor guards would view him as just another Móndyalítko, and the people of this meadow would view him as an outsider who'd married in.

He could see that Amelie was visibly shaken by everything that had just transpired, but he was thankful to Céline for having broken up the crowd and redirected their attention.

"You all right?" he asked Amelie.

"That was our aunt," she said quietly. "And Céline had to tell her that our mother is dead." She looked over to Helga, still holding Alondra. "I didn't expect so much so fast."

"Neither did I," he answered truthfully.

Helga caught his eye, and he walked over, motioning Amelie to follow.

Gently pushing Alondra up, Helga said, "Amelie, this is my sister."

Amelie's troubled expression shifted to a mix of interest and sympathy. "Oh, I am glad to meet you." She turned as if to introduce Jaromir, but Helga cut her off.

"Alondra, this is Amelie's husband, Jaromir Fawe."

For a moment, he was taken aback. His given name

was Kirell, even though few people knew it and those who did never used it. Everyone called him by his surname. Then he remembered that some Móndyalítko often took the name of the woman's family when they married. Helga had simply combined his more commonly used name with Amelie's surname.

This made him feel even more out of control, but he understood it.

"So good to see you both," Alondra said, sniffing and wiping her face with one arm. "I never thought to meet young seers from the line of Fawe again."

"We're here to find out who did that," Amelie said, pointing to the dead apple orchard. "And to get you out of here."

Alondra nodded sagely. "Yes, yes, I thought as much. I wondered if Helga would see what was happening, but I never expected her to bring help."

Jaromir glanced at Amelie, who shrugged. Not all of this discussion was making sense.

Helga grasped her sister's hand. "How far into those dead fields can we go?"

Alondra shook her head in alarm. "Not at all. We can't leave the meadow."

Helga thought for a moment and then said, "Jaromir, take me to the edge. I want to see what I can."

Glad for some action, Jaromir looked over to see Céline and Marcus on the steps, waiting for her first patient. He trusted Marcus to stay with her.

"Come on," he said, reaching down for Helga.

She let him haul her to feet and said to her sister, "You, too."

Just as they were about to head for the edge of the

meadow, Helga stopped and her body went rigid. In alarm, Jaromir followed her gaze.

She watched a man who had moved away from the white wagon, but not dispersed with the others. He was tall and muscular, with dark hair cut short. His feet were bare. His eyes were on Céline.

"Not now, Helga," Alondra said, her tone desperate. "Don't do anything. Griffin is dead now, and Gerard leads our family, so things are different, but you stay away from Jago."

Jaromir had no idea what any of this meant, but Helga continued glaring at the man.

"Your seer has Marcus right there with her," Alondra pressed. "Nothing will happen."

Amelie's expression shifted to alarm. "What's wrong? Who's that man?"

"Jago Taragoš," Helga answered, as if that explained everything. The hatred in her voice was thick. "Lieutenant, you watch him. He's a killer."

Jaromir stepped closer. "What?"

"He's a killer, and that's all you need to know."

"Helga," he insisted, "what do you mean?"

She didn't answer, and the man called Jago turned and walked away.

"See, he's gone," Alondra said, grasping Helga's arm. "Now come to the edge of the meadow, like you wanted."

After a moment, Helga nodded to her sister. Jaromir wanted to press her but knew it would be pointless. Until she was ready to speak, he'd get nothing from her. The term "killer" was ambiguous. He himself had killed when necessary, and so had Amelie. For that matter, so had Céline once. This man named Jago didn't appear to concern anyone besides Helga, so Jaromir wasn't sure what to make of the situation.

Still, he made a mental note to find out more about Jago.

After this, the four of them walked through the wagons and made their way south toward one side of the dried meadow. Jaromir spotted an area with about sixty paces between two guards, and he led the way.

Upon reaching the edge, Helga knelt and put her fingers into the dusty soil of the dead strawberry field. "Look at this," she said.

He knelt beside her to see what she'd uncovered. About two inches beneath the dried topsoil, the dirt was dark and damp and rich. The berries should be thriving.

His eyes flew to her face. "What does it mean?"

"It means there's no doubt this is some kind of curse, something cast by a kettle witch. You saw the forested areas. Someone has targeted the crops and only the crops."

Jaromir absorbed that and stood up. He turned to Alondra. "When did this happen?"

"Eleven days ago," she answered. "But it took several more days for Prince Malcolm to come and blame us." She paused. "For some reason, he turned on a young outsider named Gallius, who'd married in to the line of Renéive. The prince had him tied to a tree and beaten and burned with irons and finally killed."

"You've no idea why this Gallius was singled out?" Amelie asked her.

"None. The prince said Gallius had been seen in the

orchard with his arms in the air, but that's nonsense. Gallius had only been with us since last year, but he loved summers in the meadow. He'd never have done harm to the crops."

Helga glanced away as if trying not to wince.

"Has anyone else been questioned?" Jaromir asked.

"Just one," Alondra answered, "but not down here. Twice now, the prince has sent soldiers to take Lilah . . . Gallius's young wife, up to the castle. I think you all must have seen her today? She's Rupert's daughter, pretty thing, a bit full of herself, but I'd never wish her any harm. Thankfully, she came back both times unhurt."

That made little sense to Jaromir. Princes normally had no reservations about using harsh methods against women when their livelihoods were at stake. It seemed odd that Malcolm had tortured the girl's husband and then simply questioned her twice.

"That isn't the worst, though," Alondra went on. "The people are starting to suspect each other now. This would be a powerful curse for an outsider to cast. What if it was one of us?"

Amelie reached out and touched the woman's arm. "If it was, my sister and I will find out, and we'll get the rest of you free."

CHAPTER SIX

Céline hurried inside the white wagon and lifted her wooden box of medicinal supplies onto the table. Opening it, she looked inside and began taking out the most commonly needed ointments, syrups, and elixirs.

Oliver was up on the top bunk. As of yet, he'd not ventured out of the wagon, and she wondered if he might be better off remaining inside for now.

Marcus stood in the open doorway watching her.

"I just saw Amelie heading off with Jaromir and Helga," she said. "If I need assistance, can you help?"

"Yes. If you tell me what to do."

Keeping busy helped to stave off the emotions running through her, and she kept seeing Sinead's stricken face. Other snippets of the exchange that had taken place out front began coming back to her, and she had a few questions before any other people began to arrive.

"Marcus, you asked if you were welcome here, but Helga did not. I assumed she was somehow driven from her people, but no one questioned her presence. Do you know why she left?"

He dropped his eyes in embarrassment. She knew he didn't care for such questions.

"I've been trying to remember for days now," he answered. "But if she left five years ago, that was the same year my own family began falling into difficulties. The only thing I cared about was hunting and bringing home food."

"So you have no idea?"

"I know there was some trouble between the Taragoš and the Ayres early that spring. Jago was accused of killing one of the Ayres, and there was a gathering of the leaders to make a judgment, and they found him innocent. If they deemed him innocent, he most likely was." His embarrassment seemed to deepen. "But I don't even remember Helga from back then. As I said, we were in difficulty ourselves, and I spent all my time either hunting or sleeping. I'm sorry."

"Don't be." She almost regretted asking him now. "You can't be blamed for seeing first to the needs of your family and spending most of your time hunting as a wolf."

What a very odd conversation.

Footsteps sounded from the steps outside the door, and Céline looked over to see a mother with two children. Both children were coughing.

Céline smiled. "Come in." She turned to Marcus. "I may need hot water. Can you build a campfire and get some started?"

After that, the time passed quickly. She'd brought plenty of cough syrup made from a mixture of honey and water that had been extensively steeped in rose petals. She treated several festered insect bites.

Marcus brought hot water when she needed some for cleaning.

For the most part, Céline thought these people were suffering most from fear and stress. She spoke with some of them and learned that the Yegor guards carried in water from a nearby stream for the horses and for cooking, but it was never enough. The shifters weren't allowed to leave the meadow to hunt, and food supplies were running low. Grain for the horses was being rationed.

Marcus listened to this with a darkening expression, but Céline continued to work as quickly as she could.

A little girl came in with a particularly concerning injury on her hand. Her father carried her and sat her at the table.

"One of the guards has a dog," he said. "She tried to pet it, and it snapped at her. The man did apologize and had the animal sent back up to the castle, but the wound has grown worse."

Frowning, Marcus leaned down to look as well. The poor child's hand was swollen and infected. Céline guessed several of the dog's teeth had gone all the way through her palm.

Picking up a bottle of poppy syrup, Céline poured a spoonful and then spoke to the girl. "I have to clean your hand, and it will hurt a little. But this will make it hurt less."

Without question, the child opened her mouth and Céline poured in the spoonful. She wanted to wait a bit to let the poppy syrup work.

"You like dogs?" she asked.

The child nodded. "'Cept ones that bite."

"You must be careful with dogs you don't know." She pointed to the top bunk. "I have a cat, and he's nice to most people."

"What's his name?"

"Oliver, and when we're done here, you can pet him if you like."

The girl's eyes glazed slightly, and Céline knew it was time to work.

Picking up the jar of adder's tongue ointment and a clean rag, she said, "All right, this might hurt a little."

She started at the heel of the girl's hand and began to work her way forward. When she finished cleaning the wounds, she put aside the adder's tongue and switched to a mixture of ground garlic and ginger in vinegar.

"This is going to sting, but it will help with the infection," she said.

The child flinched only once. She was quite brave.

Upon finishing with the adder's tongue, Céline wrapped the hand in clean bandages and spoke to the father. "Bring her back tomorrow so I can check this. The wounds will heal, but we need to stop the infection."

As the girl was too sleepy from the poppy syrup to pet Oliver, her father carried her out again.

After this, a few elderly people with painful joints arrived, and Céline switched to rubbing an ointment made from monkshood into their knees and shoulders. She was careful to wash her hands afterward. Monkshood was astonishingly good for joints, but it was poison if ingested.

Marcus helped the last aging man down the steps and then came back inside. Céline sank down on the bench to rest for a moment.

"What these people need most is a decent meal and enough water for drinking and washing," she said.

She could see he thought the same thing, only he seemed more angry than regretful.

"Marcus?" a voice said from the doorway.

Whirling, Marcus looked back toward the door. A young man stood there, hanging on the frame. He was small and wiry, with long dark brown hair tied back. He wore three small silver rings in his right ear.

"It is you!" he nearly cried.

To Céline's astonishment, Marcus's face broke into a smile. "Leif."

Like a spring-loaded coil, Leif's body sprang forward, and he embraced Marcus with a quick but fierce hug.

"I couldn't believe it when I heard," he said, moving back and gripping Marcus by the shoulders.

To Céline's further astonishment, Marcus gripped Leif's shoulders and playfully shoved him backward. Leif dashed forward again, as if to shove Marcus, and in the small space of the wagon, Marcus somehow managed to step aside.

Oliver jumped up in alarm, and Céline feared a wrestling match was about to take place.

But then Marcus laughed once and held out his hand. "Not in the seers' wagon," he said. "This is Céline Fawe."

Leif studied her curiously and then bowed his head once. "Forgive me. I'm just so glad to see Marcus."

"This is Leif Kaleja," Marcus said. "He's another shifter. A coyote, and a good hunter."

Céline had no idea how to respond to such an introduction, so she nodded back.

Leif's good-natured countenance grew more serious. "Marcus, where is everyone else? I heard you came with Helga Ayres and two Fawe seers. I know your family was banished from the meadow, but where are your parents and brother? Where are your cousins, Mercedes and Mariah?"

The happy expression on Marcus's face faded.

"Mother is dead," he answered, "and Mikolai. My father, Mercedes, and Mariah are safe, and much of the rest of the family."

"Safe? Where?"

This was what Marcus had most feared, having to make explanations, and he didn't want to talk about Ryazan.

Céline cut in. "The Marentōrs made the choice to settle in one place, and they've taken on a plot of land near Sèone. Marcus visits them frequently, but he travels with us, as the road is in his blood."

Even though this was a slight embellishment to the agreed-upon story, it made more sense. He'd never simply abandon his family.

Marcus exhaled.

"Oh, I see," Leif said. "Marcus, I'm sorry about your mother and Mikolai."

"Can you tell everyone else?" Marcus said. "I don't want to talk about it again."

"Of course," Leif said. "I'm just glad you're here, and I wish we could hunt."

Marcus's eyes narrowed, and Céline wondered what he was thinking.

"Leif," she said, "do you have any idea at all who might be responsible for cursing the croplands?"

"It wasn't one of us," he answered adamantly. "Why would anyone here destroy our own summer haven? That's why we haven't tried to overpower the guards, even after Gallius was killed. No one knows why Prince Malcolm blamed him, but the leaders of the families would rather this be solved, the curse lifted, and for everything to go back the way it was."

"Then who could it be?"

"Someone who hates Prince Malcolm, I imagine. But it wasn't one of us."

The three of them fell silent, and then Marcus slapped Leif lightly on the arm. "I need to finish setting up camp. We'll talk later tonight."

Both men left the wagon, but Leif's final words kept repeating in Céline's mind.

Someone who hates Prince Malcolm.

By early evening Céline, Amelie, Jaromir, and Helga had settled the horses and prepared the wagons for what might be an extended stay. Stairs had been set up at the back of both doors, secured cupboards had been opened, and most of the supplies unpacked from the rooftops.

Marcus had helped for a while, and then he'd vanished.

Céline wondered where he'd gone but didn't want

to call attention to his absence, so she didn't go looking for him.

The campfire had been circled with stones, and Helga procured water for tea and to make dinner. Water was limited, but Céline thought they could manage.

They had no fresh meat.

"Shall we do a lentil stew?" she asked. "And we'll need to share some of these supplies with the other Móndyalítko. People are running low."

"Share supplies?" Jaromir repeated. "With how many?"

As these words left his mouth, Céline looked up and saw Marcus walking toward them from the trees. He wore nothing but his pants again, and he wasn't carrying his shirt. Instead, he carried a large dead deer—a buck—over his shoulders. His face and upper chest were smeared with blood. As he approached their wagons, other people saw him and came hurrying over.

A few paces from the campfire, he stopped and dropped the deer. Then he crouched beside it and reached for a knife Helga had left on a cutting board.

He'd barely gripped the handle when a guard in an orange tabard came jogging over. He was young and stocky, and his sword was still in its sheath, but he pointed at the deer. "Where did that come from?"

In one swift motion, Marcus stood up. "I caught it."

Céline tensed. He looked feral and dangerous, half-naked with blood on his face and torso. His black eyes were locked on the guard. Céline had never been on the receiving end of that look, and she had no wish to be.

"Out in the forest?" the young guard sputtered. "You're not supposed to leave camp."

"I came back," Marcus said calmly.

As this was indeed the case, the guard backed away a few steps. "Well . . . don't do it again."

Marcus ignored him and crouched down to begin skinning the deer.

"Céline," he said, "spread word for the other women to come. Everyone should be able to take enough meat for their pots tonight. Give them potatoes and onions, too."

"To everyone?" Jaromir asked. "There must be a hundred people here. That will cut down on our supplics."

Céline reached out and touched his arm. "Marcus is right. These people respond to loyalty and goodwill, and they all need a proper meal."

With some reluctance, Jaromir gave in, and soon, women began arriving with cheerful, grateful faces.

"Marcus, it is so good to have you with us again," one older woman said. "But you must be careful. Some of the guards are worse than others."

Apparently, none of the other shifters had thought to try to slip out at twilight.

The deer was butchered—Jaromir helped—and sections of meat were handed out. Céline, Amelie, and Helga passed out onions and potatoes.

Soon, every campfire in the meadow was aglow with a pot of venison stew hanging on a hook.

The mood of the meadow had changed, and the voices Céline heard were almost happy, as if the guards standing at various points around the perimeter didn't matter. As the Móndyalítko finished eating, they began to migrate toward Céline and Amelie's wagons. They carried violins and small flutes.

"What's happening?" Amelie asked.

"The hour of joy," Helga answered, not seeming particularly joyful. "Time for us to entertain one another."

Céline knew that most Móndyalítko spent a good part of the year earning their living by putting on shows—music, magic tricks, fortune-telling, and such— but she didn't know how they spent their evenings.

By the firelight, a few of the men began to play their violins, and she stood frozen, listening to the beautiful strains floating on the air. Then, without warning, the pace of the music quickened, becoming wild and lively.

The pretty girl Céline noticed earlier, with the silky black hair, jumped from the crowd, nearer to the campfire, and began to dance. Again, Céline couldn't move. She just watched.

The girl's feet danced swiftly, and her hips moved in erotic circles as her skirt whipped about her on the night air.

Some of the Móndyalítko cheered and the music grew faster. Then another girl jumped forward to dance beside the first one.

Céline had spent many evenings entertaining others with stories or songs or telling fortunes, but she'd never seen anything like this. A part of her was filled with joy, but another part felt sorrow at the familiarity of it all, as if she had been part of this countless times before . . . and yet she knew she had not.

Some of the people nearby her parted to let a

newcomer through, and Céline looked over to see Sinead approaching. She was as lovely and dignified as a princess, wearing a long sapphire blue gown.

Reaching out, Céline took Amelie's hand for comfort and support. Her sister grasped her fingers.

Sinead came right to them. Her soft voice could be heard easily over the music.

"Forgive my earlier weakness," she said. "I was overcome. You are my sister's daughters, and I can see her in both your faces."

Sinead was not alone in her emotions.

Though this woman was taller than their mother, Céline was shaken by the resemblance. Until recently, she had never wondered about a possible extended family. Her parents had never mentioned anyone.

"You're not Mist-Torn," Amelie said.

Of all the things she might have said, Céline hadn't expected this.

"No." Sinead smiled. "Only Eleanor and Rayna were Mist-Torn, born three years apart. I came later."

"Who is Rayna?" Amelie asked.

Sinead stared at her. "Did not your mother tell you?"

"She never told us anything. We'd never heard the term Mist-Torn until about a year ago."

At that, Sinead appeared at a loss. "Tell me how she lived. Was she happy?"

This was a more comfortable question, and Céline answered, "I think she was happy. Our father brought her to a small village called Shetâna, and he built her a shop. She planted an herb garden and spent her days working as an apothecary. Father died first, when we were young, and she mourned him. Later, she died of a fever after tending to some villagers who'd fallen ill."

Sinead closed her eyes. "I'm glad she had an herb garden and a shop. That was all she ever wanted." Opening her eyes again, she said sadly, "Eleanor was born first, and Rayna came three years later, two sides of the same coin. Eleanor could see the future and Rayna the past, but our father was proud of having two Mist-Torn seers of such abilities in our family. He worked them both much too hard. Eleanor only wished to gather herbs and practice healing. She grew unhappy. Your father appeared one day, a handsome hunter, and the next thing I knew, my sister was gone."

Céline glanced at Amelie, thinking of the pain she would feel if she ever lost her sister.

Amelie's eyes were on Sinead.

"What happened to Rayna?" she asked.

"She died only a few years ago, of the wasting sickness. She grew tired and could not eat no matter what I cooked for her." Sinead's eyes grew distant. "Our parents were gone by then. Rayna had no children, and I have given birth only to sons. I thought our immediate family line of Mist-Torn was at an end." Reaching out, she grasped Céline's right hand and Amelie's left. "I had no knowledge of you."

This action made Céline slightly uncomfortable. She hoped Sinead did not think they'd come here to rejoin the family.

"We've come here to help learn who is responsible for this curse," she said carefully.

Sinead nodded. "Yes, I thought as much as soon as

I saw Helga. How can I offer my own help? Tonight the people are happy because they've eaten a proper dinner, but suspicion is growing, and I fear soon, accusations and blame might begin to fly."

Céline thought on this and wondered if anyone here had tried to launch her own investigation. "How many seers are there in camp?"

"Until your group arrived, only two," Sinead said, sounding regretful. "Normally, there would be more, but the prince imprisoned us before some of the families had arrived. Upon learning what had happened, most wisely turned back. We've had only two shifters as well, and neither of them can rival Marcus on a hunt. I'm glad he's come."

"What can your seers do?" Céline asked, hoping they might be some help.

"Neither has a power like yours. Agnes Renéive can tell when a person lies or tells the truth, which could be useful, but she is aged and cannot leave her bed. Charis Džugi can place herself in a trance and see an immediate crisis as it plays out, but as you know, that power has its limits, too."

Céline wondered what she meant by that last part.

"No one knows why," Sinead continued, "but fewer and fewer Mist-Torn are being born. That's part of the reason I was so overcome to see two fine young women of Fawe with lavender eyes. It was like a miracle."

Céline could feel Amelie shifting uncomfortably beside her. Neither sister wished to be viewed as a miracle. They were only here to help.

"You can assist us," Amelie said suddenly. "You said

suspicion among the people here is growing worse? Tonight, could you go around and let it be known that if anyone comes to us tomorrow morning, we can read them and clear their name? Of course, only the innocent will come to us, but it will help us whittle down the list and restore some trust . . . and possibly help press the culprit, if there is one here, to try to escape or do something drastic. That strategy has worked for us in the past."

"In the past?" Sinead asked.

Amelie didn't answer the question, and Céline asked Sinead, "Will you do this?"

"Of course."

As the evening wore on, Amelie wouldn't dare admit to anyone, even Céline, but she struggled with the almost overwhelming feeling that she had lived like this before, that she spent countless nights by a campfire to the sound of violins.

The journey here, sitting on the wagon's bench on the open road, had felt so familiar, and now, here in the encampment, everything that came before in her life was beginning to feel like a dream.

This life, here with the Móndyalítko, was the one that felt real.

She was almost sorry when the hour grew late, and people began to drift away, heading for their wagons. Soon, there was no one left by their own small fire except Helga, Céline, Jaromir, Marcus, and herself.

But she was weary, too, and found herself yawning.

Céline saw this. "Time for some sleep."

They had both turned toward the steps of the white

wagon when Helga stopped them. "Where are you going?"

"To bed," Amelie answered.

"Well, a few changes need to be decided," Helga said.

"Such as?"

"We told everyone that you and Jaromir are married. He'll need to sleep with you."

Amelie went still.

Jaromir had been crouched by the fire, but he stood up. "What?"

"Can't have people wondering," Helga explained. "You two can take the white wagon. Céline and I can take the smaller one. Marcus likes to sleep outside."

At the prospect of sleeping alone in a wagon with Jaromir, Amelie tried to choke out an argument and her voice failed.

Thankfully, Céline stepped in. "I don't think either Amelie or the lieutenant would be at ease with that arrangement. I agree that he must sleep in the same wagon, but I suggest that he and Helga simply switch. He can sleep on the bottom bunk of the white wagon, and we will continue to sleep on the top bunk. Helga, you can take the smaller wagon. I trust you won't mind Marcus's company if he chooses to sleep inside on occasion?"

"Nope, I don't mind."

"Then that settles matters," Céline said.

Amelie took a breath of relief.

The mid of night approached, and as Céline lay by her sister on the top bunk, sleep eluded her again. She wasn't remotely troubled by Jaromir sleeping directly below them. In fact, the trade-out with Helga had proven preferable, as Jaromir didn't snore. He slept in silence.

But Céline was growing more and more weary from a lack of sleep, and the soft pull at the back of her mind would not allow her to rest.

For nights now, she'd continued to fight it, to ignore it, to push it away.

Finally, exhausted, she moved from under the blanket and dropped lightly to the floor.

Neither Jaromir nor Amelie stirred. Oliver was asleep on a cloak on the table. He raised his head but made no noise.

Céline couldn't help a wave of guilt. She was the one who'd insisted upon remaining with her sister. But Amelie was sound asleep and so was Jaromir. They would sleep until morning when it was time to rise.

And Céline could no longer continue to fight herself.

Slipping from the wagon, she walked toward the smoldering remains of the campfire. Marcus lay there on one blanket, covered with another, but at her approach, he sat up.

Somewhere, he'd recovered his shirt. She'd seen him wearing it earlier but didn't remember when.

"I'm so tired," she said. "I just want to sleep."

"Have I offered anything else?"

He held open the top blanket, and she went to him, moving inside his arm. They both lay down, covered by the blanket, and he drew her close as he had before, with her back up against his chest.

All the tension and restlessness drained from her body. She felt her eyes closing as she finally began to drift off.

"Thank you," she whispered.

He kissed the top of her head. "Sleep."

That was the last thing she remembered until morning.

CHAPTER SEVEN

Amelie's eyes opened as light filtered in through the windows of the wagon. She felt something warm pressed up against her, but when she looked down, it was only Oliver curled against her side. Céline was nowhere in sight.

Had her sister risen early and gone outside already?

Amelie peeked over the side of the bunk. Below, Jaromir lay on his back with his sinewy arms thrown over his eyes. She couldn't tell if he was still asleep.

Carefully, she maneuvered around Oliver, swung her legs over the side, and landed lightly on the floor. Jaromir took his arm away.

"Céline must have gone out already," Amelie said. "I'll go and see."

He nodded. "I'll be right out and get the fire started."

The strangest thing about this was that it did not seem strange at all to be speaking to him while he was half-undressed and lying in the bed below hers. Just over a week ago, it would have seemed unthinkable.

She slipped out the door and down the steps.

When she turned toward the dead campfire, she stopped.

There, on a blanket on the ground, Marcus and Céline both lay asleep. He had them covered with a second blanket, but her back was pressed against his chest, and his right arm was holding her in while he used his body to keep her warm.

Worse, the sight didn't seem wrong or even odd. Amelie was struck by the sensation that she'd seen this image many times before.

As she walked toward them, Céline opened her eyes and raised her head. The sisters looked at each other for a long moment. Then Marcus stirred and sat up, wrapping the blanket around Céline's shoulders.

After stretching his arms, he stood, nodding once in greeting to Amelie. He behaved as if Amelie seeing him waking up beside Céline was nothing out of the ordinary.

The door to the wagon opened, and Jaromir stepped out.

"We're out of water and firewood," Marcus said to him.

"How are the people here getting more?" Jaromir asked.

Marcus scanned the perimeter of the meadow. "I think from the guards."

"Let's go and see," Jaromir said.

Both men headed off.

The sisters were alone, and Céline pulled the blanket tighter.

"I haven't been able to sleep," she said. "Somehow I knew I could sleep out here . . . like this."

So she was having unexplained sensations, too.

Amelie went over and sat down. Céline wrapped the blanket about them both.

"I feel like we're living different lives," Amelie said, "in a different world, and everything from before was just a dream."

Céline pressed closer. "To me, this all feels like the dream of a life I lived somewhere before, and my real life is waiting for me back in Sèone."

"What's happening to us?"

"I don't know."

They sat together until the door of the blue wagon opened and Helga stumped down the steps.

"At least we know what we'll be doing today," Céline said quietly.

Yes, they did. They would both be reading the Móndyalítko and taking note of who was coming to them and who was not. Well, at least hopefully that was what they would be doing, so long as Sinead had been successful the night before in spreading the word.

Jaromir waited through part of the morning.

Today, it was time for him to begin his own task here, but he wanted to make sure the sisters' attention was completely engaged first. Thankfully, that didn't prove difficult.

Céline took the white wagon, and Amelie took the blue one, and by midmorning, people were coming to see them—to be read.

Once this was well under way, Jaromir went to the front outer side of the blue wagon, crouched, and reached around the wheel to where he had secured a burlap sack and his sheathed long sword on a ledge under the wagon. He'd taken care of stowing these things before starting this journey.

As he withdrew the objects, he found Marcus standing beside him.

"What are you doing?" Marcus asked.

Jaromir remained crouched. "Getting ready. I need to speak to Prince Malcolm on my own. He's the key to stopping all this."

Marcus leaned closer, examining the objects Jaromir had withdrawn. "And you need a sword to speak to him?" He didn't sound challenging, only curious.

"I need to be an officer in service to Prince Anton of the house of Pählen." Jaromir paused. "Do you trust me?"

Marcus appeared to consider the question. "Yes."

"Good. I need your help." Jaromir pointed to the north side of the meadow, toward a heavily forested area. "See that guard?"

"Yes."

"Can you distract him long enough for me to slip into the trees?"

Again, Marcus considered the question. "Yes."

He was an unusual man.

Without another word, Marcus headed off north, walking past the line of wagons until he reached the perimeter. Jaromir came behind him, keeping some distance between them and staying close to the wagons.

He expected Marcus to stop and engage the guard with some kind of question, but instead, Marcus continued moving, as if he intended to walk right into the trees.

Startled, the guard hurried over to cut him off and an argument began. Jaromir heard the word "hunting" and a loud refusal, but he didn't wait to see the outcome. With the guard's back to him, he darted between two trees and found himself in the forest outside the meadow.

After that, he made his way through the trees until a line of them spread to the east. He remained out of sight as long as possible, but within a quarter league of the castle, he knew he'd have to emerge and walk openly up the dried path of the apple orchards toward the front gates.

However, he didn't come out of hiding just yet.

First, he knelt and removed the contents of the burlap sack: his wool shirt, chain armor, tan tabard, and two sealed letters from Anton.

As Prince Malcolm had only been in power for five years, Anton knew little to nothing about him. He could be as dangerous as Anton's brother, Damek, for all they knew. So he'd ordered Jaromir to visit alone and gauge the man's nature before allowing Céline or Amelie anywhere near him.

Quickly, Jaromir stripped off the loose shirt and vest he'd been wearing. He dressed as himself, stood, and strapped on his sword. Finally, he stuffed both letters inside his shirt. He hid the sack and his clothing under some brush and then strode out onto the path.

Out here, he would see the full depths of the devastation of the crops. Everything was dead for leagues. It made him wonder if this curse was reversible. Even if he and the sisters managed to find the culprit, could anything be done to save this province from ruin?

Before coming here, he'd not realized the extent of the damage and the potential harm it could do to both the food supply and the economy of southeast Droevinka.

He approached the castle wall and walked up to the gates. The gates were open, but several guards patrolled from inside the courtyard.

He stopped before entering and found himself facing a guard with a shaved head and a white scar running from the center of his forehead to his right temple. The guard looked back at his tan tabard in some surprise. Visiting soldiers were probably rare.

Jaromir nodded to him. "I bring a message to Prince Malcolm from Prince Anton of the house of Pählen."

The guard seemed lost for an answer. Then he turned his head and called out, "Sir?"

"What is it, Ayden?"

Boot falls sounded, and a stocky middle-aged soldier strode into view from the left side of the gate. He seemed about to further question the scarred guard, Ayden, when he saw Jaromir.

"This man says he has a message for the prince," Ayden explained.

The newcomer sized Jaromir up and then touched his chest. "Captain Renald."

A response seemed in order. "Lieutenant Jaromir."

Renald looked around. "Where's your horse?"

"I left it below, near the meadow."

"If you have a message for my lord, I can take it."

Jaromir shook his head. "Prince Anton instructed me to place it in Prince Malcolm's hands myself, along with a few words not written down."

This was not unusual and the captain would know it. He probably would have been surprised if Jaromir had simply handed over the message.

Renald motioned Jaromir inside, and the two men began walking toward the castle. It was a pleasant construction of light gray stone with two slender towers on the north side and two wider towers on the south end.

Nothing Jaromir had seen so far gave him reason to be overly concerned about Prince Malcolm. The guards were disciplined, but no one appeared to be living in fear of making a mistake. This suggested they were treated fairly and that they respected authority here as opposed to fearing it. That was a good sign.

Renald led Jaromir south to a large set of doors. There, the captain stopped, and a slightly worried expression crossed his face. "At this time of day, I'm not certain . . ." He trailed off. "Wait here."

It was unusual for an officer carrying a message to be told to wait outside, but Jaromir nodded.

The captain was gone for some time, and when the doors opened again, an impressive-looking man emerged. He was tall and broad-shouldered with short silver hair, wearing a leather hauberk. He looked to be about fifty, but his features were even and his face showed few lines.

The captain came out behind him.

Prince Malcolm assessed Jaromir.

"You're one of Prince Anton's men?" he asked immediately.

"Yes, my lord."

"And what message does he send to me? My son is ill and my lady is distraught, so my time is limited."

"The message is to be conveyed in private."

Malcolm looked distracted and harried—and who wouldn't be with his crops failing?—but his eyes narrowed in interest and he pointed to an alcove in the bottom of the nearest tower. "In there."

Jaromir followed him into the alcove, and as soon as they were alone, he reached down the front of his shirt. He had to make a quick decision regarding which letter to produce. One was a false note explaining that Anton would be visiting the area soon to meet with some merchants here, and that he hoped to stay here at the castle. He also requested the pending visit be kept a secret out of security concerns. This first letter made no mention of Malcolm's current situation or of Céline and Amelie's presence.

The second letter was an admission that Anton knew of Malcolm's plight, along with an announcement that he'd sent help. Jaromir was to pass over the first letter if he deemed Malcolm to be dangerous.

In this moment, he had little to go on. This prince had brought about a man's death during an interrogation, but many princes had done that. Now Malcolm seemed more concerned about his wife and son than anything else.

Grasping the second letter, Jaromir held it out.

Malcolm broke the seal, read the contents, and looked up in shock. "You brought two seers?"

"One sees the future and one sees the past. They have helped my lord three times now to solve seemingly unsolvable issues. When he heard of your plight, he sent them to you."

"How did he find out?" Malcolm asked in alarm. "I haven't sent word to anyone yet. I would rather resolve this without it becoming common knowledge."

That was understandable, but in truth, Jaromir still had no idea how Helga had learned of the situation here.

"No one in power knows except for my lord," he assured him, "and as I mentioned, he has two seers in his service. He only wishes to offer you assistance."

Somewhat relieved by this news, Malcolm sighed. "It was one of those Móndyalítko down in the meadow. I've been providing them with water and firewood, but once their food runs out, someone will talk. While I appreciate Anton's offer, I can resolve this."

"What if it wasn't one of the Móndyalítko?" Jaromir asked.

"Who else could it be?"

"Anyone. Anyone with a grudge against you and the ability to either cast or hire someone to cast a curse. Do you have no enemies at all?"

Malcolm stared at Jaromir as if this had never even occurred to him. Perhaps he was none too intelligent.

"Today, the seers are reading anyone in the meadow who will volunteer," Jaromir added, "and there is no telling what they might learn. May I bring them up this evening to give you a report?"

Malcolm appeared intrigued by this idea, but he said, "I don't know how much time I'll have. As I said, my son is ill."

"One of the seers is Prince Anton's personal healer. She's an apothecary, and she would be honored to look at your son."

"Prince Anton's healer?" Malcolm breathed out through his mouth. "All right. Yes, bring them both before dark."

"You'll need to send a few guards down for us. They are both pretending to be part of the group down there to win trust and cooperation. So am I." He motioned to his tabard. "I have other clothing."

If Malcolm found this odd, he didn't show it. "I'll send two men at dusk."

With a nod, Jaromir turned away.

He had set things in motion. If there was someone up here on castle grounds responsible for placing the curse, Céline and Amelie would find out.

Amelie spent the morning sitting at the small stationary table in the blue wagon as one person after another came in to be read. Helga was outside, helping to manage things, and she decided who would come in to see Amelie and who would go and see Céline.

This experience was different from readings Amelie had done in the past. For one, she didn't have to convince anyone that she wasn't a charlatan. She had nothing to prove. No one expected her to put on any kind of "show" or play the mystic seer.

The Móndyalítko people simply came in, bowed to her politely, and then grasped her hand. She'd close her eyes and latch onto their spirits and see images from their past.

By late morning, she'd seen nothing to give her any

indication that anyone was responsible for placing the curse, but she hadn't expected to find something of that nature. These people wanted their names cleared, and they believed in her ability to place them beyond suspicion.

Still, the scenes she did see only served to make her feel more lost in this world. Most of the images were of laughter and travel and lively performances. She was coming to envy such a life of movement and freedom and lack of responsibility beyond survival, companionship, and enjoyment.

However, there were some difficult moments.

She saw one memory of a young woman sitting with a dying father while her brother ran to a nearby town for a healer, and when the brother returned, he wept as he related that no one could come to help a group of vagabonds.

The Móndyalítko faced hardships, too.

Freedom had a price.

She'd never done so many readings in a row and was beginning to grow tired when Helga appeared in the door.

"I'll need a rest soon," Amelie said.

"I thought as much," Helga answered. "Can you do one more? Then you should quit for the day."

"Yes."

The thought of quitting for the day was a relief.

"Now, you get in there and do as your father says!" Helga ordered someone as she moved to stand aside.

A girl of perhaps eighteen came slowly through the open door.

Amelie remembered seeing her upon their arrival,

and of Alondra mentioning her later, and then seeing her dance last night. She was the daughter of Rupert, who had welcomed them, and she was the wife of the man who'd been killed under interrogation.

She seemed to both sway and glide at the same time. She was small and slender with black silky hair hanging down her back. Her skin was pale, and her large eyes were black. Her mouth was heart-shaped and tinted red. She wore a deep burgundy skirt with a white blouse so low-cut it exposed a good deal of the tops of her perfectly rounded breasts. Her ears were adorned with several silver rings.

"You're Lilah?" Amelie asked. "Your husband is the one who was killed. I am sorry."

Not far through the door, Lilah stopped. Her expression was petulant, and she ignored the condolence.

Instead, she looked Amelie up and down, and whatever she saw didn't please her. "I suppose you think you're making yourself stand out, cutting your hair like that," she said. "But most men won't like it. They like long hair."

Amelie couldn't help being startled by the young woman's manner.

"I never gave it much thought at all," Amelie answered. "Why don't you sit down so we can finish this?"

Lilah's petulance only grew. "I don't *need* to be read. My father is the leader of the line of Renéive, and we are above such things as this petty curse. I won't forgive him for forcing me to submit to this like some common Klempá."

Amelie hadn't noticed any bigotry among these

people themselves, but Lilah appeared to view herself as far above some of the other families.

"Do you want to leave?" Amelie asked. At this point, she'd rather the girl did walk out.

With a roll of her eyes and a huffing sound, Lilah sat in the chair across the table and assessed Amelie again. "You do think you're awfully pretty, don't you? Well, I wouldn't try stealing any of the men here or you'll find your high-blown status won't save you. There are other women as pretty as you, and they fight for what's theirs."

Oh, for goodness' sake. Lilah might be a startling beauty, but she was proving to be one of the most unpleasant people Amelie had met in some time.

"Give me your hand," Amelie said, reaching out.

Grasping Lilah's fingers, Amelie closed her eyes and focused on the spark of Lilah's spirit and then upon the source of the curse. She'd become more adept at focusing her powers of late. If Lilah had anything to do with the devastation of the crops, the mists would show those images.

The first jolt hit her almost instantly, and Amelie braced herself.

When the second jolt hit, she experienced a familiar sensation, as if her body was being swept along a tunnel of mist. For a moment she forgot everything but speeding backward through the mists all around her as they swirled in tones of grays and whites.

Her ability worked slightly differently from Céline's in several ways. While Céline could only see someone else's future as an observer, if Amelie wished, she could bond with her target and see the past through his or her eyes. In these cases, the people Amelie read could be just as conscious as she was of the scenes being replayed, and afterward they were aware of exactly what she'd seen. The people Céline read never had any idea what she was seeing. The two sisters had discussed these differences, and Céline guessed they might be because the past was set in stone, and the future could still be changed—that she was just seeing one possible line unless something was done to alter it.

This time, Amelie did not bond with Lilah. She wished to be only an observer. When the reading was over, Lilah would have no idea what images from the past Amelie might have seen.

The mists vanished.

Amelie found herself standing in a lush orchard of trees laden with apple blossoms. The sun shone overhead. But she had no time to notice much of her surroundings because of the shocking sight directly in front of her . . . along with the sounds.

A tall, naked man was pumping away on a slender, dark-haired girl beneath himself: Lilah. The man's pale backside moved up and down rapidly as he breathed loudly in wild abandon.

Lilah alternately moaned and gasped and cried, "Oh, my lord, faster!"

Amelie looked away, beyond embarrassed even though she wasn't truly here and neither of them would be aware of her presence.

Their mutual sounds grew even louder, and then the man gave a great cry. After a moment, Amelie dared to glance back to see him lying beside Lilah while stroking her face. He was a large man with broad shoulders and silver hair.

"My love," he whispered.

"My prince," she murmured. "Malcolm."

Inside the vision, Amelie froze. Lilah was cavorting with Prince Malcolm?

"I would make you my own," he said into her ear. Then he reached for his pants and partially dressed himself.

She ignored her clothes but stood up, letting him see her body in the sunlight.

As lovely as she was in her skirt and low-cut blouse, her naked body was unbelievably beautiful, with flawless skin, small curving hips, and plump, high-set breasts. She stretched her arms over her head as he drank in the sight of her.

"Is that not our plan?" she said sweetly. "For you to make me your own?"

Reaching out, he ran his hand up her leg to her hip. "Yes, my love. But even if I free myself of my wife, you still have a husband."

"That can be solved." She knelt before him, leaning over to brush her lips against his chest. "And you will marry me?"

"Of course I would. With all my heart."

At that point, Amelie looked all around herself. As far as she could see, the land was lush, showing a wealth of colors in greens and white blossoms and ripening strawberries. Though Amelie knew herself to be somewhat naive in the ways of men and women, she was knowledgeable enough to know that whatever Prince

Malcolm said in the moment, it was all pillow talk. Men of his station did not put aside their noble ladies to marry a Móndyalítko mistress.

Lilah began moving her mouth lower, passing it over his stomach . . .

To Amelie's great relief, the image vanished, and she felt herself swept forward on the mists, but only for a moment.

When the mists cleared, she found herself standing near a fir tree at the edge of the meadow.

The landscape had changed, and the orchards and berry fields were dead. The first image she'd seen had taken place before the curse. This one had taken place after.

Lilah pressed her back against the tree and ran her hands down her sides. She was fully dressed now, but her blouse was pulled down even lower than normal, and half her breasts were exposed. She faced a guard in an orange tabard who had joined her just inside the tree line, so they were out of sight of anyone in the encampment.

The guard's head was shaved, and he bore a prominent scar from the center of his forehead to his right temple.

"Why do you put me off?" he asked. "No one will know, and I can tell you want me."

"Ayden," she said softly. "I do want you, but *I'll* know. I'm married. No matter how badly he treats me, I am his wife."

"He mistreats you?"

"Yes, but that isn't the worst." She drew a ragged breath. "The day before the curse . . . I saw him in the apple orchard, chanting, with his arms in the air."

"What?" Ayden's eyes shifted back and forth as he stepped closer. "You saw this yourself."

She nodded. "I swear."

"Then I can have him arrested and questioned."

Reaching out, she touched his chest. "Will you take part in the questioning?"

His body went still. "I can," he whispered.

"All sorts of bad things could happen during a questioning, couldn't they?"

This time, he nodded.

With a promising smile, she turned and slipped away from him, running back into the encampment.

The image vanished and the mists closed in.

Amelie was reeling from what she'd just seen, but she was pulled forward for only a moment again when the mists cleared and she found herself in a well-furnished room with stone walls.

To her chagrin, she was once again forced to endure the sight of Prince Malcolm on top of Lilah, as they both gasped and grunted away.

This time, they were on a bed.

Thankfully, Amelie had arrived at the very end of the amorous portion of the encounter, and after a loud cry from Malcolm, he fell to one side, holding her with his right arm.

"My love," he whispered as he'd done in the previous image.

"I must say," she giggled. "It's quite a pleasure to be arrested by you. I do hope you arrest me again soon."

Amelie felt slightly sick to her stomach as she remembered Alondra relating that Lilah had been taken up to the castle twice for questioning and returned unharmed both times.

"You are a most pleasing prisoner," he returned, smiling. Then his face grew more serious. "I am sorry about your husband. I only wanted to know the truth. I would never have killed him. My man, Ayden, was overzealous. He should not have put on that gauntlet. Now I don't even know if we've caught the true culprit."

"I doubt it was Gallius who cast the curse," Lilah said. "Even if he was involved somehow, he wasn't Móndyalítko."

"He wasn't?"

"No, he was a merchant's son who fell in love with me. Where would he learn such a powerful spell? But you'll catch whoever is responsible. I know you will, and the land will be profitable once more. You'll not lose your fortune."

He kissed her mouth. "So you are not too distraught about Gallius's death?"

"He was cruel, and my father insisted on the marriage. You did me a service, and now I am free to love you."

His guilt appeared to be assuaged. "A service? I saved you?"

"Yes," she murmured. "You saved me. Touch me again. I love to feel your hands on my skin."

The scene vanished.

Amelie hoped the images would end after this one. Her mind was racing. But when the mists cleared, she found herself standing near the front end of a Renéive wagon in the encampment.

Lilah came around one side, and Ayden suddenly appeared from the trees.

They were alone, and he caught her arm.

"What do you think you're playing at?" he demanded. "You haven't come to see me once."

"And why would I come to see you?" she returned.

Astonished, he let go of her. "You asked me to kill your husband, and I did so we could be together. What is the matter with you?"

"I never did any such thing, and if you know what's good for you, you'll never speak of it again." She tilted her head. "I'm with Prince Malcolm now, and he's in love with me, so you should watch your step."

Ayden's face went nearly as pale as his scar. "You're with Prince . . ." He stepped away, and his eyes narrowed. "And what if I tell him it was you who first brought Gallius to my attention?"

She looked him up and down scornfully. "What did you tell him in the first place? That it was you who spotted Gallius in the orchard with his arms in the air? Is that why the prince let you conduct the interrogation? How do you think he'll react when you change your story? If you breathe a word of my name, I'll say you're lying. I'll tell him you've been bothering me, putting your hands on me. I might even let on that you killed Gallius on purpose because you've lost your head over me. Who do you think he'll believe?"

Ayden's breaths quickened as he listened.

"You won't say a word," she whispered slowly. "Because if you do, you'll be the one who suffers and not me. Now get out of my way."

The mists closed in.

Amelie felt herself being rushed forward, and as the mists cleared again, she was sitting at the table in the blue wagon with Lilah watching her carefully.

"What did you see?"

For an instant, Amelie was speechless. Normally, when anything of importance was revealed, she or Céline kept it a secret until they could discuss it together regarding what it might mean or how it might be used.

But this . . . she had seen so much.

"Nothing," she finally managed.

Lilah sat back in her chair. "Do you think me a fool? I can see your face, and it doesn't look like you saw nothing." She leaned forward again. "But I know you can swear that I had nothing to do with cursing the crops, because I didn't. And you'd be wise to keep anything else you saw to yourself."

Standing abruptly, she walked out of the wagon.

Céline's morning proved somewhat frustrating.

While she certainly didn't expect to see a revealing future vision of a kettle witch casting a spell over a bubbling cauldron, she *did* hope to glean something of use.

One by one, Helga sent people in to be read, and Céline welcomed each one warmly before conducting a reading. But most of the images she saw were of the almost immediate future: women cooking dinner for what appeared to be this evening's meal or men playing violins by a fire.

She saw nothing to indicate that anyone here was involved in whoever had cursed the crops or even a hint that events would soon change for either the better or the worse.

It was as if the mists wished to show her nothing but a state of equilibrium. What did this mean? Was she being told to take action? To do something herself? She longed for guidance and hoped she would see something more useful.

The mists had never let the sisters down yet.

There was a reason for everything they saw or did not see.

As the morning went on, she felt herself beginning to grow weary. She'd never read so many people one after the other like this.

As she finished with a man who'd shown her images of nothing more than attempting to get more water from the guards—for his horses—that afternoon, she sat back in her chair, feeling the edges of exhaustion.

He looked at her calmly.

"Am I cleared?" he asked.

"Yes, I saw nothing of importance. You were trying to get more water for your horses."

He shook his head. "This is a bad business, and some of the men are ready to overpower the guards."

For the first time, Céline really looked at him. He was large with salt-and-pepper hair and a mustache. She realized he was the one who so often escorted her aunt Sinead. Was he Sinead's husband?

"Could they?" Céline asked.

"Of course. We have men and weapons, and with Marcus here, we have three shifters now. The prince posts twelve guards at most. It would be simple."

Céline remembered Marcus's friend Leif mentioning something like this, too. "Why haven't you?"

"Because the prince would probably send more soldiers after us. They would catch us, and things would escalate. No matter the outcome, our summers here would end. None of us wants that. We would rather resolve this. I want to know who is responsible, even if it's one of us."

Unlike Leif, this man didn't appear convinced of the innocence of all the Móndyalítko.

"Do you have any idea who it might be?" she asked.

"No, and that's what troubles me."

Perhaps he'd introduced himself upon entering, and perhaps not. Céline had met so many people this morning she couldn't remember. This man had a quiet power about him—and possibly a good deal of common sense. "I'm sorry," she said. "What is your name?"

He smiled slightly. "Terrell Fawe. I am your uncle by marriage. You've yet to meet your cousins, who are an unruly pack of young men."

"You are Sinead's husband? Oh, again, I am sorry. It's been rather a long morning."

"I can see that. Do not apologize."

She liked him. She liked her aunt. She wondered about the pack of unruly cousins. Unfortunately, this budding affection and curiosity did not make things easier. She had no intention of remaining here once this crisis was over.

He stood. "Take a rest. Even a Mist-Torn can't go on all day."

After he left, she rubbed her temples, thinking perhaps it might be a good time to take a rest.

Helga appeared in the open doorway. "I thought

I'd have you clear Alondra, and then you should stop. You can start again tomorrow."

As Céline's head was beginning to ache, she didn't argue. "Yes, do bring Alondra, and afterward, I think I will stop."

"I'll have to go find her."

The short break was welcome, and Céline stood to stretch her back. She faced the bunks and saw Oliver asleep on the top bunk. Except for "doing his business," he'd hardly gone outside since their arrival, and she'd been bringing his food and water in here. Perhaps the unfamiliar camp was too much for him.

Helga had been gone only a few moments when a shadow filled the interior of the wagon. Oliver awoke and jumped to his feet, hissing.

Céline whirled toward the doorway.

A large form, a man, stood there, blocking out much of the light. He entered and she recognized him from her arrival yesterday. He was tall and muscular and moved with a grace similar to Marcus's. His hair was dark and cut short. His feet were bare. He wore loose pants and a loose shirt.

"I came to be read," he said softly.

Something about him made Céline nervous, and she wondered how long Helga would be.

Oliver's hissing grew louder.

"Stop," she said to the cat. "It's all right."

His hissing dropped to a low snarl.

Céline drew herself up. "I had planned to read Alondra next and then stop for the day."

"Alondra can wait. I want you to clear me. I am Jago Taragoš."

Something about the way he spoke suggested his name should mean something to her and that he was accustomed to getting his way. But if he wanted only to be cleared, she thought this might be the fastest way to get him back out of the wagon.

"Come and sit, then," she said, taking her chair again.

He approached and sank down, watching her. His eyes moved over her face and hair. "I've never seen a young seer from the line of Fawe, but I've heard stories. They weren't wrong."

She had no idea what he meant and wasn't about to ask. "Give me your hand."

"Nothing would please me more."

He didn't sound remotely flirtatious. His expression was dead serious. After glancing once more toward the door for Helga, Céline reached out and took his hand.

Closing her eyes, she focused on his spark of spirit and on whoever had placed the curse. The first jolt hit quickly, and she braced herself for the second. The mists closed in, swirling in tones of gray and white, and she felt herself rushed forward in time.

The journey was brief.

When she opened her eyes, the mists cleared and she found herself inside a well-furnished wagon. The curtains were made from amber silk, and the table was of polished cherry wood. Small crystals hung from the ceiling over the beds.

Sunlight streamed in through the windows.

Jago was there with a smaller, older man.

The other man was dressed in a loose silk shirt

tucked into black pants, and his high boots looked expensive. Céline had seen him about the camp but had not spoken to him. His gray hair and thin mustache were both carefully groomed.

"I'm telling you, Father, it is time to leave!" Jago said. "Marcus will do as he's told if the leaders agree. So will Leif. These guards would be nothing to us."

"The leaders won't agree," his father answered, "certainly not Sinead or Rupert, and no one will resort to violence without their consent."

"And what of you?" Jago challenged. "Have you become so tame?"

The intended insult had no effect. "I've no wish to destroy our welcome here."

Jago turned away angrily. "But you should! We spend our summer picking apples and berries. Don't you feel shame? It's time to leave these tame summers in the past and live like Móndyalítko."

His father moved closer to him, jerking him back by one arm and looking into his face. "You will do nothing without my instructions. Do you understand? I have saved you time and time again from your own excesses, but this is different. There is too much at stake."

Jago opened his mouth and then closed it again. He argued no more.

The mists closed in.

When they vanished, Céline was back at the table looking at Jago.

"What did you see?" he asked.

"Nothing that would implicate you," she said, although she wasn't entirely certain about that. It seemed he hated summers in this Yegor meadow and was willing to go to some lengths to make certain the Móndyalítko would never be welcome here again.

"What did you see?" he repeated.

She wanted him to leave. "I saw you arguing with your father. You wanted to use Marcus and Leif and some of the other men to attack the guards and leave the meadow."

Surprise flickered across his impassive features. He leaned forward with interest. "What did he say?"

"He said no."

Céline stood up. "But nothing in the vision suggests you had anything to do with placing this curse. You are cleared."

Her words and actions were a dismissal.

He stood as well but made no move to leave. "Are you with Marcus?"

"I am here with Marcus, Helga, my sister, and her husband."

"You know what I mean."

"Could you please leave so I can prepare to read Alondra?"

He stood between her and the door. "I am not married at present, and the star of Fawe is fading. You could join the Taragoš, join with me."

Was he seriously proposing marriage? He'd only introduced himself a short while ago. Céline decided the best way to handle this was to continue attempting to end the discussion. "Please allow me to prepare for the next reading."

His expression darkened as if she'd insulted him. "That is your answer? I offer you a connection to

Taragoš and *that* is your response? Do all Fawe women have such poor manners?"

This was something she'd heard before. It was hardly uncommon for a man to describe a woman as "poor mannered" if she rejected his proposition.

"Please go."

He didn't move, but the skin over his cheekbones drew back, and his face began to change. Short black hairs appeared to sprout from his skin. His eyes turned yellow and his ears grew smaller and slightly pointed like those of a cat.

Jago was the third shifter.

With a sharp inhale, Céline stepped backward just as Oliver launched off the top bunk, landing on the table. As opposed to hissing, he let out what sounded like a mewling scream that must have carried a good distance.

With his right paw, he slashed at the air in front of Jago and continued to scream.

"Get away from her!" someone shouted.

Céline looked past Jago to see Helga in the doorway, brandishing a large knife.

"You get out of this wagon and away from her."

Oliver stopped his screaming.

Jago's face shifted back to that of a man, but when he looked at Helga, hatred shone from his eyes. "Or you'll what?"

"I'll call out for a wolf."

"You think a wolf frightens me?"

Without hesitation, Helga turned her head. "Marcus!"

Apparently, Jago was more concerned about

Marcus than he cared to admit, because he strode for the door.

Helga stood aside and let him pass.

Then she ran inside and grabbed one of Céline's hands, inspecting her manically. "Are you all right? Did he hurt you?"

"Helga, I'm fine. He didn't hurt me."

But something about him had left Céline very unsettled.

Marcus ran up the steps and stopped in the doorway. "What's happened?"

"Nothing," Céline answered quickly. "Just a possible . . . nothing."

He frowned when he saw the knife in Helga's hand.

Helga's body was shaking.

Jaromir made his way back through the forest and down the encampment. He stayed hidden in the trees until reaching the north side of the meadow. Then he changed his clothes and found a space beneath the root of a fir tree to hide his armor, tabard, and sword.

After making a mental note of the exact location, he picked up a few small branches on the ground, went to the tree line, and began making noise.

A guard down the perimeter heard him and came jogging over. "What are you doing?"

It was the same guard who'd welcomed them yesterday upon their arrival.

Jaromir did his best to appear puzzled by the question. He held up the branches. "I saw these and thought to gather them."

"You aren't supposed to leave the meadow."

"I haven't."

The man looked around. "Where did you come from?"

Pointing to the nearest wagon, Jaromir said, "From over there."

Frowning, the guard sighed. "I didn't see you or I'd have warned you off. Next time, ask me and I'll fetch the branches for you. My lord has ordered no one should leave the perimeter of the meadow."

Jaromir couldn't help noting the regret in the man's voice. He didn't care for this assignment.

"All right, I will," Jaromir said, and he walked back into the meadow carrying the branches.

Upon hearing howling and shouting, Amelie ran from the blue wagon, jumped over the steps, and hit the ground.

Alondra stood on the ground near the white wagon, and Marcus stood in the doorway. Amelie ran to him, bounding up the steps.

"What's wrong?" she asked.

He shook his head, and she pushed past him. Inside, she found Helga holding a knife in one hand and Céline in the other. Oliver was on the table with his fur standing up and his tail the size of a small bush.

Helga's body was trembling, but no one appeared to be hurt.

"What in the world has happened?" Amelie demanded.

"Nothing," Céline answered, helping Helga to sit on

the lower bunk. To Amelie's surprise, Helga let her. "I had a visit from the third shifter here in camp, Jago Taragoš. It seems he is some sort of large cat. Oliver didn't care for him and sounded the alarm."

"Oh." Amelie had a feeling there was more to the story than this, but Helga was white as a sheet, and so it seemed best to follow Céline's lead by trying to play the situation down. Looking around, she asked, "Where's Jaromir?"

"I haven't seen him," Céline answered. "Helga, can I get you some tea?"

"No. I don't want tea."

Amelie turned to Marcus, who still stood there helplessly. "Where's Jaromir?" she repeated.

To her surprise, Marcus blushed as if the question were a difficult one. "I . . . I will go and look for him."

He vanished.

Men.

Alondra entered, wringing her hands, and she went back to sit with Helga. "Not to worry. Jago is gone."

"Amelie, would you close the door?" Céline asked tightly. Once the door was closed, she turned back toward the bunks. "Helga, please be good enough to tell us whatever there is between you and Jago. If there is some danger that we don't know about, you cannot keep it to yourself."

Helga wouldn't answer, and Alondra shook her head once at Céline. When Helga refused to speak, nothing would move her.

With a sigh, Céline looked back to Amelie. "Did you see anything useful in your readings?"

"As a matter of fact, I did."

Going to the table, Amelie sat down and began to tell the other three women what she'd seen of Lilah and Prince Malcolm . . . and the guard Ayden.

Even Helga began to listen with growing interest as Amelie recounted one scene after the next.

At one point, Alondra gasped. "Lilah said Gallius mistreated her?"

"Yes," Amelie confirmed. "Is it not true?"

"Goodness no. If anything, she mistreated him. He was a wealthy wool merchant's son who fell for her so hard he married her against his father's will. I think she believed the father would forgive them, but Gallius was cast from the family and cut off from his allowance or inheritance. Rupert took him into the family, but I think Lilah was disappointed by how it all turned out. She places a good deal of stock in her beauty."

"You think?" Amelie asked sarcastically.

"She seemed to believe she'd married into money."

So Lilah had lied to both Malcolm and Ayden about Gallius being cruel.

"But to get her own husband killed?" Céline asked, aghast. "You think her capable of that?"

"It's what I saw," Amelie said. "Or at least she provided a reason for his arrest and put the idea to kill him in Ayden's mind."

"So those two times she was arrested," Alondra asked, "she was really . . ."

"Up in the castle in bed with Prince Malcolm," Amelie finished.

All four women were silent for a while, and then Céline asked, "Can anyone see how this might help us?"

"Not yet," Amelie answered, "but I saw all of that for a reason. Céline, did you see anything of use?"

"Not much." She glanced over at Helga in concern. "I did see what I believe to be a near-future image of Jago arguing with his father. Jago is ready to attack the guards and escape. His father said no, and he said it quite adamantly. He also suggested that the other leaders would never sanction such action."

"Silvanas has always been cautious," Alondra put in.

"He looks out for himself," Helga added bitterly.

"So Silvanas is the leader of the Taragoš family? And Rupert leads the Renéive?" Céline asked. She appeared to grow thoughtful. "But the line of Fawe is led by Sinead, and the Marentõrs also pass leadership down the female line. Why are some families led by men and others by women?"

"Tradition," Helga answered, seeming a bit more like herself now. "The families go back for hundreds of years, and the Móndyalítko follow tradition."

The group fell silent again, and then Helga asked, "So, are we going to say anything about that little vixen getting her husband killed and bedding Prince Malcolm?"

"Not yet," Céline answered quickly. "We don't know how it's connected to the curse, and we may need to use such information against her or Prince Malcolm later."

The door to the wagon opened, and Jaromir leaned inside.

"Where have you been?" Amelie asked.

"Up at the castle," he answered as if he were discussing the weather.

She stood up. "You went to the castle without telling us? How . . . how did you get out of the meadow?"

He waved the question off as if it were unimportant. "I slipped out into the trees and then walked up to the gates. But I delivered a letter from Prince Anton, offering Malcolm your services, and he wants to speak to you both. He's sending an escort before dusk."

"What?" Céline asked. "You never said anything about bringing a letter from Anton. Why would the guards even let you inside the courtyard?"

"I looked like myself, wearing my armor, tabard, and sword. I hid them under a wagon and brought them along." He seemed impatient at the questions. "None of this matters. Just be ready to go at dusk."

"Why didn't you tell us any of this before?" Céline asked.

"Prince Anton's orders. He wanted me to make certain Malcolm wasn't a danger first."

As Amelie stood staring at Jaromir, she felt heat rising into her face. He'd come here with his own agenda—dictated by Anton—and hadn't breathed a word. He'd brought a letter, his armor, and his sword hidden somewhere. He'd slipped away today without telling anyone.

On the journey here, she'd spent a week, sitting beside him on a wagon bench chatting about the route and the scenery, thinking him a partner in this venture, and all that time, he'd kept her in the dark about his own plans of what he would do once he got here.

She couldn't speak.

She thought he'd finally begun to view her as an equal in these ventures, not merely as a tool to be used in the service of Prince Anton.

"Bring your medicines when we go up," he said to Céline. "Malcolm's son is ill."

With that, he pulled the door closed and disappeared from sight.

CHAPTER EIGHT

For Céline, the afternoon passed slowly.

Amelie wasn't speaking to Jaromir, and to make matters worse, he didn't appear to notice. Something was troubling Marcus as well, and he kept finding things to do such as brush the horses or maintenance on the wagons.

As he was needlessly cleaning one of the wheels, Céline crouched down beside him.

"What's wrong?" she asked.

He wouldn't look at her. "I helped your lieutenant slip out of camp today . . . as his distraction. I didn't quite realize the situation."

Was that all that was bothering him? He'd helped Jaromir slip away?

"It's all right," she said. "He's very good at getting people to do what he wants."

"But now he says that you are all going to be taken up to the castle tonight, and I'm not to go. I don't like it. Does he think he can protect you alone?"

"Oh." She paused. "Please don't worry. He wouldn't be taking us if he thought there was any danger."

"But he doesn't know. How long was he up there today? Less than an hour?"

She had no words of comfort to offer him, and she had no idea how to quell Amelie's anger, but in truth, she was greatly relieved that Jaromir had gained them entrance to the noble family living in that castle.

The roots of any real secrets or any grudges would most likely be found up there.

Shortly before dusk, she had just gathered her box of medicinal supplies and walked down the steps of the white wagon when three Yegor guards rode in on horses.

Amelie and Jaromir were ready and waiting outside.

The lead guard called out, "Where is the healer?"

Céline stepped forward. "Here. My sister and her husband are to accompany me."

He frowned at the word "husband" and glanced at Jaromir but said nothing.

Their aunt Sinead, however, saw all of this and came hurrying over in alarm. "What is this about?" she demanded of the guard.

Quickly, Céline moved to her. "I think one of the guards down here told the prince about a newly arrived healer. Prince Malcolm's son is ill, and I've been called up. It would be best if Amelie and Jaromir accompanied me."

Sinead listened to this and calmed somewhat. "Would you like me to come, too?"

Céline smiled. "No, thank you. We'll be fine." She couldn't help being touched by her aunt's concern.

Turning away, she started for the castle.

The guards remained on horseback but kept their

mounts at a slow pace so Céline, Amelie, and Jaromir could walk.

The journey was short, and they passed through the open gates and into the courtyard. A middle-aged guard approached and dismissed the horsemen.

"Captain Renald," Jaromir greeted him. "These are Prince Anton's seers."

The man blinked several times. "Where is your uniform?"

"Hidden. In the encampment, we're all passing ourselves off as Móndyalítko. Has Prince Malcolm told you who we are?"

"Yes."

"We needed to earn trust in order to conduct a quiet investigation."

"Céline and I *are* half Móndyalítko," Amelie bit off, correcting Jaromir.

He ignored the comment, and so did the captain.

"This way," Renald said.

He led them through the main doors of the castle. Inside, there were passages running left, right, and straight ahead. He took them down the center passage, which emptied into a large hall.

Three people stood before a dead hearth. It was still too warm to require a fire.

Céline rapidly assessed all three people as they turned.

The first was a tall man with wide shoulders wearing a leather hauberk. He was about fifty, with silver hair and a handsome face. This must be Prince Malcolm.

Beside him stood an elegant woman of perhaps thirty. She was slender with white-blond hair that hung loose, held back at her forehead by a simple sliver tiara. Her eyes were vivid blue and her skin ivory. Her face was a tad narrow and her nose perhaps a bit long, but she stood with a straight, dignified quality that reminded Céline of Sinead. Her velvet gown was emerald green and cut to show her narrow waist.

Her expression was unreadable.

The hall's third occupant was a young woman of about eighteen. Dressed in red silk, she could not have been more different from the woman in the center. This younger woman was short and curvy. Her chestnut hair was piled on her head to add a bit of height. She had a face that most likely showed every emotion that passed through her head.

As Céline, Amelie, and Jaromir entered the hall, she was staring at them in open curiosity until her gaze fell upon Amelie. Then she frowned and glanced at the prince as if concerned.

Prince Malcolm stepped forward.

Before he could speak, Jaromir said, "My lord, may I present Céline and Amelie Fawe, seers to Prince Anton?"

Malcolm's gaze brushed over Céline and stopped on Amelie. After a moment, he seemed to remember himself and nodded. Half turning, he said, "This is my wife, the Lady Anna, and my daughter, Jenelle, from my first marriage."

Céline filed that information away. It seemed he'd been widowed and then remarried someone at least twenty years younger than himself.

Lady Anna moved up to join her husband. Her feet seemed to glide beneath her gown. As with the captain who'd first greeted them, beneath her calm veneer she showed a flash of alarm at the sight of the three people in her hall dressed as Móndyalítko.

"May I know which one of you is Prince Anton's physician?" she asked.

Her voice was carefully modulated, but Céline heard the underlying confusion.

Instinctively, Céline pitched her own voice to sound exactly like that of a lady of Anton's court, and she answered. "That would be me, my lady. Please forgive our attire. My sister and I have Móndyalítko blood on our mother's side, and Prince Anton felt it might be wise for us to play upon this. He advised us to join the encampment in an attempt to win trust and coopera-tion." With a smile, she gestured toward Jaromir. "I'm still not accustomed to seeing the lieutenant without his armor and sword. It's all been rather disconcerting."

None of this was precisely true, but it was some-thing Lady Anna would understand.

Upon hearing Céline's tone, diction, and explana-tion, Lady Anna smiled in return. "Oh, I do see. I'm sure this has been difficult for you, and I thank you for coming." The smile reached her eyes, and her voice was warm. Then she said, "I've only just left my son a few moments ago so that I could come and meet you. Might we go to him now?"

"Yes. I hope I can offer some help."

Lady Anna looked to Amelie and Jaromir. "Too many visitors overwhelm him. Please wait here with my lord." She then turned to Jenelle. "Do you wish to come, my dear?"

Jenelle's eyes shifted once again between Amelie

and Prince Malcolm. "No, I think I'll stay. You can give me a report when you return."

Céline wondered what Jenelle might be thinking, but she also heard a clear connection between the two women. Anna might be her stepmother, but they appeared to get on well.

Lady Anna led the way, and Céline fell into step beside her. They walked back down the center passage and turned right. From there, they made their way to the base of a tower.

As they began to climb, Céline asked, "Can you tell me what ails your son?"

"It is his breathing, and it has troubled him all his life. My brother had the same ailment as a child and grew out of it. I hope the same for Lysander."

Lysander.

Céline liked the name. "Is he worse at some times than others?"

"Yes, summers are the worst when the air turns hot, but this year he fell so ill when . . ."

"When the curse began?"

Anna nodded. "I'm not sure what the connection could be unless it is the quality of the air. It has been so dusty." She paused and stopped Céline. "Over the years, my husband has allowed several physicians to see Lysander, and some of the experiences have been troubling. One man actually bled him before I realized what was happening and put a stop to it. I'll not have any of that nonsense near my son."

Céline's opinion of Anna was rising by the moment. "I don't believe in any of that nonsense, either, and I will do nothing without your permission."

"Very well, then."

They emerged on the second floor and stopped at the third door on the right. Anna opened it and walked in first.

"I've brought someone to see you," she said.

Following her, Céline found herself standing in a child's bedroom. There was a toy barn and horses and little soldiers in one corner. The only occupant Céline saw at first was a maid in a white apron who bowed to Anna.

"How has he been, Jane?" Anna asked.

"The same, my lady."

Céline then saw a small white-blond boy in a large bed. He looked to be about eight years old. He was pale with dark circles under his eyes. When he attempted to breathe, he drew the air in through his mouth instead of his nose, and he made a wheezing sound. Céline had seen this before.

Quickly, she went to the maid. "Jane, could you please send to the kitchens for a teapot of boiling water and a large bowl?"

Jane looked to her mistress.

After a moment, Anna nodded and Jane left the room.

Céline went over to Lysander, put her box on the floor, and sat on the bed. He watched her with some trepidation, and she had a feeling that his mother had not been exaggerating about his experiences with physicians. Perhaps he knew a healer of some kind when he saw one.

"Hello, Lysander," she said. "I am Céline, and I promise not to do anything you won't like. I need to listen to your chest with my ear. May I do that?"

Still watching her cautiously, he nodded.

Leaning down, Céline put her ear to his chest. "Try to breathe for me."

Though the wheeze was audible, she heard nothing rattle. He was not congested, and the wheeze was due to the effort it took him to draw breath. His air pipes were constricted.

Sitting up, she said, "Could you open your mouth?"

He did, and she could see his throat was raw and sore from the sheer effort of breathing.

"We're only going to do two things today," she said. "I know you will like the first. The second won't be fun, but I promise it won't hurt at all."

She could see him relaxing. She spoke the truth, and he was beginning to trust her.

"What is the first?" he asked.

"I want you to drink a little of a syrup that I make."

Moving to the floor, she opened her box and took out a bottle. Holding it for Lady Anna to see, she said, "This is nothing but water steeped and then resteeped in a large jar packed with rose petals. Afterward, I mix the water with honey, and it creates a soothing elixir for the throat."

Most children liked the taste of this, and it made them feel better if they had a cough or sore throat.

"Can you help him to sit up?" she asked.

Anna came over to help, moving the pillows and helping her son while Céline took a wooden spoon from the box.

Lysander was an agreeable boy, and he drank down three spoonfuls as she offered them.

"I'll leave this with you," Céline said to Anna. "If his throat becomes sore, give him several spoonfuls."

The door opened and Jane came back in carrying a heavy teapot and a bowl.

"Set the bowl on that table," Céline instructed. Looking around, she picked up a spare blanket at the end of the bed. "Lysander, do you think you could sit in your chair for a short while?"

"Why?" he asked, taking a wheezing breath.

"I'm going to have you sit and lean over that bowl. Then I'm going to pour water into the bowl and settle this blanket over your head. Steam will come off the water, and you'll breathe it in."

"That's all?" he asked.

"That's all."

"You believe that will help?" Lady Anna asked.

"I do."

Anna and Jane both helped Lysander out of bed and to the chair. Céline poured the hot water into the bowl and then put the blanket over the boy, covering the bowl and trapping as much of the steam as she could.

"Breathe as deeply as you can," she said.

She could hear him trying, and after a few moments, the wheezing lessened. A short while later, it stopped, and she could hear him breathing without much labor.

Lady Anna heard this, too, and her blue eyes widened.

Céline kept the blanket over Lysander until the water ceased to give off steam, and then she lifted it. He was breathing normally through his nose without laboring through his mouth. His face had more color.

Lady Anna helped him back to bed. "Do you feel better?"

"Yes, Mama."

She looked to Céline. "Steam?"

"His ailment is not uncommon, especially in children. You mentioned your brother had this and outgrew it? Dry air or sometimes overexertion causes difficulties with their air pipes. Steam will usually help relax their pipes and allow them to breathe more easily."

Lysander laid his head on the pillow and seemed exhausted. Hopefully, he could sleep now.

Lady Anna came to Céline. "I don't know what to say. You would not believe some of the things I've been told to try."

Unfortunately, Céline would.

"I haven't healed him," she said, "only given him some relief."

"Yes, but you've given us something that works when he becomes this ill."

Céline was almost embarrassed. The lady behaved as if she'd performed a miracle.

It was time to use the goodwill she'd gained.

"If Lysander is able to sleep, perhaps we should go back to the hall and discuss . . . the other matter."

With a final glance at her son, Anna answered, "Yes."

As Céline walked back into the hall with Lady Anna, she noted the relief on Jaromir's face at the sight of her.

Malcolm and Jenelle walked to Anna, and the three began conferring in low voices.

Céline used to the opportunity to go to Jaromir and Amelie by the hearth. "Is everything all right?"

"I've been attempting to make small talk until your return," Jaromir answered tightly, glaring at Amelie. "And I've had no help."

Ugh.

Amelie was still angry with Jaromir, but Céline hadn't expected her to leave him high and dry in this situation.

Before any of them could speak again, Malcolm strode over. "My lady says you have been of great assistance, and that Lysander is sleeping easily."

"I didn't do much," Céline answered. "But sometimes simple things work best."

"Indeed." He studied her face more closely. "We decided to wait to speak of other matters until you and my lady returned. Could you now tell us more of this business of you as Anton's seers? What exactly does that mean?"

Céline knew to make this sound as matter-of-fact as possible, and again, to invoke Anton's name. "Amelie can touch people and see images of their past. I see images of their future. Prince Anton has engaged us three times to find the cause of various issues for his family. In all three cases, we succeeded. That is why he sent us to you."

"And how exactly did he learn of my . . . issue, as you so politely put it? I'm facing complete ruin, and I'd like to know how word spread to the southwest region."

This was an awkward question, and she decided to fall back on partial honesty. "I am not entirely certain, my lord. Prince Anton has a Móndyalítko woman, from the line of Ayres, employed at Castle Sèone. I believe someone sent her word."

While this answer didn't appear to satisfy him entirely, his concern was probably a matter of keeping his current plight as private as possible until it could be solved—if it could be solved. If a message was sent to a Móndyalítko woman in Prince Anton's employment, from Malcolm's perspective, that might be the only leak.

"And in your time in the encampment, what have you learned so far?" he asked.

Lady Anna and Jenelle came closer to listen. Céline was not certain what to make of Jenelle. She was quiet, but she also seemed poignantly aware of everything happening in this hall.

Turning her attention to Malcolm's question, Céline braced herself. She was about to launch into a gamble she'd been considering all afternoon. "We've learned nothing in regards to who is responsible for cursing the crops. Today, our purpose was mainly to clear the names of those people who wished to be pronounced as innocent. But . . ."

She let the word hang in the air.

"But what?" Malcolm pressed.

"One thing became clearer and clearer to both Amelie and me as the morning passed. The Móndyalítko we've read all wish to resolve this crisis as badly as you do. They spend the better part of the year on the road doing performances for money. They've no wish to lose their summer haven. Why do you think they have not attacked your guards and left the meadow?"

"Attacked my guards?"

"There are a hundred people down there. They

have strong men and weapons. You have twelve guards posted at a time."

"If they tried that, I'd send soldiers after them."

"And they know it, and the situation would escalate, and even if they managed to overcome the soldiers, they'll have made an enemy of you. That's the last thing the leaders of the families want. They want the crops growing and healthy again. They want the trust between you and themselves reestablished."

Malcolm's brow wrinkled. "What is it you're suggesting?"

"Join forces with them. Free them. Call off your men. Let the Móndyalítko fish in the stream and fetch their own water. Let them collect firewood. Let them hunt in the forested areas and take their horses farther afar to graze."

"What? No. They'd pull out by morning, and then I'd never know who placed the curse or how to reverse it."

"They would not, not if you go down and speak to the leaders yourself. Ask for their help. Ask that no one leave until this is resolved. They will work with you. They will watch their own and see who might try to escape. If you ask the leaders for their help and show trust in them, you will solve this much faster than treating them all as suspect criminals."

His eyes were locked on her face, and she could see his hope begin to rise. Then he glanced away. "Things may have already gone too far. There was an incident. I'm sure you've been told. I had a man questioned, and he was killed. I didn't intend for it to happen, but it did. You think those people will be able to get past a death?"

Céline hated herself for sounding as if she discounted Gallius's life, but there were many other lives at stake. "I do. He wasn't Móndyalítko. He'd only married in to the line of Renéive last year. These people are pragmatic, and as I told you, they want to resolve this."

"Even if one of them placed the curse? And who else could it possibly be?"

It could be anyone, she thought, but didn't say it.

"Yes. Even if it proves to be one of them," she answered. "Free them and ask the leaders for their help. I promise you will receive it."

Malcolm looked to his wife. "Anna, what do you think?"

"I think this is very good counsel," she answered.

Slowly, he nodded to Céline. "All right. I'll go back down with you tonight."

CHAPTER NINE

Shortly after arriving back at the encampment, Jaromir could still hardly believe what Céline had accomplished. The scene taking place down here in the meadow also gave him new insights into Malcolm.

The man was gifted with charm.

He called everyone—including his own guards—to the largest campfire in the center of the wagons, and he announced that he'd been wrong to imprison the Móndyalítko for the past twelve days and that all guards would be pulled off tonight. Additionally, he would be sending grain for the horses and food supplies for the people to supplement what they could provide for themselves via hunting and fishing.

Jaromir hadn't expected him to be clever enough to take Céline's idea and embellish it.

There were no cheers in answer to his speech, but many people nodded in relief as the news began to sink in.

After this, Malcolm moved into the crowd, speaking one by one to Rupert, Sinead, Silvanas, and the leaders of the other families. Though he apologized with what sounded to be true sincerity to Rupert over the death of Gallius, he was wise enough not to offer any sort of compensation, which would have been taken as an insult.

Rupert didn't offer absolution in return to the apology, but he took Malcolm's hand when it was offered.

"He's much better at this than I'd expected," a soft voice said to Jaromir's left.

He looked down to see Céline standing at his shoulder.

"I agree," Jaromir answered. "He's the one who wronged them, but the moment that grain and those food supplies arrive, they'll be grateful to him."

"Even I didn't think to suggest that."

"No, but you thought up the rest of it, and you posed it to him perfectly. Sometimes you still manage to amaze me."

She raised one eyebrow. "A little cleverness amazes you?"

Realizing how condescending he'd just sounded, he smiled in apology. "No. Sorry."

She smiled back at him and then turned her eyes to the crowd. Malcolm was standing with Lilah, Rupert's beautiful daughter. Céline's smile faded.

"Those two are sleeping together," she said quietly. "And she was the one who arranged to have her own husband arrested."

He started with a jolt. "Are you certain? Malcolm seems so attentive to his wife. He even asked for her counsel."

"Yes, I'm certain. Amelie saw it."

"When?"

"This morning."

"And I'm just hearing about it now?"

"You are no one to complain about the lack of sharing information."

At that, a rush of anger passed through him. Neither Céline nor Amelie had a right to chastise him for following Anton's orders.

The anger passed, and he looked around, seeking Amelie. He hated being at odds with her. Nothing felt right when there were hard feelings between them. In all his life, he'd never once cared if one of his mistresses was displeased with him. Amelie wasn't even his mistress, and yet he couldn't help suffering over her opinion of him. A part of him wished he could alter this and live in a state of not caring.

"Where is she?" he asked.

"I'm not sure. I saw her speaking to Sinead's husband a little while ago, but you know her, and it's best to leave her alone until her temper eases. If you try to force her into telling you why she's so angry—and I think you know the answer—the two of you will just end up fighting."

Before he could respond, Marcus came walking up. He reached out for Céline, embraced her quickly, and let her go.

"What was that for?" she asked.

"We have you to thank for this," he said. "I know it." He glanced toward the forest. "I wanted to tell you that now we've been freed, Leif and I are going hunting. We may be gone half the night."

"Of course," she answered, and then she looked through the crowed. "I haven't seen Helga. Do you know where she is?"

"In the blue wagon," Marcus answered. "She's been in there alone since you left. Something troubles her."

"I know it does." She started to walk away. "I'm going to go and speak with her. Marcus, be careful hunting, and, Jaromir, remember what I said about Amelie."

As she left, Marcus followed her with his eyes. "There is no one else like her," he said.

Jaromir could not disagree. "No, there isn't."

With that, Marcus broke into a jog, heading for the trees.

Standing alone, once again, Jaromir scanned the crowd for Amelie. He didn't see her, but many people were moving now, heading out for water or firewood. Prince Malcolm was still speaking to some of the family leaders.

As Jaromir turned, a flash of blue caught his eye, and he saw Amelie slip from the crowd and walk swiftly toward the white wagon. She climbed the steps and disappeared inside.

He breathed in and out a few times and then, unable to stop himself, he started after her.

Alone inside the white wagon, Amelie sank down onto the lower bunk. Oliver was asleep up top.

She knew she should be glad that Céline had managed to free the Móndyalítko trapped here—or at least free them to a point. She wasn't sure what would happen if the culprit was not rooted out soon, but for now, the

people were no longer confined to the perimeter of the
meadow.

And she was glad.

She wasn't bothered that her sister hadn't said anything earlier about making an attempt to convince
Prince Malcolm tonight. For all Amelie knew, the idea
might have come to Céline in the moment.

Céline's mind often moved swiftly.

But standing near Jaromir in the hall had been difficult. Her anger with him had faded enough to be
replaced by worry.

He didn't trust her.

He didn't see her as an equal.

What did that mean for them?

Annoyed with herself, she pushed this last thought
away. There was no *them*.

The door to the wagon opened, and Jaromir came
inside. He closed the door behind himself, and as soon
as she saw the expression on his face, her anger flooded
back. She'd seen that look before. It was his "You are
in the wrong for questioning my authority and you need
to realize it right now" look.

She hated that look.

"You want to tell me what's wrong?" he asked, but
his voice was full of challenge, as if any response she
gave wouldn't be worth the air she'd used to breathe.

He was so tall his head nearly touched the ceiling,
and without his armor, tabard, and sword, he almost
was like a different person, as if his uniform had become
part of her mental image of him.

But he wasn't a different person. He was the same
Jaromir.

"Why should I bother, when you already know, and you don't really want to hear anything I have to say?" she answered.

His light brown eyes narrowed. "I know you're sulking because I followed Prince Anton's orders."

"Sulking?" She jumped to her feet. "You think I'm sulking like one of your spoiled mistresses? You sat beside me on a bench for a week, letting me believe that you and Helga had come up with a plan to help us join with the Móndyalítko, to become part of their group and earn their trust. You let me think this was the *only* plan." She could feel herself shaking. "And all the while, you had a sword, your amor, and a letter from Anton hidden under one of the wagons so that you could carry out an entirely different plan. You let me sit there like a fool!"

He'd gone still, watching her. "I never see you as a fool, but you aren't the head of Anton's military. You are one of his seers, and we have different functions."

"Not on a task like this! When we're this far from Sèone, Céline and I are sometimes all you have! What if you'd run into trouble up at the castle? What if you'd been arrested? The only person who even knew you'd gone up there was Marcus, and he had no idea why. We'd have been blind." She choked once and looked away.

"Amelie . . . ," he said, sounding shocked now, as if none of the scenarios she just mentioned had ever occurred to him.

"You don't see me as a partner," she went on, hating herself for the tremble in her voice, "and you never will."

He closed the distance between them in three steps

and held her face in his hands. "Don't say that. I do see you as a partner. I do. But I have to protect you."

To her endless shame, she sobbed once. "And who's going to protect you?"

His breathing was ragged, and then his mouth pressed down hard on hers. Clutching at his shirt, she kissed him back, too lost to even speak anymore. His mouth opened, and she responded, moving her lips with his.

This had happened once before, up near the Ryazan mines. Only then, she had pushed him away even though she hadn't wanted to.

Tonight, she couldn't bring herself to stop this. She didn't want to stop it.

His hands slipped from her face to her back and he pulled her closer, letting her feel the strength in his body. His lips moved from her mouth to brush her cheek.

"Amelie," he whispered.

The longing in his voice reverberated through her until she found his mouth again, kissing him with the same longing and need she'd kept locked away inside her.

Without taking her mouth from his, she sank back down on the bunk. He drew away long enough to jerk off his vest and shirt. Then he lay down beside her, stroking her face with one hand.

"Amelie," he whispered again.

Céline entered the blue wagon quietly and closed the door behind herself.

Helga sat at the small stationary table staring into space. Céline sat down across from her. Without thinking, Céline reached over to grasp one of Helga's hands.

Instead of pulling away, as she might have done, Helga gripped down on her fingers.

"I heard quite a ruckus going on out there," Helga said. "Sounds like that prince had a change of heart?"

"Yes."

"And he's just forgiven, as if Gallius never died?"

"I think the leaders of the families are trying to see a larger picture."

"They always do," Helga said bitterly, "no matter who dies."

"Please tell me what happened to you. I know it must have been something terrible to make you leave Alondra and leave your people. Does it have to do with the Taragoš, with Jago?"

"It's an ugly story."

"I want to hear it. I need to hear it."

Helga pulled her hand away and crossed her arms. Her sharp eyes seemed a thousand miles away. Then she began to speak. . . .

CHAPTER TEN

Helga

When my power as one of the Mist-Torn manifested, I was only seventeen, and my family rejoiced.

Before that, I had few attractions that any of my people might value. I was short with wide hips and a stocky build. I was considered somewhat bad-tempered. My face was pleasing enough and my hair was a dark, rich brown, but I couldn't sing and I certainly couldn't dance.

I did tell a good story.

Even so long ago, I remember those times as if they were yesterday, traveling through each year with my father, mother, and younger sister, Alondra. There were five wagons in our caravan, and my uncle, Gaelan, was the leader of our group.

He and his family lived in the largest of the wagons, and his eldest son, Griffin—who was one year my senior—was fated to be our next leader when his father passed. I never trusted Griffin. He'd always struck me as someone who would do what best served himself, but tradition is tradition, and the Ayres were led by the eldest male, followed by the son of the eldest male.

Who was I to question tradition?

I was happy then. I loved my parents and my sister, and my spirit thrived under our yearly cycle. We spent the autumn camped outside the great city of Kéonsk, with hundreds of other wagons and farmers and merchants, for the great harvest fair. All through autumn, we put on shows of music, dance, and magic for the people visiting the fair, and they'd throw money into our hats. We used these funds to resupply.

In early winter, we rolled southwest, through a series of towns or large villages, one after the other, where we'd entertain people weary of the cold gray skies and hungry for amusement. Uncle Gaelan had carefully arranged invitations from the town councils or leaders years ago. I learned as a girl that my people weren't always trusted and sometimes even turned away—or chased away—and that we needed a proper invitation.

In the spring, we'd begin the long journey southeast, to Yegor, where we summered in a meadow with other families in their caravans, and we harvested crops for the prince in exchange for our welcome.

Not all Móndyalítko families lived by such a cycle. Some traveled far and wide, to other countries like Bela and Stravina, and they varied their adventures each year. But my uncle preferred a safer routine, and my parents followed his judgment, for he'd always kept us fed and safe.

I first felt the nag at the back of my head during the early days of the Kéonsk fair in my seventeenth year. At the time, I had no idea what it meant, but when it didn't go away within the hour, I grew alarmed and told my mother.

She went still, staring at me.

"Tell me what you feel," she said.

"It's like an itch, but not an itch, as if I've forgotten something, and I must remember what it is, but I can't."

Hope flooded her face. She grasped my hand, leading me up inside our wagon. There, she lit a single candle and set it on the table.

"What are you doing?" I asked.

"Come and sit." Her voice trembled. "I believe you have your grandmother's gift."

I nearly gasped. Among the members of our caravan, we possessed no Mist-Torn and no shifters. This was an embarrassment to my uncle. My grandmother had been Mist-Torn, but she'd died when I was young.

With the vanity of a seventeen-year-old, I liked the thought of taking my place as the only Mist-Torn witch in my family. Foolish girl.

"What do I do?" I asked my mother.

"Focus on the flame and on the prompt in your mind, repeat this litany in your thoughts to help you concentrate: *Blessed fire in the night, show me what is in the sight, show me what brings fight or flight, blessed fire in the night.*"

"But it isn't night. It's broad daylight."

"The words will simply help you to focus."

I did as she instructed, eager to prove her right, that I was indeed Mist-Torn. This caused some distraction at first, but then I focused on the flame, on the nag, and on the litany, repeating the phrases in my mind.

The wagon around me vanished, and to my shock, I

found myself surrounded by a sea of white and gray mists. They cleared, and I was standing in a field that I recognized. It was not far from the vast campground of the Kéonsk fair. It was a place our men sometimes took our horses to graze.

I saw three horses grazing and a fourth one was sniffing something on the ground. Moving closer, I looked down at the prone form lying in the grass. It was Uncle Gaelan's youngest son, Gustavo. His eyes were closed and his head was bleeding. When I looked at the horse beside him, I saw red on its right rear hoof. Gustavo must have startled the creature somehow and been kicked.

The mists closed in, and the scene vanished.

I was once again back in the wagon.

"Mother!" I cried. "Gustavo is hurt. He's been kicked in the head, and he's lying in the small field where we take the horses to graze."

She didn't wait or bother to answer. Running outside, she called to the men, who began rushing for the field. The next few hours were a blur of activity as Gustavo was found and brought back and his wound tended to and everyone worried for him.

But in the early evening, my mother, father, and Uncle Gaelan came to me, and I could see their excitement.

"How is Gustavo?" I asked.

"He will recover thanks to you," Gaelan answered. "We reached him in time."

He'd never spoken to me with such respect. He rarely spoke to me at all.

"Your mother tells me you felt the prompt and looked into the flame and saw Gustavo," he went on. "Is this true?"

"Yes."

"She is Mist-Torn," my mother added.

"Your own mother is long gone," Gaelan said to her. "Can you guide Helga yourself?"

"I can."

My uncle was pleased, beyond pleased.

And so a new world began for me. My mother explained how my grandmother's abilities had worked. They were twofold. The first possibility involved the mists reaching out to me, telling me that something was amiss or needed to be seen. This was the case with Gustavo. Such prompts mustn't be ignored.

The second ability was for me to read individual people who might come with a question. I could focus on another place or person and see exactly what was happening in the moment. I knew well that seers from the line of Fawe, with their lavender eyes, often saw the future and the past, and at first, their gifts seemed more useful to me.

How many people wanted to know what was happening someplace else right *now*?

"You'll see," my mother said. "A good number."

I soon learned she was right.

My uncle set me up in the largest, finest wagon—his own family's wagon—a few mornings later. I wore a new red velvet dress with gold hoops in my ears. He then walked around the fair announcing that the line of Ayres boasted a seer who could read the present.

Not long after, people began arriving.

I was nervous. I'd seen other Móndyalítko women who were not Mist-Torn put on mesmerizing shows as they pretended to read futures. I was no show woman. I simply sat at the table and waited.

The first man to enter the wagon appeared to be a farmer. He looked askance at the silk cushions and hanging crystals, but he had a kind face.

"How can I help?" I asked, as my mother had taught me.

"When I traveled from my farm to bring the first half of the harvest to the fair," he answered, "I left the other half in the fields for my sons to bring in. But bad weather threatened. Can you see my farm and tell me if the rest of the harvest has come in safely?"

At once, I was at ease and began to see how useful my powers could be to other people.

"Come and sit," I said to him.

My mother had explained what I should do, but this was the first time I'd put this ability to the test. Reaching out, I grasped his hand and closed my eyes, and I focused intently on the spark of his spirit and the image of his farm.

The wagon vanished, and the mists closed in. When they cleared, I stood on the outskirts of a mown wheat field. To my right was a cheerful cottage with a thatched roof and just beyond that was a large barn where I could see young men working. All the fields in my sightline had been cleared of their crops, and the wheat was bound and ready to be threshed.

The mists closed in, and I found myself back in the wagon. I was pleased to give him good news.

"The harvest is safely in, and I saw your sons working with the bound wheat in the barn. All is well."

He thanked me with a smile and paid me well.

This went on all morning. Some of the news I delivered was not so pleasant. One woman sought to see if a sick friend left behind had recovered from her illness, and I saw that the friend had died.

By noon, I'd grown weary, and Uncle Gaelan called the readings to a close, but he was pleased when he counted the coins I'd earned.

That night, everyone made a fuss over me. I didn't have to help with the cooking, and I was served dinner first—and only the best portions.

I might have let some of this go to my head.

Strangely, even though Alondra was my sister, and therefore naturally placed in a position of rivalry, she held no resentment toward me at all and only rejoiced in my elevation. She was a sweet soul and ever mindful of the feelings of others.

Perhaps it would have been better for her to inherit my grandmother's gift.

It was Griffin, my uncle's eldest son, who would someday be our leader, who frowned that night when I was served dinner as I sat by the fire like a spoiled princess expecting her proper due.

"I don't see why Helga suddenly has no duties," he said, "and gets the best cuts of meat simply because she sat in a wagon all morning doing something that requires no skill or effort on her part."

His words stung a little because they held truth. A kettle witch often underwent years of study to cast spells, and the women of my family who read or pretended to read fortunes were all practiced in how to put on a show for each patron and to listen and tell people what they needed to hear.

My ability was natural. It required no study and no skill.

But my uncle turned on Griffin angrily. "Hold your tongue! Your cousin earned more in a single morning than the entire family has earned at the fair so far this year. You should be thankful we have a Mist-Torn among us, and we can hold our heads higher. Next autumn, we'll be given a camping spot at the front of the fair, closest to the city. Mark my words."

Griffin glowered at me, but he obeyed his father and held his tongue.

The next morning, Gaelan once again set me up in the largest, finest wagon, and I went to work. For the first time, I wavered in my joy and my pride as I wondered how many days in a row I'd be expected to sit in my red velvet dress and my gold earrings and earn coins as a seer.

That morning also showed me the pain my gift could bring to someone else, and I never quite recovered from understanding the power I held.

Early on that day, a woman in a peach silk gown stepped carefully inside the wagon and looked at me. I could see desperation and fear in her eyes, but the rest of her face was calm and guarded. She was nearly fifty, but she must have once been quite beautiful, and the remnants were still visible in her blue eyes and small straight nose. Her near-black hair was piled elaborately on her head, and only a few strands of gray showed.

Moving closer, she sat down across from me, and I could see the tiny lines in her face.

Before speaking, she held up a fat pouch and slid it across the table. I knew she was going to ask me to see something difficult.

"How can I help?" I asked.

She opened her mouth once, closed it again, and then tried for a second time. "I live inside the city walls. As a young woman, I was married to a man old enough to be my father, and I served him well as his wife. He died last year, leaving me well provided for, and this year . . . this year, I married a man younger than myself." She closed her eyes as if making a confession. "He is handsome and perfect, and all I've ever dreamed of. I've tried to convince myself that he loves me. In recent weeks, I've come to fear he is . . . cavorting with my maid. I hope I am wrong, but I must know. This morning, I dressed myself as you see and announced I was going to visit a friend and that I would be gone for hours." She paused. "Can you see what is happening right now, inside my home?"

I shifted uncomfortably in my chair. I didn't want to do this.

Still, I didn't see how I could refuse, and I understood her reasons for wanting to know. Reaching out, I grasped her hand and focused on the spark of her spirit and on her husband and on her house. By this point, I'd learned to feel exactly when I made the connection.

The wagon vanished, and the mists rose. When they cleared, I found myself standing in a lavishly decorated bedroom.

I faced the bed.

A tall man with sandy blond hair and hawkish features lay naked upon a cream silk comforter. Beneath him lay a smallish woman with large breasts and wavy red hair. She was perhaps seventeen.

His hand stroked her stomach as he kissed her.

"This is too brazen," she whispered, pulling her mouth away. "Not in the mistress's bed."

"Yes, in her bed," he whispered back. "It's now my bed, too, and you deserve the feel of silk beneath you."

He kissed her again, harder this time, and she gave in, kissing him back.

The mists rose and vanished, and I was once again in the wagon, facing the woman in the peach gown. My expression must have betrayed me, because hers crumpled.

"It's true, then?" she choked.

I didn't want to answer, but she deserved to know. "I saw a blond man in a bed with a cream-colored comforter. He was with a red-haired girl."

The woman closed her eyes again, and I don't think I'd ever seen such grief. This was my first real glimpse into a world outside my own. This lady had spent much of her life married to a much older man, and then when she finally believed it was her turn for some happiness, it was only to learn the man she'd married by choice was unfaithful.

"I've been a fool," she said. "Everyone told me, but I didn't want to believe."

"What will you do?" I asked. Until then, I'd not allowed myself to be drawn into actual conversation with the people who came to me, but I wanted to know.

She opened her eyes as if considering my question. "Nothing. I will do nothing. I will say nothing."

Standing, she nodded to me once, but her face was still lined with pain. "Thank you."

She left, and I wondered how I would be able to carry on for the rest of the morning. I somehow managed, and later, Uncle Gaelan was stunned when he counted the contents of the single pouch alone. He kissed the top of my head. His action made me feel guilty, as if we were profiting from the suffering of others.

For the remainder of that autumn, I spent mornings doing readings, and for the rest of each day, I was petted and spoiled, and I had no other duties whatso-ever.

When the fair broke up and we pulled out, heading southwest, I could hardly contain my relief. While traveling at least, I would be given a reprieve. My parents' standing had improved greatly among the family, and our wagon now rolled second in line, right behind Uncle Gaelan's.

That winter, we followed the same path as always, passing from one town or village to the next—always invited, expected, and welcome. My reputation grew during those cold months, and I did more readings than I could count. I never ceased to be surprised by how many people wished to know what was happening in the moment in a different location, but most of the reasons were similar in nature: checking on an ill relative or friend, checking crops or livestock on a family farm some distance away . . . or attempting to learn if a spouse or lover was faithful.

I seldom felt the nag again, as this only appeared

to occur during an emergency of which I must be made aware.

And anyway, Uncle Gaelan was more interested in the money I earned by reading people.

In the spring, we headed east, and I was given a true rest.

As we rolled into the meadow beneath the castle of Yegor, my life returned *almost* to what it had been before. Though word of my new standing spread quickly among the other families, most of our people would not require my abilities, and I once again returned to daily duties like any other Móndyalítko woman. As opposed to feeling resentful, I welcomed the mundane tasks: cooking, tending chickens, washing clothes, and cleaning the wagons. Alondra and I chatted away like the sisters we were, and I was thankful not to be sitting in a hard chair reading strangers all morning.

Soon, we were harvesting strawberries, then raspberries, then blueberries, and finally apples. We fished in the streams and snared rabbits, and some of the other families' shifters brought down the occasional deer to be shared. Life was good.

In the autumn, we rolled out of the meadow and headed back for Kéonsk.

By the time of our arrival, just as always, large numbers of farmers, merchants, and other Móndyalítko converged for the fair, far too many to be allowed inside the already crowded city.

Wagons, tents, and market stalls were set up outside, overseen by a city administrator called Master Rolfo. He was lord of the fair back then, but this position altered every decade or so.

Just as Uncle Gaelan had predicted, we learned that Master Rolfo had kept a prime spot for our five wagons, just outside the west entrance of the city. Nobody could miss us there. Rolfo didn't do this out of kindness, but after the previous year, I was now considered quite a draw. It was clear that a number of people would come to see me and then would spend money at the merchant stalls.

The city took a portion of all money earned at the stalls.

Once again, I became "the seer" each and every morning. I can remember being called "the great Helga." I had no duties. I was petted and spoiled and served dinner first. The lure of this had worn off, though, and my mind kept drifting back to the days of summer when I'd stood in the sunshine picking blueberries.

I earned a good deal of money that autumn.

In early winter, we left Kéonsk and began our winter visits.

For the next five years, nothing much of note happened. Then in the autumn of my twenty-fourth year, we took our place in Kéonsk once again for the autumn fair. By this point, I was resigned to my fate. The family thrived with fine clothes, good food, new wheels for the wagons, and several new horses. Most of our comforts were entirely due to me.

It never occurred to me to try to alter the arrangement.

One evening, I was resting in our family's wagon when a knock sounded upon the door. Surprised, I got up to answer it and found myself looking out at a solider wearing the red tabard of the Väränj—the city guards. He was of average height and build, with short brown hair and brown eyes. There was nothing about his appearance to make him stand out . . . and yet when his eyes held mine, I sensed an old soul inside him.

"Yes?" I asked for lack of anything else that came to mind.

"Are you the seer?"

I wanted to sigh. "I only do readings in the mornings. Come back tomorrow."

"I can't. I'll be on duty. Please."

His voice held an edge of desperation, and I couldn't send him away. Stepping back, I let him in. I'd never done a reading in my own family's wagon before.

"What is it you need me to see?" I asked.

"My family lives to the south. I received a letter from my sister this morning, telling me my mother was ill, dying, and that I should come. But the letter was delayed, and it's now weeks old. If my mother is still ill, I'll request leave and set out tomorrow. If she is well . . . or if she has died, I'll remain here at my duties, write back to my sister, and go home when I can. But I need to know."

As with his appearance, his request was nothing out of the ordinary, but I could hear the emotion in his voice. He was torn between family and duty.

We both sat, and I took his hand. His fingers felt warm and weathered in my own. I focused on the spark of his spirit and on his home and on his mother. The mists closed in.

When they cleared, I found myself standing by a

small family graveyard. A fresh grave had been recently dug, with a wooden marker that read ELIZA PORTER, LOVING MOTHER.

The mists closed in again and faded, and I sat looking at the soldier.

"I'm sorry," I said, and I was sorry. "If your mother is Eliza, I saw her grave. She has passed over."

He drew a ragged breath and closed his eyes.

His hand was still in mine, and I gripped down more tightly on his fingers. Something about him moved me.

"Don't go back into the city," I said. "You shouldn't be on your own. Stay with us and have dinner. There'll be music afterward, and you should have others about you."

His eyes opened. "What's your name?"

"Helga."

He nodded. "I'm Saul."

I liked his name.

He did stay for dinner, and I sat with him, offering whatever comfort I was capable of, which wasn't much, as by nature I am not a giver of comfort.

The following night, he came back and brought me a bouquet of late-season roses. No man had ever brought me flowers. The next night, he brought a small box of almonds rolled in sugar and cinnamon.

I was being courted.

We walked among the wagons and closed stalls in the darkness, talking softly of small things, and soon we found ourselves drifting through the trees on the edge of the encampment until we reached the meadow where Gustavo had been kicked those years ago.

Slowly, Saul sank down to sit on the grass, and I sank down beside him.

He kissed me gently, and I kissed him back. There was no question of what we both wanted. With the same gentle movements, we removed each other's clothes, and I lay back in the grass.

I loved the feel of his hands and his mouth.

I was in love.

That was a sweet autumn of stolen moments. We both performed our duties by day and slipped away at night whenever possible, exploring each other's bodies and whispering soft words to each other.

Even then, we both knew it was the fleeting love of a season. I would never be a soldier's wife, and he would never resign his post and join a band of traveling Móndyalítko.

That is not to say that parting didn't cause us sorrow, but when winter set in, I kissed him good-bye, and our wagons rolled southwest, leaving him behind.

I hoped to simply hold the memories in my heart.

But Saul left me with a good deal more than memories, and about a month later, I began throwing up my breakfast. Before long, it was clear I was with child. Thankfully, among my people, this caused a woman no shame, and a new life was reason for celebration. My mother and Alondra both sought to care for me through the most difficult months as my body grew more unwieldy. I found that I didn't like being pregnant and vowed to never put myself through such an ordeal again.

In early summer, just as the raspberries ripened in the fields of Yegor, my pains began.

I was lucky, and my labor was brief, and with the help of my mother and Alondra, I delivered a baby girl into the world with a fair amount of ease.

I named her Renata, and her birth was the last moment of ease she ever gave me.

She came out screaming and didn't stop for nearly a year. Even with other women helping when they could, I got little sleep and neither did anyone else in my wagon. I felt worn and exhausted much of the time.

Almost as soon as she could form words, Renata used them to tell me when she didn't like something— and she didn't like much. She was picky about food and clothing and the blankets on her bed.

As the years passed, and she turned six, this only grew worse.

She looked a good deal like me, with a stocky build and thick dark hair, and my mother often said, "Oh, Helga, don't be hard on her. She reminds me a good deal of you."

"Of me? Was I so difficult?"

"Don't you remember?"

I did not. Did Renata take after me?

Somewhere in her childhood, though, I came to realize how much I loved her. I loved her small hands and her serious face, but she also caused me great trials. Renata was born to be disappointed. She often looked at me with great expectation, as if waiting for me to do or provide or produce something wonderful, and I never had a single clue what she wanted or expected. For her tenth birthday, I made her a beautiful doll, and she only sighed when she saw it.

"My friend Onya's mother gave her a new dress for her birthday."

"Did you want a new dress? You should have asked."

She sighed again. "You know I'd never *ask* for anything."

This was the way of our life together, her looking at me in expectation, and me never once living up to whatever it was she wanted—as I never knew what it might be.

When she reached the age of sixteen, she began to prove very useful to the family. Renata worked hard. She was a fine cook and seamstress. She sang like a dove and helped with performances. I was proud of her.

She was prone to bad dreams, though, and would sometimes crawl into bed with me and let me hold her. These moments filled me with love. But in her waking hours, she never stopped looking at me with a challenge of expectation that I could never understand or meet. Perhaps the fault was mine.

However, in her twentieth winter, she proved to be an anchor for me in time of tragedy and change. We stopped, as always, at a town called Salihorsk, only to be told that an illness had struck, and we must be careful. We settled our wagons outside town and only went in to conduct performances.

We should have moved on.

Within days, my mother fell ill with a fever and a red rash on her face, and my father followed soon after. Mother died first. Other members of our family fell ill, and in the end, it was the youngest and eldest we lost, including Uncle Gaelan.

Griffin was now our leader. By then he'd been

married for well over a decade, with two young sons, Gerard and Gersham.

I was so lost in mourning my parents, especially my mother, that I didn't think much on the change in leadership. Alondra was no better. She had loved our mother so. It was Renata who cooked meals and cared for us and kept her sharp eyes open.

"You look out for Griffin," she whispered to me one night. "He does not value you as Uncle Gaelan did."

She was right, and I paid mind to her words.

Everything was different now. One generation had been wiped out in a single winter and replaced by the next. In the end, though, Griffin's disdain for me proved not such a bad thing, for I had no interest in pleasing him, either.

When we reached Kéonsk for the following autumn fair, he came to me. "You can do your readings in the morning, but I see no reason why you should be excused from other duties or be treated any differently from anyone else."

I nodded. "Fine. If I'm like anyone else, then I can decide when I wish to do readings and when I don't. And I'm not doing them every day."

He frowned, but he was the one who'd started us down this path.

After that, I set my own schedule and spread word for when people might visit. I had less privilege under Griffin, but a good deal more freedom, and I much preferred this.

I never forgot Renata's loyalty and how she'd cared for Alondra and me over that dark winter.

Then, in Renata's twenty-second summer, in Yegor,

I noticed a change in her, and she was not as attentive as usual to her duties, often distracted. I wondered about the cause until I came around the side of a wagon one day and saw her holding hands with a young man from the line of Kaleja. The expressions on both their faces could not be missed.

They were besotted.

I was happy for them, happy for my girl. After that one autumn so long ago, I never saw Saul again and heard later that he'd been reassigned, but the glow of those months never left me completely, and I was glad for my Renata to bask in the same happiness.

I wondered where this would take them. Her falling in love with a young man from one of the families was different from me falling for a Väränj soldier. Renata's attachment could end in marriage.

As the summer ended, though, I noticed Renata becoming agitated and looking around a good deal, as if seeking him out and not finding him. I saw them together one day, and he appeared uncomfortable, but then I made out her face. She looked at him with the same demanding expectation with which she so often looked at me. Only a person already lost in the throes of great love can endure that look on a long-term basis.

He was not such a man.

When we rolled out of Yegor in the autumn, I knew Renata's sweet affair had ended badly, and I tried to be kind to her. She appeared so lost and confused, but how could I explain the problem? Few people wished to live their lives as a constant disappointment to someone else. If I'd tried to explain this, she wouldn't have understood.

With another month, though, it was clear that her brush with love had left her with more than memories, just as mine had.

She was with child.

The prospect of a new life filled me with joy, and I saw my girl blossom as well. She appeared to forget her young man—whose name I cannot remember—and prepare for the birth of the child. Alondra was equally excited.

The three of us now traveled in our family wagon, and soon there would be a fourth. How could we not be pleased? The months swept by.

In the very early spring, we'd not yet begun the journey for Yegor, and we were encamped in a village in the southwest. In the afternoon, I'd gone into the village to purchase some bread and cheese, and then I stopped at a tavern to buy a small jug of red wine to bring home as a treat.

I'd just reached the bar when I felt the nag at the back of my head. It was strong, and fear washed through my stomach. There was a lit candle on one table, and I dropped into a chair, staring at the flame.

Blessed fire in the night
Show me what is in the sight
Show me what brings fight or flight
Blessed fire in the night

The tavern vanished and the mists rose. When they cleared, I saw my Renata lying on her back in a bed in our wagon. Her face was a mask of agony, and she cried out.

Leaving the bread and cheese behind, I ran.

When I reached our wagon, Alondra and our cousin Matilda were both there with Renata. Matilda had delivered many babies and was considered our family's midwife. When I saw her face, I went cold.

She came from the bunk and met me at the door.

"Renata's pains have come early, and the baby is breech. I've tried, but I cannot turn it. I will keep trying."

I pushed past her and went to my girl, kneeling and grasping her hand. "It's all right."

She gripped down on my fingers. "Mama, it hurts."

My stomach lurched, and I'd have done anything to take her pain into myself. "I know."

That was the longest night of my life.

After hours and hours of torment, Renata finally gave birth to a breech baby—a tiny girl. With unspeakable relief, I laid the baby on my daughter's chest. "What shall we name her?"

"Jolene," she whispered. "I always wanted to be named Jolene."

I smiled. "Jolene."

Within moments, Renata began to bleed and there was nothing any of us could do to stop it. All my relief changed to panic as I tried to help Matilda, but the bleeding did not stop, and my daughter died while I was helpless to do anything.

My Renata was gone.

I don't remember much of the weeks that followed. There is only so much anyone can take, and I had neared my limit. A parent should not outlive a daughter, and the world seemed a dark place.

I later learned that Alondra had cared for Jolene in those early days. One of the young women from our caravan was nursing a baby, and Alondra went to her for help. It was months before I came back to myself to lend a hand, and I was ashamed that Alondra had been so burdened alone.

"It's been no burden," she assured me. "Jolene is a dear child."

And she was.

She rarely cried, and she learned to laugh early. We soon moved her to drinking bottles of goats' milk and cared for her entirely by ourselves. It hurts to admit this, but I did not love her then. I think a part of me blamed her for Renata's death, even though I knew such feelings weren't fair.

A year passed.

I remember the day I came to love her.

She walked early. She did everything early. At just past a year, she was a tiny thing, smaller than any other baby her age, and yet she was nearly running.

One day, I took her outside with me so I could do some washing, and I set her on the ground. In a flash, she was off, racing for the hens pecking at the earth. With a squeal of laughter, she scattered them, and then she turned and looked at me and threw her arms in the air and laughed again.

"Mama!"

I went to her swiftly and scooped her up. Her face was alive with delight.

"Grandmama," I corrected, for I'd never overlook Renata or allow her to be forgotten.

The child put both her hands on my face and

something changed inside me. She was an odd little thing who took delight in small pleasures and who loved to laugh.

"Jo," I said.

In that moment, the name Jo suited this tiny ball of joy in my arms, and that name stuck with her for life.

Jo was as different from her mother—or from me—as fire was from frost. As she grew, she remained slender and small boned. Her eyes were so light brown they glowed. Her hair was thick and light brown as well, unusual for our people. Her skin was ivory. She was the prettiest little thing I ever saw.

She loved everyone and everyone loved her.

By the time she was five, she was the center of my world. She was delighted by everything and always made me feel like a good grandmother. I disliked leaving her with Alondra even long enough to conduct my readings—but I did.

The years passed, and she grew from a pretty child into a beautiful girl. She sang and danced and told stories and became quite a draw in our performances. Some people simply liked to see her. She was like a woodland sprite.

In the night, she and I talked about many things.

"Do you mind having to do so many readings to earn money for the rest of us?" she whispered.

No one had ever asked me this before.

"No," I answered. "I have the gift, and I need to use it. Do you mind singing and dancing?"

"I love both," she whispered back. "But I love telling and hearing stories more."

She did love stories. She was a terrible cook and couldn't sew a stitch, but no one minded. Her lithe body rarely stopped moving unless she was asleep. She seemed to run everywhere.

In her seventeenth year, we traveled along a southwest road in late winter and stopped near a stream to make camp. I was just lighting a campfire when she came to me with a queer expression.

"Grandmama?"

I jumped up, fearing she was ill. "What's wrong?"

"Something is bothering the back of my neck . . . like an itch but not. I don't know what it is."

Hurrying over, I took her arm and ushered her inside our wagon. I didn't want anyone else to hear. Quickly, I lit a candle and set it on the table.

"What's happening to me?" she asked.

"I think you have the gift. Sit. Focus on the flame and on the nag at the back of your neck and repeat the same string of words in your mind. They'll help you focus."

I gave her the litany, and she stared at the flame. I'd never seen this happen in someone else before and I watched without speaking. Suddenly, her face went blank, and then she sucked in a loud breath of air.

"Grandmama!" she cried. "I saw upstream. A horse has died in the stream and is rotting. The water flowing our way is contaminated. Don't let anyone drink it."

I leaned forward long enough to say, "Don't tell anyone you saw this. Not yet."

Then I rushed to spread the warning. Thankfully,

no one had used any of the water yet. Our men traveled upstream, pulled out the dead horse, and collected buckets of clean water from above.

I let everyone think it was me who'd been shown the image.

Alone with Jo, I asked her, "Do you want to let everyone know? We can, but life will change for you. You'll have a more respected place, but you'll also have to live as I do, using your gift to earn money."

She looked at me, and I could see in her sweet face that she was torn. "Would I be able to help you? To take some of the work from you?"

"Probably not. Griffin would set you up in a different wagon."

She hesitated. "Could we keep the secret a little longer, then?"

This was what I'd wanted. I wanted to protect her. "Yes," I assured her. "As long as you like."

So our family had another Mist-Torn, but Jo and I kept it to ourselves for now. I wanted her to enjoy her youth a little longer.

In the late spring, when we arrived back at Yegor, though, I began to realize there would be new problems to face. At seventeen, Jo was so unbelievably lovely and so full of life that every young man from every family in the meadow began to take notice.

One of them was always stopping by with wildflowers or sweets until I ended up chasing them off. Jo handled them as she handled everything, with a warm smile or laugh, but no encouragement. As of yet, no one had stolen her heart.

That summer was the first time I saw Jago Taragoš following her with his eyes. The other young men were a nuisance, but nothing more. Jago worried me. He was a valued shifter, a panther, but his expression often held no emotion at all.

I mentioned my worries to Alondra by the fire one night.

She glanced over at him. "There's little he can do besides look at her. He was married two years ago."

Was he? I tried to remember and then did. Yes, he'd married a girl from the line of Džugi.

"Which one is she?" I asked.

Alondra's eyes scanned the families, all by their fires for the evening. "That one, with the shiny hair."

The young woman was pretty, with a fine figure and black silky hair. But as I watched her, I noticed she seemed nervous, afraid of her own shadow, and Jago never once glanced in her direction. He only watched Jo.

I didn't like it.

Throughout that summer, I sometimes did see Jago looking at his young wife, but his eyes held no pleasure. Her nervousness only grew worse, and he watched her with discontentment, like a toy he'd once wanted and now wished to toss away.

For the first time, I was relieved when the summer ended and we rolled onward to Kéonsk. We forgot about Jago Taragoš and enjoyed the autumn fair. I took Jo shopping inside the city several times and bought her some new clothes and new curtains for the wagon.

She loved to shop.

The winter proved mild, and we enjoyed our travels southwest.

Only when we traveled back to Yegor the following spring did my worry over Jago Taragoš turn into something more.

Upon our arrival, he was waiting and he greeted Jo by kissing her hand. She was polite but drew away from him quickly and came to me. I glared at him. Jo was eighteen that year, and I was sixty-four, but I was not weak or stooped, and I could still stare down a shape-shifter.

"It's all right," I said to Jo once he'd left. "He's married and can't bother you much."

I was wrong. Shortly after this, Alondra came back from having greeted some of our friends.

"Jago's no longer married," she said. "His young wife is dead."

"Dead?" I asked.

Alondra nodded tightly. "In the winter, she went to fetch water by herself. No one knows why. She was attacked by an animal and killed. Her throat was clawed."

Alondra's eyes were bleak. She wouldn't say it. No one would say it, but I knew what had happened. Jago had tired of his wife, and he had sent her off for water, and he'd killed her.

Now he was after Jo.

I readied for the battle that would come.

Jago wouldn't approach Jo first. He'd go to Griffin, but I was ready. The next morning, Griffin came to our wagon. He was sixty-five now and showing his age. He embraced Jo lightly as he smiled at her.

"I have good news," he said. "Jago Taragoš has asked for your hand. He'll be the next leader of that family, and this is a wondrous opportunity for you, for our own family to be so connected."

Jo shrank back and looked to me.

I stepped up. "She's no wish to marry him."

Griffin frowned in confusion. "You don't?" he asked her.

She shook her head. "No, Uncle. He frightens me."

"Why?"

"Why?" I echoed. "Because he's a half-mad shifter who killed his own wife when he got tired of her. We'll not send our Jo down the same path."

Griffin's eyes widened. "Helga," he admonished. "You mustn't say such things. That tongue of yours will cause us trouble." But he was uncomfortable now and backing away. "Still, Jo, if you don't wish to marry him, no one will force you."

"I don't," she stated in a clear voice.

Griffin was soon out of sight, but I could see Jo was still slightly shaken.

"Don't worry, my girl. Alondra and I aren't the only ones in the family who'll stand by you."

And this was true. Griffin might be petty on some counts, but he had two fine sons, Gerard and Gersham, now in their thirties, and they were both devoted to Jo as the brightest light in our family, calling her their "little cousin" with affection. Gerard was the elder. He was strong and quite good in a knife fight.

That night, as we all ate dinner by our fire, Jago Taragoš came striding up with an angry expression.

Jo pressed against me, but Gerard stood up, and Jago stopped.

"What do you want, Jago?" Gerard asked.

Griffin went pale with what appeared to be embarrassment, but he remained seated.

"I want to speak with Jo!" Jago spat.

"Then speak," Gerard said.

Growing angrier, Jago looked down at Jo. "I am free now, and I have asked for your hand. Do you understand what that means? I will be the leader of my family when my father passes. You would be my wife. The line of Taragoš is far above the line of Ayres in wealth and standing." He appeared truly puzzled. "You cannot mean to refuse me?"

With Gerard standing beside her, Jo spoke in a steady voice. "I've no wish to marry anyone right now. Of course I am honored by your offer, as would any girl among the families. Please ask another."

"I want no other. I am free now. You cannot mean to refuse me."

"She said no," Gerard broke in. "Show proper manners and accept her answer."

Among the Móndyalítko, once a woman said no, a man was expected to walk away. But Jago took a step closer to Jo and snarled down at her. "This is your final answer?"

"It is," she answered. "I cannot marry you."

His eyes flashed in hatred and disbelief as he looked at her. I could see his mind working, how he saw her now. He had made himself free—ridding himself of a wife—and he'd probably been envisioning Jo in his bed for months.

The way he saw it, she was a cold, heartless girl who'd spurned him and spurned his family.

With one last snarl, he whirled and strode away.

Turning, I held Jo in my arms. "It's all right," I said. "You were brave, and I think the worst is over."

She leaned into me, and I was angry now myself. A sweet creature like Jo should not have to face down the likes of Jago Taragoš.

For the next few days, I kept a close eye on Jo, never letting her out of my sight. Then the sky clouded over and a spring rain began. We all thought it would pass soon, but it grew heavier throughout the day until finding dry firewood for cooking became difficult.

In the late afternoon, Gersham formed a small party from our family to go out in the wooded areas and gather branches so we could dry them. Jo went along to help, but I didn't worry. She was safe with Gersham.

I set about cleaning and cutting some trout that Gerard had caught earlier that day, in preparation for a pot of fish stew. This took me a while, and I'd just started in on the potatoes when Gersham came jogging up to the wagon, looking all around.

"Is Jo not here? She's not come back?" He sounded alarmed.

A knot began growing in the pit of my stomach. "What do you mean? She was with you."

Gerard came striding over. "What's happened?"

Gersham's alarm turned to agitation. "We were gathering firewood, searching under the brush to find anything still dry. Jo wasn't far from me, but I was digging beneath a shrub, and when I came up, she was gone. I looked around there, and then I came back."

Without warning, the nag at the back of my head hit harder than anything I'd ever felt before.

I didn't bother to go inside and light a candle.

"Where?" I shouted. "Show me where."

He turned and began to run. Gerard ran beside us. Even at the age of sixty-four, I could still run when I needed to, and we broke through the trees. I was sick with fear, and my body moved on panic alone.

Gersham reached the place where he'd lost Jo, and the three of us fanned out.

"Jo!" I called. "My girl! Where are you?"

I headed toward the stream, looking down and to each side as I hurried. Somewhere inside me, I *knew* . . . I already knew, but I couldn't accept it.

When I saw her lying near the stream, I stopped, and a cry of anguish burst from my mouth. Gerald came sprinting from my left, and then he, too, stopped. Slowly, I walked forward and looked down.

My beautiful Jo lay with slashes across her face and her throat torn open. With another cry of anguish, I sank down beside her. I had no words.

Gersham came running up.

"He did this," Gerard whispered. "That shifter." His voice rose. "He'll pay. I'll brand his face myself."

I couldn't think of revenge or punishment or anything besides the sight of Jo on the cold ground. I was numb.

"Oh, Helga," Gersham whispered.

Gerard wore a coat. He stripped it off and wrapped it around Jo, lifting her body and holding it to his chest.

"Tonight!" he spat. "I'll brand his face and see him banished tonight!"

That time, his words got through to me. Our people had no death penalty. In the case of a terrible crime, like this, the criminal's face was branded with a circle, and then he or she was banished for life. Any Móndyalítko who saw the brand would know the mark of a murderer. No help or shelter would be given for any reason.

Looking at Jo's body in Gerard's arms right then, I couldn't bring myself to care about Jago's punishment. Our brightest light had been snuffed out in an instant all because she'd said no to a violent man. Nothing that happened to Jago would bring her back.

But I would care soon. I would care very much.

Gerard strode back into camp with tears running down his face.

Alondra saw us coming . . . saw what he carried and fell to her knees. "No!"

"Father!" Gerard shouted.

Griffin came out of their wagon, and when he saw what Gerard held, his face went ashen.

"It was Jago," Gerard went on. "You call a meeting of the leaders now! There will be justice tonight."

Griffin stared at him. "Give her to me."

I almost stepped in. I didn't want Griffin carrying my Jo to a meeting of the elders, but of course he had to. He had to show them what had been done.

Gerard passed her body over. Her throat was still bleeding, and I looked away. I did not think I could take so much pain.

"Everyone stay here," Griffin ordered.

For a moment, I thought Gerard would argue, but he held back. Griffin walked off, carrying Jo, and a meeting of the leaders was called. This was how we worked.

The leaders would be informed and then discuss and then vote on the outcome. Sometimes others would be called to testify. This system had served us well, and I knew there could be no doubt of Jago's branding and banishment. Griffin had seen what had happened when Jo refused Jago.

Also, though no one had dared accuse Jago openly, some people believed he had killed his own wife.

Tonight, after this, Jago would be gone. It troubled me to loose him upon the world, branded or not. But as I said, this was the worst punishment our people would deal out to one of our own.

I went to Alondra and drew her to sit with me by the dead campfire.

Gerard and Gersham sat beside us, and we waited. There was nothing else we could do until Griffin returned to tell us that the sentence had been passed. As more time ticked away, I became troubled. This should have been a quick vote. There was no doubt of Jago's guilt.

"What is taking so long?" Gerard asked, speaking my own thoughts.

Finally, Griffin came walking back to us down through the line of wagons. He steps were slow.

"Where is she?" I asked. "Where is our girl?"

"Sinead is preparing her. . . . We did not think you or Alondra should be faced with such a task tonight."

Gerard stood up. "I want to brand Jago myself."

Griffin glanced away. "There won't be a branding."

I felt the blood draining from my face. I didn't think I'd heard correctly.

"There is no proof," Griffin went on quietly. "Rupert demanded some sort of proof. A witness to the crime. Something of Jago's left behind at the scene. Anything. Jago is the Taragošes' shifter. He is their hunter. As leaders, we cannot deprive them of him without proof."

"But he did it," Gerard said in disbelief. "Let me go and testify to the leaders."

"Nothing you can say will provide proof."

"You know he did this. Father, you voted to banish him?"

"There is no proof," Griffin repeated. "And banishing someone like Jago is not an easy task." Then his gaze turned hard as he studied his son. "And there will be no blood revenge, either, or you'll be the one wearing the brand. Do you hear me?"

As these words sank in, I realized what had happened. Rupert did not wish to lose his son or to lose the Taragošes' only shape-shifter, their hunter. He must have not only demanded hard proof that Jago had murdered Jo, but probably hinted that any attempt to brand and banish Jago would result in more violence that no one wanted.

The cowards.

Alondra wept softly, and Gerard wouldn't look at his father.

I was dead inside, shattered. I had outlived my daughter and now my granddaughter. The justice of my people—that I had so long believed in—didn't exist. I had no place here anymore. I couldn't wake up tomorrow and see the leaders of the families going about their morning business as if they'd not let a murderer go free to live his life while my sweet Jo would be buried in the ground.

In the night, as Alondra slept, I donned a cloak, packed a satchel with clothes, food, and a little money, and I walked out of the meadow. I kept walking. I know I should have told Alondra. I should have said good-bye at least, but I was beyond speaking at that point, and I cared for nothing besides leaving my old life behind.

I walked, heading west.

Within a few months, my money ran out, and I could have used my gift to earn more, but I wouldn't. I turned my back on all things Móndyalítko. Summer turned to autumn, and I continued west. I slept outside much of the time unless I could find an abandoned barn. There were days when I didn't eat.

I knew my family would be in Kéonsk soon, but nothing could tempt me to rejoin my people. Whenever I closed my eyes, I saw Jo's bright, loving face staring back at me.

Sometimes traveling farmers or merchants would offer to give a ride, and I accepted, even taking charity in the form of food by their fires. But my hair and clothes grew dirtier, and I began to resemble the aged mad-woman I felt to be on the inside.

One night in midautumn, I found myself on the streets of a town, and I was so hungry that I stood on a corner and begged for pennies. A few people were kind, and I was able to buy a bit of cheese for dinner. Once the thought would have shamed me, but not anymore. I was beyond caring.

A few days later, I was walking down a road when two farmers offered to take me to the village of Sèone, where they were heading to sell their crops.

I'd never heard of Sèone, but I had nowhere else to go, and I was grateful for the offer of a ride.

We rolled along through the day, and then the driver pulled up the wagon. "There it is," he said. "Castle Sèone."

I turned to look and blinked at the sight. A moat the size of a river surrounded an enormous hill, almost a small mountain. Not far from our wagon, I could see a gatehouse with an open portcullis at the end of a retractable bridge across the moat. A wall—with numerous barbicans—stretched from both sides of the gate all the way around the area at the bottom of the hill.

On the other side of the gatehouse was a road leading about halfway up the hill to yet another gatehouse set against another stone wall that encircled the hill at that point. At the top of the hill stood a castle.

This place would be difficult to breach.

"We're going in there?" I asked in alarm. Once inside, would I be allowed out again?

But no one answered me and before I knew it, we started forward again, across the bridge. As we entered the gatehouse, a few guards waved us through.

We kept going and passed through the second gatehouse to the inside of the high stone wall . . .

And there, I looked around in surprise.

We entered what appeared to be a thriving town built all around the castle above. People and animals and dwellings of all sorts stretched out as far as I could see. A smithy and a tannery stood just ahead. Cobblers, weavers, candle makers, bakers, and butchers hawked their wares. But more that than, I saw a vast number of what looked like homes to my left, and all the people looked well fed.

"They all live here inside the castle wall?" I asked the driver.

He frowned at me in puzzlement. "Of course. It's safest here inside the wall. Prince Anton protects his own."

That was the first time I heard Anton's name.

When the farmers reached the market, I climbed from the back of the wagon and looked about. Walking past a few stalls, I hungrily eyed fresh bread and fruit, but I had no money.

A woman with two small children looked at me, and I knew how shabby and filthy I must be. She came to me, carrying a canvas bag. "Here, my dear," she said, pulling out a loaf of bread. "Take this and go sit yourself over there." She pointed to a line of shops with awnings. "No one will mind."

Wordlessly, I took the bread and she drew out two apples as well, passing them over. Then she shooed her children down the street. Grateful, I took the bread and apples and found a place beneath an awning to rest.

This was my introduction to Sèone. The villagers here thrived, and so they were given to kindness to the old madwoman with wild hair who appeared one day and took her place near the market. I never went hungry.

Several people stopped by me each day with gifts of

food or coins or a new blanket. There were several public wells for water, and I never went thirsty, either. As it was midautumn and already growing cold, I had no idea what I'd do when winter arrived, but I lived day to day.

The problem with that was . . . now that I was no longer starving or walking endlessly, I had too much time to think.

Was this how I would spend the remainder of my life? As a beggar woman on the street? Me? Who'd once been a great seer of the line of Ayres? One night when I closed my eyes, I didn't see Jo's bright face looking back.

I saw Renata. She shook her head at me.

The next day, I was so ashamed of what I'd become that I moved locations and found a place near the walkway up to the castle. I leaned back against a stone pillar and wondered what it might be that Renata would have me do.

Footsteps sounded, and I looked over to see a tall man walking toward me. He was proud. I could see that in his bearing. There was a sheathed long sword on his hip. He wore chain armor over a wool shirt, with a tan tabard over the armor. His hair was pulled back at the nape of his neck. The goatee around his mouth suited him.

He struck me as someone who thought well of himself.

At the sight of me, he asked, "What are you doing out here, old woman? You should move on."

His tone was arrogant.

Another arrogant man who thought the world owed him everything.

Suddenly, all the anger from the past months that I'd never expressed welled up inside me, and I found my voice, my own again after so long.

"Don't you 'old woman' me! You think you can go bossing people around because some prince gives you armor and a little power? Underneath that tabard you're just like everyone else, probably half as smart, and that swagger doesn't give you leave to ask me my business or tell me where to go!"

He stopped walking. Then he came over and crouched down. "Do you know who I am?"

"I couldn't care a rat's tail who you are. Only thing I see is some cocky soldier who likes to throw his weight around and needs to be taken down a peg or two."

This left him in shock, and he was quiet for a little while. I glared at him.

"I'm the new commander of Prince Anton's guard," he said finally. "And you're right. Some of this has gone to my head."

I wavered. Maybe I'd been wrong about him. Maybe.

"No one has talked to me like you just did in some time," he said, and then he pointed up at the castle. "I'll make you a bargain. If you come with me, I'll give you your own room and a job. You can live and work and eat there as long as you like. In exchange, you call me out when you see me getting above myself. No matter what I say, you'll never be afraid of me, and you'll . . . as you put it . . . 'take me down a peg or two.' Deal?"

It took a moment to absorb his offer. My own room and a job. A home.

Closing my eyes, I saw Renata again, and this time, she nodded.

I looked at the soldier. "Deal."

CHAPTER ELEVEN

When Helga stopped talking, Céline had no idea what to say.

So many revelations coming all at once were difficult to take in.

Helga was Mist-Torn. All this time, she'd had her own innate power and had never given a hint.

Worse, Céline had been warned the story was ugly, but the raw nature of it was almost overwhelming. To lose Renata in childbirth was terrible enough, but to lose Jo in such a senseless and violent manner . . .

"Oh, Helga. I'm so sorry." At least she understood why the older woman had not been able to speak of these things. "I never meant to bring it all back like this."

"You had to know."

"So, after meeting Jaromir, you spent five years working up at the castle?"

"Yes, and I learned things were not so smooth in Sèone before he came. I'd never tell him what I really think of him. It would go to his head."

Céline's mind flashed back to that morning, to the

sight of Helga holding a knife and calling for Marcus when she'd found Jago in the wagon. Céline shivered. Though Jago had made her uncomfortable, she'd had no idea.

"Does Jaromir know about Jago?" Céline asked.

"He knows some, but no one who matters knows all of it except for the leaders of all the families, and they'll do nothing."

"Well, Jaromir should be told everything."

"You do it. I can't talk about it again."

The weight of the incredibly long day and all its events suddenly weighed down upon Céline.

"Helga, please get some rest," she said. "Again, I'm sorry for putting you through this, but I do thank you. It helps me so much to know."

Helga nodded once without speaking.

"I'm going to go and check on Amelie," Céline said. "Will you be all right?"

"Of course."

Céline wasn't so sure Helga would be all right, but she did need to check on her sister. With a final pat of Helga's hand, she stood up. "Crawl into bed and get some rest."

Turning, she left the wagon and breathed in the night air, trying to push some of the long story from her mind to contemplate pieces in small doses as she could let them in.

The camp was nearly empty now, with most of the people having gone inside their wagons to sleep. Marcus sat by the campfire nearer to the white wagon. Wearing no shirt or boots, he watched her approach.

"How was the hunting?" she asked.

"Good. We brought back a deer." He paused and then motioned to the white wagon. "I wouldn't go in there."

"Why not?"

"Because Amelie and Jaromir are in there to-gether."

Céline shook her head. "What do you mean?"

"I mean that I think they are together. Leave them be."

As she walked to him, her eyes widened. "You mean . . . ?"

He nodded.

How did he know that? Perhaps he sensed it? Céline looked to the wagon. In truth, she'd known this was only a matter of time. The pull between her sister and Jaromir was so clear that nearly everyone saw it but the two of them.

Slowly, Céline sank down beside Marcus. The fire burned low.

"Where's your shirt?" she asked.

"I can't remember where I left it. I'll find it tomorrow."

He spread one blanket on the ground and shook out another one to cover them. As with last night, Céline was so exhausted she tried to tell herself that there was nothing unusual about any of this, about sleeping on the ground with Marcus.

But tonight, instead of pulling her up against his chest, he used one hand to gently push her down onto her back, and then he lay down with his face directly above hers. She looked into his dark eyes for a long moment.

Lowering his head, he kissed her. The pressure was soft, as if he wished to savor it, and the feeling was so familiar she almost wept. Somewhere, at some time, they had kissed and made love and slept by a campfire many times.

Moving her hand up to his chest, she kissed him back, taking comfort in the warmth and strength and familiarity of his body. It would be so easy to lose herself in this, to let it go on as she forgot everything else but the connection with him.

A small tinkling bell rang in the back of her head.

This was no sweet season of love as Helga had enjoyed. If she gave herself to Marcus, it would mean a good deal more. He'd be destroyed if it started and then ended.

With her hand on his shoulder, she pushed carefully. "Stop."

He stopped, staring down at her face. "Why?"

"You know why."

There was another face, a different face between them: Anton.

Marcus didn't even pretend ignorance. "I can give you things he can't."

This conversation hurt, and she tried to look away.

"Marriage," he went on. "Children. You could live with me out on the homestead. I could live with you at the shop. I don't care where we live."

This day had already been too much, and she closed her eyes. He was right. Everything he said was right. Her mind drifted to the picture he painted. He could marry her, raise children with her, build a life with her.

Anton could not.

And yet Anton was adrift and alone, and somehow

she knew that if she cut him off and married Marcus, Anton's last vestige of any hope for internal peace would die. She couldn't do that to him. She couldn't do it to herself.

Also, no matter what Marcus said, he wouldn't be happy living in Sèone. He might think so now, but after a few months of being trapped inside the city walls, he'd be desperate for acres of forest. He'd long to shift to his wolf form, to run, and to hunt.

No wife, no children, could ease that.

Céline might have lived many lives with him before this one, but all the visions and images of these lives were in the open air on the open road, sleeping by a campfire.

In this current life, she lived in Sèone and her heart belonged to Anton.

With regret she couldn't express, she crawled out from beneath Marcus and got to her feet. "This isn't fair to you," she said, "me sleeping in your arms. It's not fair."

He flinched.

She hadn't meant to hurt him, not ever.

Turning, she went to the blue wagon and slipped inside. Helga was asleep in the bottom bunk. Without bothering to undress, Céline climbed into the top bunk and lay there restlessly for the remainder of the night.

The following morning, Amelie opened her eyes to find her head resting on Jaromir's chest.

The night came rushing back.

In the darkness, it had been so easy to lose herself

in him. She'd never known the pleasure men and women could give to each other, and some of the sensations she'd experienced still left her reeling.

But now sunlight filtered through the windows, and she lifted her head. She'd never seen his bare chest and arms up so close before and couldn't help taking in the sight now. His forearms showed tight sinews, and he had scars on one shoulder and down across his rib cage.

He opened his eyes. "Good morning."

His voice was so casual and welcoming that it caught her off guard, but then she realized this was nothing new to him. He'd probably awoken with more women than he could remember.

It was new to her.

"You all right?" he asked, as if reading her face.

"Yes."

She was naked and didn't want to remain in the bunk but also didn't want to climb out. Why should she be embarrassed? She and Jaromir had exchanged every possible intimacy in the night. And yet she was embarrassed.

Again, as if reading her expression, he sat up and reached for the top bunk, pulling down another blanket.

"Here."

Gripping it, she wrapped it around herself and climbed from the bunk, picking up her clothes. When she glanced back, his eyes were filled with concern.

"You're not sorry?" he asked.

"No," she answered instantly. "I'll never be sorry."

He smiled and leaned back.

After dressing quickly, Amelie left the wagon and went outside.

She found Céline already up, attempting to get the fire lit.

"Where's Marcus?" Amelie asked.

"He went for water." Céline's voice sounded strained, and her eyes met Amelie's. "Are you and Jaromir . . . ?"

"Don't ask me yet. Please. I don't know what we are." It was then that she took a good look at her sister. Céline's clothing was rumpled and wrinkled, and her hair was in a tangle. "How was your night?"

Céline sighed. "So much happened. Amelie, I have so much to tell you."

The door to the white wagon opened, and Jaromir emerged. Amelie quickly crouched to help Céline with the fire.

"What's the plan for this morning?" Jaromir asked, stretching. "More readings?"

His question brought her skidding back to reality. This was the start of their second full day here—as their day of arrival hadn't counted for much—and they were no closer to learning who had placed the curse.

"I'd like to go back up to the castle," Céline said, "on the excuse of checking on Lysander. The key to finding whoever cast this curse lies in rooting out the motive, and it's most likely that someone is trying to hurt Prince Malcolm or one of his family members."

"Agreed," Jaromir said. "I'll go up with you."

"All right," Amelie agreed. "I'll stay and do readings down here. I can at least clear more people and try to take note of who doesn't want to be read."

Jaromir glanced at Céline and motioned with his hands at her clothing. "You might want to . . ."

She looked down at herself and then touched her

tangled hair. "Oh yes. I'll need a fresh blouse, and I'll see if Helga packed any other skirts."

Marcus came walking back with a bucket of water. He avoided looking at Céline.

Amelie couldn't help wondering why.

After Céline spent a little time changing clothes and tending to her appearance inside the wagon, she gathered up her box of medicinal supplies.

Though she hadn't slept well, she was glad to be launching back into their investigation first thing today. She didn't want to think on what had passed between her and Marcus in the night.

She'd done the right thing by leaving the fire and sleeping in the wagon with Helga, but the right thing was often the most difficult.

Opening the wagon door, she looked down to find Jaromir waiting for her.

"Ready?" he asked.

"Is Amelie all set up?"

"Yes, she's in the other wagon, and Helga is already gathering people for her to read."

The mention of Helga brought back other aspects of last night. Walking to the fire, Céline spoke directly to Marcus. "Would you stay in camp, near to Amelie, while we're gone? Don't let Jago Taragoš anywhere near her."

Jaromir had followed, and he frowned. "Why?"

Céline knew this couldn't be put off. As succinctly as she could, she told them the last part of what Helga had related last night, the part about Jago. Jaromir's mouth dropped halfway open.

"What?" He turned to Marcus. "You knew nothing of this?"

Marcus looked abashed. It probably bothered him that this had happened right under his nose those years ago, and he'd been living his life between hunting and sleeping at that age to the point that he'd remained unaware of possible murder among his own people. "I remember something . . . and I told Céline what I did remember—but things had become difficult for my own family around that time, and I didn't pay attention to much else."

Céline defended Marcus. "It's not his fault. It seems that everyone involved tried to hush it up quickly."

"Poor Helga," Jaromir said. Then he frowned again. "She should have told us the details sooner."

"I don't think she could," Céline answered, and looked to Marcus. "You'll watch out for Amelie while we're gone?"

"Yes."

Céline and Jaromir set off, leaving the meadow and walking east, up the road toward the castle.

"When we arrive," Céline said, "could you leave me to go in on my own? I want to see the women this morning, and women will tell each other things they wouldn't say in front of a man."

He didn't answer, but she took his silence for agreement, and when they arrived at the gate, they were ushered through without asking.

Jaromir noticed a few guards playing dice across the courtyard. "You're sure you want to go in alone?"

"Yes, I'll be fine."

"All right. I'll see what I can learn out here." He

pointed to a door on the south end. "That one leads past the kitchen. You'll be closer to the tower if you want to check on the boy."

He walked over and joined the dice game.

Céline went to the door he'd pointed out and shifted her box to one hand so she could let herself in.

Within moments of passing through, she saw a large kitchen to her right, and she recognized a girl standing at the stove. It was the young maid she'd met in Lysander's room.

"Jane," she said.

The young maid looked over and smiled. She pointed to a large teapot on the stove. "Miss Céline, how good of you to come. You're here to see Lysander? I was just heating this to bring it up to him and Lady Anna. It seems to help so much."

"How many times have you put him over the steam?"

"Only once more since you left yesterday, but he's having a little trouble this morning." The water wasn't boiling yet. "You go on up and tell them I'm coming. Do you remember the way?"

"Yes, I think so."

Céline set off down a short passage toward the base of a tower. She passed a few doors and stopped outside one of them when she heard a gasping sound. Was someone hurt?

"Faster!" a female voice moaned.

Céline felt her face going red as she realized what was happening on the other side of the door.

A man gave a cry, followed by more gasping. "My love," he said. "My Lilah."

It was Prince Malcolm's voice.

Going tense, Céline was torn between fleeing and listening. Malcolm was in a side room of the main floor of the castle with Lilah while his wife sat upstairs with their sick son.

"You do love me," Lilah said. "You want to spend your life with me."

"You know I do. You make me young again."

"Put your hands on me here," Lilah said, "and promise we'll always be together."

"I promise."

A moment later, some of the gasping began again. Céline drew away, hurrying down the remainder of the short passage for the stairs. Was Malcolm serious in his promise? Did he intend to set Lilah up as a permanent mistress? Did Anna know about any of this?

Somehow the threads of these details must be important. She simply didn't see how yet.

Upon reaching the base of a tower, she began to climb and emerged on the second floor. Walking down that passage, she stopped at the third door on the right and knocked lightly.

"My lady?"

Opening the door, she looked inside.

Both Anna and Jenelle stood by Lysander's bed, and both women turned to see Céline.

Lady Anna smiled. "Miss Céline. You are most welcome. Come and see how your young patient fares."

She appeared just as impeccable as the day before, standing straight with her white-blond hair held back at her forehead by the same simple silver tiara. Céline couldn't help feeling respect for this woman. Even in the face of several trials at once, she maintained such dignity.

Beside her, Jenelle wore a butter yellow velvet gown that set off her chestnut hair. She assessed Céline carefully.

Jane entered the room, carrying the steaming teapot. The bowl was still on the table, but it had been emptied. "We should do this before the water cools."

Céline agreed and went to the bed. "Good morning, Lysander. Did you sleep any better last night?"

"Some," he answered, climbing out of bed on his own. His color was better today and the dark circles beneath his eyes had faded. "I like the honeyed cough syrup you brought."

"I thought you might."

He was wheezing a bit and breathing mainly through his mouth, so she led him to the chair and covered his head with a blanket while Jane poured the water. Céline held the blanket while he breathed in steam.

Afterward, she helped him back to bed.

Jenelle watched her throughout, and this caused Céline to ponder the young woman. Though Anna's dignity was admirable, she was also a carefully guarded person in her manner, and therefore a poor source for information. Perhaps it was time to get to know Malcolm's daughter a little better.

"I just came to stick my head in and check," Céline said to Anna. "Please send for me if you need anything."

"I thank you," Anna answered. "And I will."

Taking in her elegant face, Céline tried not to think about Malcolm and Lilah downstairs. Instead, she looked to Jenelle. "Would you mind walking me out? I got a little turned around on my way in."

Jenelle raised an eyebrow. "I wouldn't mind at all."

After a polite farewell to Lady Anna and Lysander, Céline followed Jenelle out into the passage and fell into step beside her.

"I assume you wish to speak with me on some matter," Jenelle said. "You hardly strike me as the type to get 'turned around.' But I warn you, if you want to speak with someone frank, I bring new meaning to the word. I'll tell you anything you want to know if you can lift this curse."

Céline assessed the young woman as quick-witted, but her voice also held notes of bitterness and disappointment.

"I rather did want to talk to you," Céline admitted. "My sister and I are no closer to learning anything of use. I wondered if you had any insights."

"Me? I know nothing of the Móndyalítko down in that meadow."

"Well, there is nothing to prove it's one of them. Does your father have any enemies among the nobles?"

As she walked, Jenelle tilted her head as if this had not occurred to her before. "I don't see how. He's rarely in the same room with other nobles. My father hates social occasions with people of his own class. Five years ago, my uncle, Prince Kristoff, died without an heir. My father was named prince, and we moved here. Since then, we've hardly gone anywhere, and he only invites people to visit when there's no other choice. He prefers living in his own little world."

Again, she sounded so bitter.

"When did your own mother die?" Céline asked suddenly, hoping to throw Jenelle off balance.

"When I was seven, but I barely ever saw her and don't remember her at all. From what I understand, she and my father were not a happy couple. He married Anna soon after. She must have been nearly twenty then."

"Does it bother you to have a stepmother?"

At that, Jenelle offered a short, sharp laugh. "If you believe that, you are a very poor seer. Anna is the only one who makes life bearable. Before all this curse business, and then Lysander falling so ill, she was planning to take me on a trip to Enêmûsk, so I might finally . . . attend a few dances and events."

The source of Jenelle's bitterness became clearer. She was unmarried, and it seemed her father was doing nothing to amend that. Lady Anna took more of an interest.

"Anyway, as a child," Jenelle said, "I felt sorry for Anna when she married my father. She and I are first cousins."

Céline stopped walking. "Pardon?"

"You didn't know? My mother and her mother were sisters. When my mother died, Father asked for Anna's hand, and he got it. There's no blood connection between them, so her parents didn't object. Anna got rather pushed into it, though. She'd always viewed him as an uncle, and I've heard rumors that she was already in love with someone her own age."

"Pushed into it? You mean she was pressed into the marriage?"

Jenelle nodded. "That's what the older servants all

say, but if it's true, she's made the best of things. That's what Anna does . . . make the best of things. I'm not so inclined." She paused. "And my father did make her the princess of Yegor. She'll always have that."

Again, these details were important, but Céline couldn't see how they fit together in regard to having anything to do with the curse.

"And Anna did something my mother could not," Jenelle went on. "She gave my father a male heir."

More bitterness.

"Does he worry for Lysander's health?" Céline asked.

"I think he does sometimes, whenever he can tear himself away from his newest Móndyalítko whore."

Céline stumbled, almost dropping her box of supplies. "You know about him and Lilah?"

"Is that her name? There's a new one every summer. Thank the gods Anna has no idea, but he picked up a taste for camp girls some years ago and can't seem to get enough. It's disgusting."

Goodness. Jenelle had not been exaggerating when she called herself frank.

So Malcolm had been bedding Móndyalítko women for years? Did he make them all the same promises he'd made to Lilah? Céline mulled this over. It could give any jilted or forgotten woman in the camp a motive.

Jenelle led her to the front doors of the castle, and a guard there opened one.

Céline looked to Jenelle. "I must thank you for the talk. You have given me a good deal to consider."

Jenelle's face was serious. "I hope you can solve this. Selfish as it sounds, I want to go to Enêmûsk, and

Anna won't leave Father or Lysander while things are in this state."

Was this her only concern?

"Do you want to know if you'll meet your husband soon?" Céline asked, hoping for an opportunity to read Jenelle. "I could see your future and tell you."

Startled, the girl looked at her eagerly, and then the expression faded. "No. Sometimes I feel like I'm barely getting through the day now. If you tell me this will continue to go on, I don't think I could bear it. I want the hope."

She turned and walked away.

Jenelle certainly knew her own mind.

With her thoughts busy, Céline went out into the courtyard. Jaromir spotted her, made his excuses to the dice players, and came striding over.

"Well?" he asked. "Did you learn anything new?"

She hesitated. "Possibly."

CHAPTER TWELVE

B ack inside the blue wagon, Amelie's morning was proving tediously similar to yesterday. The Móndy-alítko who came to see her were all looking to be cleared, and the images she saw were mundane in nature. But sooner or later, the possibilities would be narrowed down—at least among the people here.

As she finished her fourth reading of the morning and bade a middle-aged man good-bye, she wondered how Céline and Jaromir were faring. This thought led to a flash of images from the night before, of things she'd done and said to Jaromir when they were alone in the darkness.

The images were certainly not unpleasant, but she pushed them away. She needed to focus.

When she looked over at the open doorway, a striking young woman of about nineteen was looking in at her. Amelie had seen her around camp but didn't know her name. She was small with slender shoulders, a small waist, and curving hips. Her black hair was pulled up into a tail at the back of her head, and it still hung to the center of her back. She hovered there in the doorway, seeming nervous.

"Come in," Amelie said.

The girl didn't move. "My father told me I had to come, that I had to be cleared."

"You'll need to sit down for me to do that."

Finally, the girl came inside, still watching Amelie with caution.

"What's your name?" Amelie asked.

"Miranda, from the line of Klempá."

"I'm Amelie."

"I know who you are."

She didn't sound accusing, only nervous, and Amelie's interest began to pique. Up close, Miranda was quite lovely, with graceful, slender hands and straight white teeth.

"I'd rather have your sister read me," she said. "Is she not here?"

"No, she's gone up to the castle to check on the prince's son, but I can clear you if that's all you're after."

At the mention of the prince, Miranda glanced away. With a look of resignation, she held out her hand. "Very well. My father wants this done today."

She clearly had something in her past she wanted to hide, and Amelie had no wish to expose anyone's personal secrets, but Miranda was the first person to see her who'd been reluctant to be read.

Grasping the girl's hand, Amelie focused on the spark of her spirit, on the past, and on anything that might be related to the curse. The first jolt hit, and she braced for the next one. Then she felt herself being pulled backward through the swirling mists.

When the mists cleared, she saw herself standing in a small room with stone walls, facing a bed. Prince Malcolm was stretched out on the bed, half-covered by a blanket. Miranda lay beneath him, half-covered as well, and he was stroking her hair.

"My sweet girl," he whispered.

She beamed up at him. "I've never loved anyone as much as you. Do you promise it will always be like this?"

"Always. Ask me for anything and it's yours. I'd give you the world."

He leaned down and kissed her.

The mists rose again, and Amelie found herself moving quickly through a barrage of scenes of the two them in bed or in the woods on a blanket or once alone in the orchard, always touching and kissing, murmuring promises and words of love.

Then the mists closed in, and when they cleared, Amelie found herself inside a shabby wagon. She remembered the Klempá were among the poorer of the Móndyalítko. Miranda stood facing a woman about twenty years older than herself.

"The harvest is over," the older woman said. "We leave tomorrow, and you'll come with us. He wants you gone."

"You're wrong!" Miranda cried. "He loves me. He doesn't want me to go. He said he'd keep me here with him, that he'd find a way."

"Don't be a fool," the older woman said. "Men like him will say anything to get what they want." She held up a pouch of coins. "He came down this morning and gave me this."

Miranda stared at the pouch. "He gave you money?"

"He wants you gone."

The mists closed in, and Amelie felt herself being pulled forward in time.

When they cleared, she stood in the Yegor meadow, only it was lush and green, and the apple trees to the east were covered in white blossoms.

It was spring.

Numerous wagons were settled and several were still pulling in. At least a year had passed.

Looking toward the tree line, she saw Miranda furtively slip into the forest, and she followed. The girl moved like a deer, easily passing through heavy brush until she came to a clearing and peered through.

Her body went stiff.

It was effortless for Amelie to follow—as she wasn't really there.

Stepping up beside the girl, Amelie looked into the clearing. From what she'd already seen, she recognized this clearing as a place Prince Malcolm and Miranda had often met.

Now Malcolm lay on a blanket on the ground with Lilah.

"My sweet," he murmured.

Hidden in the trees, Miranda put her hand to her mouth.

The mists closed in and Amelie was rushed forward again. Then she was sitting in the wagon, facing Miranda.

Both women remained silent for a few breaths.

"Did you see?" Miranda said finally.

Amelie was almost lost for words. "You . . . you were with the prince the last summer?"

"He loved me. He thought I was perfect."

Amelie was not given to pity, but as she drew her hand away, she said, "I'm sorry."

"Am I cleared?"

While Miranda certainly had motive enough to lash out at Prince Malcolm and try to ruin him, if she'd been the one to cast the curse, the mists would have shown this.

"Yes," Amelie answered.

Without another word, Miranda got up and left. Amelie sat there, thinking. Last spring and summer, Malcolm had had a love affair with Miranda and then paid her family to take her away at the end of the harvest, and now this year, he'd turned his attentions to Lilah.

When Amelie had read both young women, the mists showed details of the affairs.

Why?

Movement in the doorway caught her eye, and she looked over to see Céline coming in.

"Can you take a break from readings? I have a good deal to tell you."

"Of course," Amelie answered. "Close the door."

Céline closed it and came over to sit. "I'm not sure where to start." She appeared weary, and Amelie wondered if she'd slept at all.

"Why don't you start with whatever happened last night?"

Nodding, Céline launched into a story about Helga that was difficult to hear, but when it was over, Amelie understood a few things much better.

"Helga's Mist-Torn?"

"Yes, and I'm nearly certain that's how she learned of what was happening here."

Poor Helga, to lose her daughter and granddaughter. No wonder she hated Jago Taragoš.

"You think it really was Jago?" she asked Céline.

"I do, but I don't think he has anything to do with the land being cursed."

"So, what happened up at the castle?"

Céline related of hearing Lilah and the prince in a side room of the castle, but then she moved to a more interesting conversation with Jenelle about Malcolm.

"She claims he chooses out a new girl from the camp every summer, and he's been in power for five years."

Amelie sat straight. "I just did a reading for the girl he picked last summer. It was awful. He convinced her that he loved her and then got rid of her once the harvest was in."

Céline blinked. "Truly? Then she has a motive."

"It's not her, but . . . what about the girls who came before her?"

This was the first solid lead they'd encountered. If Malcolm had been convincing one girl each summer that he loved her, and then he discarded her and blatantly chose a new love the following year, there could be several women here driven to hurt him.

"Who was the girl you read this morning?" Céline asked.

"Miranda Klempá."

"Do you think it's possible that once she came to terms with the truth, she might have learned which other girls from among the families came before her?"

"It's possible, but she's rather tight-lipped."

Céline stood. "I'll go and talk to her. We need to find out one way or another."

Amelie agreed Céline should try. For some reason, people often told her their secrets.

"I'll come right back," Céline said, and then she headed for the door.

When Céline stepped outside, she looked over to see Helga and Jaromir both crouched by the fire. Helga was pouring Jaromir a mug of tea. Marcus stood a few paces behind them.

"Should I fetch someone else for Amelie to clear?" Helga asked.

"No," Céline answered. "We need to follow up on something first and discuss it."

"With what?" Jaromir asked.

"I'm not entirely certain yet, but I need to speak with someone alone. I won't be gone long."

Jaromir frowned—as he felt strongly about being told everything immediately. But this was a delicate matter, and she had no intention of embarrassing Miranda further without need.

Marcus came closer. "Should I walk with you?"

After last night, she had no wish to be drawn into a conversation with him just yet. "No, thank you. I'm not leaving the camp. Could you point me toward the Klempá wagons?"

She knew he felt rebuffed, but he pointed down the line of wagons. "Last group before the trees."

"Thank you."

Turning, she walked toward the edge of the meadow

and made her way down the front side of the wagons. Most of the activity in camp took place on the back sides—which faced inward—and she didn't wish to be seen and stopped along the way.

Here, near the edge, she was alone and had time to think about what she might say. If Miranda knew the names of the other young women Malcolm had seduced, would she share them?

This was the first genuine motive she and Amelie had uncovered.

Her thoughts were so preoccupied that she was nearing the end of the line of wagons, almost to the Klempá, when she noticed a shadow up ahead. Then someone large stepped from beyond the side of wagon and stood in her path.

She froze.

It was Jago Taragoš.

Glancing around, she saw that they were alone here, with the trees to her right, a wagon to her left, and him blocking the way forward.

"I saw you leave your wagons and come this way," he said.

Everything Helga had told her came rushing back. "Yes, I have someone to visit. Please do excuse me."

She stepped forward, hoping he would move aside, but he didn't, and when she tried to step around him, he cut her off.

"I would speak with you," he said.

"As I told you, I have a visit to make."

His eyes narrowed. "Show me the manners of hearing me out."

There he was, insulting her manners again. Did he truly think this was the way to impress a woman?

"I had no idea there were any Mist-Torn seers from the line of Fawe," he went on, "young and beautiful. I spoke poorly at our first meeting. I thought to impress you with my family name and standing." He took a long breath. "But you must understand that I am free. I am not married, and I have much to offer."

Céline suddenly wondered if he'd ever taken another wife. Nearly six years had passed since the death of his own and five since the death of Jo. If he hadn't remarried, it was most likely because for all their silence on the question of Jo's death, none of the families wished to hand him one of their daughters. No wonder he was so attracted to the idea of a young seer like herself who simply appeared one day. He probably saw her as a new prospect. Surely he must have known Helga would warn her?

Or perhaps he was so self-delusional that he'd convinced himself that he bore no guilt?

"Consider my offer," he said. "I am a hunter and a good provider. I will someday, possibly soon, be the leader of the Taragoš. As my wife, you'd have a place of honor and status." His voice lowered. "And I would cherish you with all my heart and all my body."

Staring at her, he genuinely appeared to think his words would melt her resolve. His expression was open and vulnerable, and that made him more dangerous. She had to put him off without angering him.

"Jago . . . ," she began. "I'm honored by your offer, but I have a home in Sèone, and I will be returning there. At present, I have no wish to marry anyone."

His features flattened in surprise. "That is your answer? After what I just said?"

She took a step back, wondering if she could dash around the wagon and run for a more populated area.

"I don't wish to offend you," she said.

"But that is your answer? A refusal?"

When she didn't speak, his eyes narrowed further, and his expression shifted to a mix of anger and blame. She remembered what Helga said about the way he'd viewed Jo after her refusal, that she was nothing more than a cold, heartless girl who'd spurned him and his family.

Before she could think or move, he darted forward, closing the distance between them in seconds. One of his hands closed over her mouth, and the other hand lifted her off the ground as he dragged her rapidly into the forest. She tried to struggle, but the strength in his hands was incredible, and she could only feel herself being half carried, half dragged across the forest floor. Was this how he had caught Jo? By snatching her away when Gersham had crawled under a bush to look for firewood?

A few moments later, he stopped moving and shoved her away. She caught herself on a tree and looked back wildly.

His eyes were alight with rage but also with hunger and pleasure, as if he'd been longing to do this and denying himself. Though it was daylight, the sky was overcast and scant light penetrated through the dense trees.

"Run," he whispered, pointing deeper into the forest.

As he said this, his hands were no longer hands. Short black fur was sprouting from the skin on his arms, and his hands had become claws. His face began changing, and he dropped to all fours as more fur sprouted from his body.

In the span of a few breaths, Jago was gone. A great black cat, the size of a small pony, stood in his place, snarling, exposing white fangs. His breeches fell away on the ground behind him as he rushed forward. His shirt had ripped during the transformation, but shredded pieces still clung to him.

He'd positioned himself between Céline and the meadow.

Whirling, she had no choice but to run the other direction, toward the stream.

Back at the campfire, Helga poured another steaming mug of tea and handed it to Jaromir—who already held a mug in his right hand.

"Take this in to Amelie," she said. "If the sisters are taking a break to follow a lead, I'm sure she could use a bit of tea . . . and some company."

With a nod, he took the mug and headed off for the blue wagon.

Craning her head, she glanced back at Marcus, who stood behind her with a fairly miserable look on his face. Poor thing. In spite of her well-warranted opinion of shifters, she couldn't help liking him. He was one of the good ones. "You want some tea?"

He shook his head.

She was about to tell him to come and sit down when

a nag so strong that it caused pain hit the back of her head. She gasped and fell forward. In a flash, Marcus was beside her, holding her up.

Shoving him off, she grabbed a small stick from the fire and pulled it out so she could focus down upon a small flame.

Blessed fire in the night
Show me what is in the sight
Show me what brings fight or flight
Blessed fire in the night

The scene around her vanished and the mists closed in. When they cleared, she was in the forest, and she could hear the sound of the rushing stream. An instant later, Céline, her face awash with terror ran past, catching her skirt on a bush and jerking it loose as she ran on.

The sounds of raging snarls came from behind her. . . .

Gasping again, Helga turned to Marcus. "It's Céline! She's somewhere by the stream and Jago's after her. Go! Go!"

Before the final word left her mouth, he was sprinting for the tree line almost faster than she could follow with her eyes. Reaching into her boot, she withdrew a long hunting knife and stood up. Common sense told her to call out for Jaromir and then run.

"Jaromir! To the stream! Céline's in trouble."

Then she ran after Marcus, moving much faster than anyone might expect.

*   *   *

Amelie tensed slightly when Jaromir came into the wagon alone with two steaming mugs of tea. His company was not unwelcome, just the opposite. She simply hoped that he didn't want to "talk" about things or ask questions about how their relationship had changed.

At present, she wasn't sure she had any answers for him.

"Tea?" he asked, holding up a mug.

She nodded. "You should stay anyway. When Céline comes back, I'm hoping we might actually have a short list of suspects."

"Really?"

"Yes. Apparently, Prince Malcolm has been—" She was cut off by the sound of Helga shouting outside.

"Jaromir! To the stream! Céline's in trouble."

Dropping both mugs, Jaromir ran for the door, and Amelie followed. He jumped over the stairs and landed on the ground, looking all ways.

"I don't see Helga!" he called.

Amelie ran to join him. She didn't see Marcus, either. "She said the stream! Go!"

He bolted with her on his heels.

Céline knew Jago was playing with her.

As a panther, on all fours, he could have caught her easily, but he seemed to be enjoying letting her run for now. She raced through the trees and the brush along the stream, but sooner or later, either he would catch her or she'd have to turn and fight.

She had no weapons, and even amid panic, she

scanned the ground for a stout branch or anything she might grab. Amelie always relied on the element of surprise, and Céline struggled to channel her sister's courage.

Up ahead, near a wide spruce tree, she spotted a large jagged rock. Without slowing until she was almost upon it, she grasped it as she ran past and then dodged halfway around the side of the tree to use it for partial cover. She hoped he'd keep coming without seeing what she'd grabbed so that she might land a hard blow to his head. If she even stunned him, it could give her a chance to run back toward the meadow.

But when she turned, he'd stopped and he was once again in the form of a man, naked, standing near the rushing water in the stream below.

"The line of Fawe!" he spat. "So proud. You think yourself above me, above my family. What do you think of me now?"

In a blink, he was a panther again on all fours, and he charged. With little choice, Céline stood her ground, gripping the jagged rock, ready to attempt a strike. He was coming so fast she panted in fear, already picturing his claws slashing her face and her throat.

Then . . . when he was two body lengths from her, something black dashed through a bush to her left and smashed into Jago hard enough to knock him off his feet. Both forms rolled down into the stream with a splash.

Snarls and roars and growls exploded in the air, and she ran to the edge of the bank to look down. A tall black wolf—Marcus—was still rolling through the water with the panther. The panther slashed with both claws as the wolf fought for a hold on its throat.

All Céline's instincts screamed at her to help Marcus, but she didn't know how and she dared not get in his way. Both animals moved downstream as they continued to fight.

"Céline, stay there!" a voice called.

Helga emerged from the trees, downstream, directly above the wolf and the panther. The wolf leaped off the panther, and then charged back in, going for its throat and pinning it in the stream. The panther slashed, leaving bloody wounds down the wolf's shoulder, but the wolf didn't let go and held it there, biting deeper.

To Céline's shock, Helga ran down the bank into the stream.

"No!" Céline cried, fearing for the old woman's life.

But Helga raised her large knife and drove it down right through the panther's left eye, dropping all her weight and sinking the blade into its skull.

Rock in hand, Céline ran toward the trio in the stream, but the panther ceased moving. The wolf let go and stumbled backward. A breath later, the panther shifted into Jago, who lay dead with his throat torn and a knife through his eye.

Marcus was himself again, too, but his face and the front side of his right shoulder were slashed and bleeding.

More crashing sounded in the brush, and then Jaromir and Amelie emerged from between two trees downstream. Both gripped long knives.

Jaromir's eyes dropped to the sight of Jago's body.

Céline ran for Marcus, gripping him to keep him from falling. The slashes on his face were superficial, but his shoulder was bad. Blood flowed from the two deepest slashes and ran down his stomach over his hip.

"We have to get him back," she called.

Jaromir and Amelie hurried over, and Jaromir looked down at Jago. "Marcus, you killed him?"

"No," Helga answered. "I did."

CHAPTER THIRTEEN

That night, a gathering of the leaders was called.
A large group stood around a burning campfire
at the east end of the wagons.

From what Céline understood, at the first gathering
that involved Jago, five years ago, only the heads of the
families were involved, which was part of why the story
had been so easy to hush up.

This time, everyone involved was present, and a
good number of people from the families had gathered
outside the circle to listen. Céline wondered about the
difference, but Helga stood beside her and pointed to
a middle-aged man with a muscular build.

"That's Gerard," she whispered. "New leader of the
Ayres. He and Sinead both demanded this be more
public."

She hadn't said much since killing Jago, and her eyes
were hard. Céline wondered if she even cared what
happened to her now.

Sinead and her husband, Terrell, walked straight to
Céline and stood beside her. Jaromir and Amelie stood

a short ways back. Marcus was seated on a chair to Helga's left. Céline had stitched the wounds, stopped the bleeding, and bandaged him. She'd begged him to remain in bed, but he insisted on coming to this gathering.

A slender man with graying hair stepped near the fire. Céline recognized him from her reading of Jago: Silvanas, leader of the Taragoš. His expression was strained and weary, and in spite of everything, Céline couldn't help a flash of pity. The man had lost his son today.

"Helga of the line of Ayres has confessed to killing my son," he said. "Let the judgment of the act begin."

"Céline should speak first," Sinead called in a strong voice, "and tell us what happened."

Céline had known this was coming. For some reason, she turned her eyes to Gerard, thinking on his pain and sense of helplessness the day Jo had been killed, and although she'd never met this man, she spoke directly to him.

She began with Jago cornering her alone on the outskirts of the meadow, pressing his proposal, growing angry at her refusal and dragging her into the trees. She continued with the ugly chase, her finally turning to defend herself, Marcus launching in, the fight in the water, and Helga running to finish it.

"Helga had no choice," she said. "Jago would have killed Marcus and then me."

Gerard's eyes were blazing, and he took shallow breaths. He was most likely reliving the past. Only then did Céline allow herself to look at some of the other leaders. Silvanas had gone pale. Rupert appeared uncomfortable. These people had covered up a murder five years ago, and now they were being faced with the consequences.

"Marcus," Rupert asked. "Is this what happened?"

Standing from his chair, Marcus nodded. "Yes. I almost did not arrive in time. Jago was attacking Céline, and I caught him at the last instant. He would have killed her. He had gone mad." He looked to Silvanas. "And Helga had no choice. I was already wounded when she ran in. She saved me and Céline."

With open reservation, Rupert addressed Helga. "You can corroborate what these two have testified?"

She glared at him. "I've got no call to justify myself to you. I saved a girl this time. I couldn't save the last one. I couldn't save my own girl. But that killer is dead and gone now. You judge me however you like. The gods know I've judged you."

Sinead stepped forward. Her body was tight. "I propose a judgment of self-defense or defense in the case of others. Everyone in agreement raise your hand."

Her own hand and Gerard's rose instantly. One by one, the other leaders raised their hands. Rupert was the second to last. Finally, even Silvanas slowly raised his hand.

"Done, then," Sinead said. "Helga, go and get some rest."

And with that, the gathering was over. Jago was dead, and Helga's actions had been justified.

Céline had never seen anything quite like this. It had seemed impartial and fair, but she knew from

Helga's story that a vote of consensus did not always equate to justice.

Jaromir reached out to Marcus. "You need help walking back."

"No, I can walk."

Céline glanced once more to Gerard, who nodded at her and looked sadly at Helga. To the best of Céline's knowledge, those two had not spoken to each other since Helga's arrival. Perhaps they would both find it too painful.

Then Céline nodded to Sinead. "Thank you."

This seemed awfully formal, but she didn't know what else to say.

She, Amelie, Helga, Marcus, and Jaromir headed back for their own wagons. Upon reaching them, she noticed Jaromir watching Amelie with a mix of longing and uncertainty. These scant nights here, in the meadow, away from all other responsibilities, might be the last moments of peace those two would have in some time.

"Amelie," she said, "why don't you and Jaromir head in and rest? I'm going to take Helga to the other wagon and sit with her for a bit. She shouldn't be alone. Is that all right?"

Startled, Amelie glanced at Jaromir and back to Céline. "Yes, of course."

Quickly, Amelie and Jaromir vanished into the white wagon.

"I don't need you to sit with me," Helga said.

"I know," Céline answered. Then she looked to Marcus. "Perhaps you should come with us and sleep in a bunk tonight?"

"No," he answered. "I'll sleep better by the fire."

She had no idea what to say to him. He had saved her life today. He had taken wounds meant for her.

Turning, she fell into step beside Helga, and they both climbed the short steps and entered the blue wagon, closing the door behind themselves.

Helga went straight to the back and sank down on the lower bunk.

"Does this change anything for you?" Céline asked. "Would you want to rejoin your family?"

The older woman seemed so tired. "No. That time is past. My life is in Sèone now." She tilted her head. "What about you? You know at some point, Sinead will try to talk you into staying."

Yes, Céline had expected this and was surprised it hadn't occurred yet. "My life is in Sèone, too."

Her heart was in Sèone.

Helga lay back, and Céline went over to pull an extra blanket up over her shoulders.

"I'm not a child," Helga grumbled.

"Let me take care of you a bit."

Céline crouched there by the lower bunk as Helga's eyes closed. Soon, the older woman was breathing deeply—but not snoring yet.

With reluctance, Céline rose to face the top bunk. She was exhausted, beyond exhausted, and the thought of tossing and turning up there, unable to shut off her mind, was almost too much.

Without thinking, she left the wagon quietly and walked back to their own small campfire. Marcus sat there, gazing into the flames. His dark eyes rose at her approach.

She sighed. "I know this isn't fair to you, but I'm so tired. I need to sleep so badly."

Without a word, he used his good arm to spread out a blanket, and then he lay down. She went to him and curled up against his back this time, pulling another blanket over both of them.

"I don't want to press against your shoulder," she said.

She slipped her arm around his stomach, and he grasped her hand, holding it against himself.

"Sleep," he said.

Near the mid of night, Amelie lay in Jaromir's arms, both of them still awake as he brushed his mouth over her face and neck.

She reveled in the feel of his warm, bare skin against hers, and she unconsciously ran her finger over the scars on his back. He had so many scars.

Tonight had been even more intimate and intense than last night, as she was learning what to do, what he liked, and what she liked.

The result was a revelation.

For now, she'd managed to push away all thoughts of tomorrow, and simply live for today, but she'd not been so successful with attempting to push away the past. It haunted her that this was all new to her, and Jaromir had been with so many women.

She longed to ask him one question, but she feared the answer. He was not a sweet talker and if she asked him something, he'd tell her the truth.

As if sensing something was wrong, he lifted his head with his face directly above hers.

"What is it?" he asked.

Unable to stop herself, she blurted out, "Is this . . . is it different for you from everything that came before?"

He seemed to understand exactly what she was asking him, and he didn't answer for a few seconds.

Then he said, "Yes. It's very different."

She breathed in relief and didn't press him further. For now, that was all she wanted to know.

CHAPTER FOURTEEN

The next morning, Céline helped Helga to boil some oats for breakfast, and everyone did their best to pretend the situation from the previous night was normal, with Céline and Marcus sleeping by the fire, and Amelie and Jaromir sleeping alone in the wagon.

In spite of his wounds, Marcus had gone to water the horses, and Jaromir came striding from the tree line with an armload of firewood.

He leaned over the pot. "Oats again?"

Helga offered him a withering look. "We didn't bring our own chickens along. You could try trading with some of the people here for a few eggs."

"I may just do that," he growled back. "Is there tea?"

"Here," Céline said, lifting a clean mug and pouring him a cup.

"What's the plan for this morning?" he asked, taking a sip.

Céline had been contemplating that question herself. Yesterday, before being cornered by Jago, she'd been attempting to see Miranda Klempá.

"Amelie and I thought we might be onto something yesterday." She lowered her voice. "It seems Prince Malcolm has been seducing and then discarding a new girl from this encampment every year. Amelie read one of them, but she's not the kettle witch. It may have taken another of the discarded women time to realize his pattern and become angry enough to take revenge."

He listened carefully. Helga stirred the oats, listening, too.

"We were hoping to try to put together a list of names," Amelie added. "That line of action still seems more useful than reading people to clear them. At least we've uncovered a motive."

Jaromir nodded. "Good. I agree. So you planned to start by questioning the girl Amelie read yesterday?"

"Yes," Céline answered. "It's possible she might know the names of the others. If she doesn't, we'll speak quietly with some of the leaders and see if they know anything. But we must be careful. If we're wrong about this, we don't want unfair accusations being cast."

Though she'd slept well, she felt badly in need of a bath. Later, she might take Amelie to stand guard and attempt to wash herself in the stream. But this morning, she wanted to continue attempting to put together a list of names.

"All right," Amelie said. "You start with Miranda. I'll—"

Céline never heard what Amelie planned to do, as the sound of pounding hooves interrupted them. Looking east, she saw a guard from the castle racing into camp. He headed straight for their wagons, pulled up his horse, and jumped to the ground.

It was Ayden, the guard with the scarred forehead.

"The prince's son can barely breathe," he panted, speaking to Céline. "Lady Anna begs you to come."

Céline thought quickly. During a crisis of this nature, the castle might well offer other avenues to learning the names of Malcolm's conquests, but she herself had to focus on Lysander.

"I'll need my sister and Jaromir," she said.

"They can come up on foot, but you come with me now." He jumped back on the horse and held his hand down.

Céline turned to Jaromir and Amelie. "Get my box of supplies and hurry after us."

Grasping Ayden's hand, she felt herself lifted off the ground. Swinging her leg over the horse, she sat behind him. Then they were off, racing for the castle.

Amelie and Jaromir wasted no time.

With him carrying the box, they nearly ran up the dry road to the gates of the castle, where they were passed through without question.

"Where to now?" Jaromir asked as they entered the courtyard and looked around. Céline was nowhere in sight.

"I don't know," she answered. "We should ask inside."

After passing through the main doors of the castle, they headed for the great hall. Walking through the archway, Amelie saw Prince Malcolm and his daughter, Jenelle, standing by the dead hearth . . . facing six men in shabby clothes with dusty hair. All six had an air of desperation.

A few of Malcolm's guards stood nearby, and one had his hand hovering above the hilt of his sword.

"You are not the only one facing ruin, my lord," said a man standing out in front of the others. "We're facing death if this is not turned around."

Malcolm crossed his arms. "Do you think I'm not aware of that? I swear to you that I'm doing everything in my power to find out who has done this to the land."

"But we heard you freed those tzigän in the meadow!" another man cried. "It had to be one of them, and you know it . . . my lord."

Amelie winced at both his tone and his choice of term. "Tzigän" was a derogatory term for the Móndy-alítko, and the word meant "vagabond thieves." It didn't take much for her to figure out what was happening here. These men were from Malcolm's villages. Normally, they'd all be either harvesting crops or picking strawberries for him. Their lands were as dead and dry as the lands around this castle.

They wanted answers. And who could blame them?

Just then, one of the men spotted her and Jaromir in the archway. As his eyes raked over their clothing, his expression flattened. "There's two of them now!"

All five other men turned in equal anger.

"You!" the leader shouted. "It was one of you who cast this curse!"

Amelie stiffened in alarm, and one of the Yegor guards drew a sword, but Jaromir stepped in front of her, unarmed, and faced the desperate villagers.

"I am Prince Anton's lieutenant, from the house of Pählen, here to investigate who it was who cast this curse," he said, and his voice carried across the hall.

"It may very well have been one of the people down in that meadow, but that is exactly what this lady and I are trying to learn." He spoke in the same voice he used when giving orders to his men back home. Even wearing no armor, no tabard, and no sword, he had once again become "the lieutenant."

Both the sound and his words had an instant effect, and the hall fell silent. When Jaromir talked, people listened.

"We *will* find out who did this," Jaromir said, "and we will reverse it." He pointed to some mugs and several pitchers that had been set out on the table. "But from what I understand, the prince's son is ill today, and as far as the curse is concerned, there's nothing any of you can do. Have a mug of ale and rest for a while. The best you can do is to let us solve this, and we will solve it."

Malcolm gestured toward the mugs. "Yes, Jerome," he said to the leader, "come and have a drink and let us talk. As the lieutenant says, we will solve this. Now, tell me if there is anything I can do in the interim. Do you need grain for your livestock? I have emergency stores."

The man at the front nodded tightly and finally said, "Thank you, my lord. I am sorry your son is ill."

The tension broke, and Jenelle began pouring mugs. Amelie crossed to her quickly and whispered, "Where is my sister? We brought her box of supplies."

For some reason, Jenelle was far less at ease with her than Céline, and Amelie had no idea why. Now Jenelle looked at her uncomfortably and glanced at Malcolm. In a flash, Amelie came to a realization. The girls Malcolm had chosen from among the people in the meadow had been small with near-black hair and pale skin.

Amelie was Malcolm's type, and so her presence concerned Jenelle.

"She's with Anna, caring for Lysander up in his room," Jenelle answered, and then paused. "I would take you myself, but I think I should stay with my father just now. The room is easy to find. Head down the main passage until you come to a right turn. Follow that to the base of the tower and go up to the second floor. Lysander's room is the third door on the left."

"Thank you," Amelie said.

Going back to Jaromir, she took the box. "Stay here and learn what you can," she whispered. "I'm going up to Céline."

He nodded.

She left the hall and hurried down the main passage toward the front of the castle. When she reached the right turn, she took it and walked even faster until she saw the base of the tower. At the base, the passage continued a little farther, and she heard some kind of commotion up ahead.

Curious, she continued on a little farther and found herself standing outside a busy kitchen.

"Get it hotter," an older woman ordered.

Several women were struggling to get large pots of water on top of a wide woodstove.

Amelie continued scanning the scene, and her eyes stopped at the sight of a young woman sitting at a table with a goblet in one hand and bread covered in jam in the other.

It was Lilah.

"I don't care how busy you are, Helen," Lilah said to the older woman at the stove. "My goblet is empty."

"Yes, miss," the woman said tightly. She left the stove and poured wine into Lilah's goblet.

"That's better," Lilah said, sounding imperious. Then she spotted Amelie in the doorway and her eyes widened. "You?" She set down the bread and the goblet. "What are you doing up here?" she demanded.

The women in the kitchen glanced over, and Lilah's expression grew angrier and more alarmed. Standing, she walked swiftly to Amelie and pushed her down the passage, out of sight of the kitchen.

By way of reaction, Amelie's fist clenched, and her first instinct was to drop the box of supplies and flatten Lilah, but she held back.

"What are you doing here?" Lilah repeated, her voice lower now. The alarm in her eyes had grown, and it struck Amelie that Lilah might be worried about the exact same thing that worried Jenelle.

Amelie was small and pale and pretty with near-black hair and dressed in the garb of a Móndyalítko girl.

"Not that it's any of your business," Amelie answered, "but I'm here to help Céline with the prince's son."

"Oh." Lilah released a breath. "Is that all? That sickly boy? He won't matter much soon anyway. You should leave. Get out and go back to camp."

Amelie began turning to head for the tower. "You don't have the right to tell anyone here what to do. I'm going upstairs."

"Oh yes, I do," Lilah said.

Something in her voice made Amelie stop. The rude girl sounded so utterly certain.

"I'm going to be the lady of this castle soon," Lilah went on, "and if you want a place in the meadow next summer, you'll have to answer to me."

Incredulous, Amelie looked back. "The lady?"

"It's common knowledge. Why do you think those kitchen women rush to serve me?"

"What about Lady Anna? He can't divorce her, and so you cannot be made mistress here."

"Divorce, no. But the prince is weary of her and that sickly son." Lilah smiled. "You think I'm some deluded girl, but you're wrong. Malcolm wrote a letter to Grand Prince Rodêk, asking for an annulment of his marriage to Anna on the grounds that she's not provided him a healthy heir and that as he was once married to her aunt, the family bond is too close and they shouldn't have married in the first place. Malcolm promised that in return for this favor, he would back whomever Rodêk chooses in the upcoming election."

"No," Amelie whispered. "That would disinherit Lysander. He'd be illegitimate."

"Oh yes. I saw the letter. Malcolm used his seal and sent it. Grand Prince Rodêk has no reason to refuse and a good reason to agree. It will be as if the marriage to Anna never happened. He'll marry me, and I'll give him strong sons." Lilah took a step closer. "So you'd better do as I say if you and your sister ever want to return to the meadow for the harvest." Turning on her heel, she headed back to the kitchen. "I'm going to finish my wine. I suggest you leave now."

In disbelief, Amelie watched her go.

Malcolm planned to annul his marriage to Lady Anna? Could it be true? It seemed that not only did

Lilah believe it, but the servants of the castle believed it. How far had word spread?

So far, in the internal workings of the family, Amelie and Céline had garnered many small pieces of information but nothing that fit together.

This was a piece that fit.

Quickly, she jogged for the base of the tower.

Upon arriving in Lysander's room, Céline found Lady Anna near to giving way to emotion. Her careful veneer of dignity was strained to the limit. Lysander lay in his bed, gasping for air through his mouth.

Jane was there as well. A pot and bowl of water sat on the table.

Céline hurried to the bed.

Anna's eyes held fear. "I don't know what to do. He started like this about an hour ago. The air is so dry today. There is dust throughout the rooms. We tried using a bowl of steaming water, but he couldn't sit up well enough to breathe it in."

"Have you given him any syrup to ease his throat?" Céline asked.

"Yes."

Lysander's face was nearly white, and circles under his eyes were a mix of yellow, purple, and black. Anna's fear was warranted, and something had to be done quickly. Céline fought to think. Her mind slipped back to a night when she was a girl in Shetâna, and her mother had been called to the bed of a little girl whose condition looked and sounded much like Lysander's. Céline tried to remember what her mother had done. And then . . .

"My lady! Do you have a large bathtub in the castle, something that can be carried in here?"

"Of course."

"Have it fetched. Have it brought in, and then get the women in the kitchen busy heating as much water as they can. Lysander will sit in the tub, and the water will need to be as hot as he can stand it. Some of us will hold blankets to keep the steam in, and others will need to keep heating and pouring water."

Anna listened and then nodded to Jane. "Run and give Miss Céline's instructions. See to the tub first and then go to the kitchens. Hurry."

Jane ran.

Within moments, the room was in a flurry of activity.

Several men came in carrying the tub, and they set it on the floor. Not long after this, Amelie stuck her head in the door, carrying Céline's box of supplies.

"Do you need anything?" she asked.

Something in her voice sounded odd, and looking over, Céline knew her sister well enough to know that she'd learned something she needed to discuss. Whatever it was, it would have to wait.

"Not from that box," Céline answered. "But we'll need your help soon enough."

Soon, Jane and some of the women from the kitchen came through the door, struggling with buckets of steaming water. Bucket after bucket was poured, and thankfully, the eldest woman, who was called Helen, had thought to bring a bucket of cold water as well.

Céline tested the water with her hand. It was nearly

boiling, but plenty of steam rose. Using the cold water, she lowered the temperature just enough that Lysander would not be scalded.

"All right, get him in," she said.

Quickly, Lysander was stripped down to his under-drawers, and then Lady Anna lifted him and carried him to the tub. The woman was stronger than she looked. She settled him with his back against the front of the tub.

"There, my darling," she said. "Try to lean back and breathe."

Amelie, Jane, and Céline held blankets up and around the tub to keep in the steam. The kitchen women continued to work, removing water as it cooled and replacing it with hot.

After a while, Lysander ceased gasping and his breathing began to ease.

Céline kept him in there and maintained the steady pace of work around him going on for some time. She watched the boy until he breathed normally and some of his color had returned and his eyes appeared to grow sleepy. He must be exhausted.

Still, she kept him in the steam.

Finally, she nodded to Lady Anna. "I think we can dry him and let him get some rest."

Anna appeared weary, too, but her eyes were grateful. "Thank you."

She lifted her son from the tub, not caring that the water splashed on her velvet gown, and together, she and Céline dried him, dressed him in a long-sleeved wool shirt, and got him back to bed.

He was asleep almost immediately.

"Leave the tub for now," Anna instructed the servants quietly. "Jane will sit with him while he rests. I must go and speak with the prince."

Everyone but Jane left the room.

Céline and Amelie accompanied Lady Anna to the great hall. When they arrived, they found Malcolm, Jenelle, and Jaromir waiting. There was no else besides a few guards and a few servants, who were busy clearing away some mugs and pitchers.

At the sight of Anna, both Malcolm and Jenelle went to Anna quickly as she began to explain what had happened upstairs.

To Céline's surprise, Amelie grabbed her hand and pulled her off to where Jaromir stood by the hearth.

"Listen to me," Amelie whispered, "because we may have to act quickly."

Céline had known something was coming, but she'd not expected it to be this urgent.

"Malcolm has written to Prince Rodêk seeking an annulment to his marriage," Amelie rushed in a low whisper. "He's planning to put Anna aside and marry Lilah."

"What?" Jaromir whispered back. "No. Princes don't put their noble ladies aside and marry Móndyalítko camp girls."

Once again, he seemed to have no idea how arrogant he sounded.

"It's true," Amelie answered. "The entire kitchen staff seems to know, and they're already treating Lilah like the mistress of the castle." She took a shallow breath. "If they know . . . Lady Anna could know."

Céline stared at her. An annulment would be worse

than divorce in this case. Lysander would be declared illegitimate, and Anna would have no recourse at all. If Anna knew of this plan being hatched, she had a stronger motive to hurt Malcolm than any of the Móndyalítko women.

But the curse had made Lysander so ill, and Anna was genuinely distraught. How could she have cast it? Still . . .

"What do you want to do?" Céline whispered.

"I need to read her. Now." Amelie looked to Jaromir. "Even if we have to . . ."

She trailed off, but Céline understood what she'd meant and so would he. More than once, Jaromir had held someone down while one of the sisters did a reading. In this case, they might need him to apply his strength in another direction.

Jaromir's expression was unreadable. He was capable of almost anything in the line of duty, but he'd never had to use force against a prince or a prince's family.

After a moment, though, he said to Amelie, "I'll handle it. Wait for me to tell you to move."

Malcolm, Lady Anna, and Jenelle broke up their small conference and approached the hearth.

"I am told that once again, I have you to thank," Malcolm said to Céline. "I am at a loss for words."

He appeared so concerned for his son—whom he was planning to cast off as a bastard. Could he be so heartless as to pretend this relief?

"None of us have eaten," Lady Anna said. "And I thought I would order an early lunch. Will you all please stay and eat with us? Céline, I would so like for you to check on Lysander again before you leave today."

The servants had left the hall with the mugs, and only three Yegor guards remained.

Before Céline could answer, Jaromir stepped in.

"My lord, before that," he said to Malcolm, "would you mind clearing the room? Something has come to our attention concerning the curse, and it must be shared in private."

Surprise and hope passed across Malcolm's face. "You know something? You can share anything in front of my guards."

Jaromir shook his head. "No. In private. Send them out."

Once again, he used the same tone with which he spoke to his men in Sèone. But Malcolm was a prince, and he frowned. Clearly, he didn't care for ultimatums. "I would prefer they remain."

"Then we'll say nothing."

Both Lady Anna and Jenelle began to appear uncomfortable with the scene playing out before them.

Angry now, Malcolm finally looked to his men and waved one hand. "Out."

All three guards nodded and strode from the hall.

"Well?" Malcolm demanded. "What is this news?"

By way of answer, Jaromir stepped forward and looked to Amelie. "Now," he said.

Before Céline could think or move, Amelie dashed forward and grasped Anna's hand, pulling her away from Malcolm and Jenelle.

Shocked, Malcolm started after them. Jaromir shoved him back against the wall and pinned him there. Malcolm tried to pitch him off.

He failed.

The lieutenant was immovable.

Jenelle's eyes widened in alarm, but Céline held up one hand. "Please. Please wait."

By then Amelie had pulled Lady Anna down to kneel on the floor, still gripping her hand, and both women's faces had gone blank with their eyes far away.

Amelie fought to grasp the spark of Anna's spirit.

Although it was a terrible invasion, she knew she couldn't go back as only an observer this time. She needed to see and feel the past as Anna had felt it. Merely watching events as they had played out would not be enough in this case.

The first jolt hit. Amelie fought to latch onto Anna's spirit, and when she had it, she forced it to mesh with her own. She could feel anxiety flooding Anna's mind, but she didn't let go. She struggled to see through Anna's eyes and feel what she had felt and experienced . . .

Until she was Anna.

The second jolt hit.

The room around them vanished, and they were swept backward together through the gray and white mists.

CHAPTER FIFTEEN

Lady Anna, Princess of Yegor

Anna Janvier was lucky enough to grow up in a place that she loved, surrounded by people she loved.

Her grandfather had made a fortune dealing in timber and stone and then built a manor in central Droevinka about a hundred miles south of Kéonsk. Later, her father, Henri Janvier, proved an equally skilled businessman, and as a result, when he'd made an offer of marriage to Lady Roweena Lambert, who was first cousin to the young prince of house of Hilaron, his offer was accepted.

When Roweena came to live at the Janvier manor, she brought her sister, Siobhan, with her, announcing they couldn't be separated yet. Anna's father had agreed to this arrangement without reservation. He would have agreed to anything.

He valued Roweena and was astonished to have married so high.

Some people said this went to his head, and he forgot that he was not noble himself but had risen in station via his wealth.

Henri, Roweena, and Siobhan set up house together in the manor, and the three of them got on well.

Or these were the stories Anna was later told.

Shortly after the marriage, children began to arrive.

Anna's brother, Landon, came first, then Anna, and then her younger sister, Adrienne. From the time Anna could walk, she remembered her aunt Siobhan as the most prominent person in her life, always there with either a hug or a scolding. Her father and mother were more reserved with their affections and attention, waiting to see what value each of the children might offer.

Landon and Anna took after the Janvier side of the family, slender and blond with quiet natures. Adrienne took after their mother's side, short of stature, with a mass of chestnut hair.

As a boy, Landon had difficulties with his health and was often kept indoors because of breathing troubles. Some seasons were better than others.

By the time Anna was eight years old, she'd become fully indoctrinated into Aunt Siobhan's opinions on life. Siobhan strongly believed in personal responsibility and that for every crime, there must be a punishment. She lavished love on Anna and her siblings but was also swift with justice.

This proved puzzling at times.

One cold winter, Anna was inside the manor, working on a painting of a bowl of fruit—as her mother felt it was important that she master the art of painting still lifes. Aunt Siobhan came up quietly behind her, and as Anna turned in surprise her small brush stroked red paint all across her aunt's fine fur cloak.

Anna blanched, expecting a well-deserved punishment for such blatant carelessness. Her father would have been angry. But Aunt Siobhan only reached out to comfort her.

"Don't fret. It was an accident. There should never be punishments for accidents, only intentional wrongs."

This incident stayed with Anna.

A few weeks later, Adrienne and Landon had a terrible argument in the stable when they both wanted to ride the same pony. Anna witnessed the scene. At the age of seven, Adrienne could already stand up to Landon, who was ten. They shouted at each other until the stable master solved the dispute and put Landon on the pony. Adrienne's face was dark with anger.

That evening, Landon found that his favorite toy, a carved wooden and painted horse, had been thrown into the dining room hearth, and only a few burned pieces of it remained.

He wept.

Anna knew Adrienne had done this.

Anna's parents were far too busy to notice such trauma among their children, but Aunt Siobhan was not. She gathered them by the hearth and demanded to know what had happened. Landon managed to tell some of the story of the afternoon argument.

Siobhan looked into Adrienne's face. "Did you do this? Did you burn your brother's special horse?"

With a sob of her own, Adrienne confessed, and Anna could see that she did regret her actions. Normally, she and Landon were good friends.

"You did this willfully," Aunt Siobhan said, "and there must be a punishment." She turned to leave the hall. "Wait here."

She was not gone long and when she returned, she carried a small purple silk gown. Adrienne's favorite color was purple, and she'd been longing for a grown-up dress.

"I was making you this for your birthday," Aunt Siobhan, "as I know how you wanted one."

With that, she tossed the dress into the hearth and it caught fire.

Adrienne cried out, but Aunt Siobhan made them all watch the dress burn.

Anna found this rather harsh.

Aunt Siobhan stood firm. "The punishment must fit the wrongdoing," she said.

And so Anna came to understand her aunt's view of the world better. Accidents were accidents, but harmful intent required swift retribution.

Two years later, this was driven home on a much larger scale.

Anna had sensed her father was troubled about something. One day, he took a retinue of house guards and left the manor, riding away.

Troubled, Anna went to Siobhan.

"Aunt," she asked. "Where is Papa going?"

She knew her mother would only brush her away.

"Kéonsk," Siobhan answered. "He'd been planning to cut down five acres of trees on the west edge of his lands, to sell the lumber. But our neighbor, Allard Telanger, offered a dispute, swearing those trees are on his own property. The deeds to both estates aren't clear, so your father has gone to see the magistrate in Kéonsk to let the matter be judged."

Upon hearing this, Anna was somewhat relieved.

Although she felt sorry for her father, a land dispute was not the worst thing in the world, and she was glad to have been made privy to the truth.

However, he returned with a defeated face, and at dinner, he discussed the matter openly and told the family what had happened.

"The magistrate found in favor of Telanger," he said, "which I would have accepted. Then one of the magistrate's clerks told me in private that Telanger offered a large bribe before the hearing. The ruling was bought and paid for."

Again, Anna was sorry for her father, but she had a feeling that, considering the size of their property, these five acres wouldn't be too great a loss.

In the night, as she slept in a large bed with Adrienne, both sisters were awakened by their aunt.

"Get dressed, girls," Siobhan whispered. "You have much to learn tonight."

Outside, Anna was surprised to find a horse and two ponies saddled. There was a large sack tied to the saddle of the horse.

"Mount up," their aunt ordered.

It never occurred to Anna to refuse. The three of them rode into the night alone, down the road, and then through forest. Growing weary, Anna had the feeling a good deal of time had passed.

Finally, Aunt Siobhan pulled up and dismounted.

She walked to an enormous oak tree that reached into the night sky. "Do you see this?" she asked.

Anna and Adrienne both nodded.

"This is the border of your father's land. I learned that your grandfather used this oak as a landmark when he purchased the property—or so your father told me. So the five acres behind us rightfully belong to your father, and this Allard Telanger has stolen them away through bribery. Should Telanger be allowed to benefit from his willful treachery?"

"No, Auntie," the girls said dutifully.

Intentional crimes must be punished; these were the teachings of Aunt Siobhan.

Taking down the large bag, their aunt took out firewood, an iron hook, and a cauldron. She built a fire and set the cauldron over the flame. The she drew out a water flask and poured water into the cauldron.

Other, smaller items came from the bag. "Come and look, girls."

Anna and Adrienne moved to see what she'd withdrawn.

There was a sharp knife and a leather glove. Anna recognized the glove. It was her father's. Siobhan took the knife and walked to several of the trees behind them, cutting off bits of the branches.

When she returned, she sat cross-legged before the cauldron.

"Sit with me," she said, "one of you on each side."

They did.

"What will you do?" Anna asked.

"We will do it together. Telanger's punishment must be fitting, don't you agree?"

"Yes."

"Each of you put one hand on my leg and wish your strength into me."

Anna and Adrienne both reached out, each grasping one of their aunt's knees.

The water in the cauldron boiled, and Aunt Siobhan looked up at the night sky.

"Hear my cry!" she called.

Then she looked into the cauldron.

"For the one who was wronged," she said, dropping the glove into the water.

Picking up the knife, she slashed her own hand open, letting blood run into the water.

"Life force from the one who seeks justice," she said.

Then she picked up the bits of branches from the trees and dropped them.

Closing her eyes, she whispered, "A curse upon trees won in betrayal; only those stolen from the wronged; death and disease upon the spoils, but nothing else will be touched."

With her eyes still closed, she raised her head again.

"Hear my cry!"

Her hands dropped down over Anna's and Adrienne's. Anna's hand was instantly slick with blood. "Now, girls, share your strength. Repeat my words and let your strength flow."

All three of them chanted.

A curse upon trees won in betrayal.
Only those stolen from the wronged.
Death and disease upon the spoils.
But nothing else will be touched.
Hear my cry!

Anna focused, trying to pass all the strength inside her to her aunt. Nothing about these actions seemed frightening or strange. A wrong had been done and must be addressed.

A cracking sounded around them. Letting go of her aunt's hand, Anna stood and turned. The trees behind them began to change color, fading and dying. Leaves and needles fell to the ground. Branches withered. The earth grew dry and dusty.

"All five acres will die?" Anna asked.

"All five acres, but only those," Siobhan confirmed. "Telanger will gain nothing from his bribe."

They rode home. Anna washed any remaining blood from her hands and let her aunt tuck her back in. She slept well.

The next day, their father announced that a blight of some kind had hit the five acres he'd lost, and the timber was worthless to Telanger. He had no explanation.

Anna listened and said nothing. Neither did Adrienne.

In the days that followed, Anna asked Siobhan where she had learned to cast such spells, and her aunt smiled as if remembering something important.

"Like you, my parents were too busy for children, only mine hired someone. She was the wisest woman I ever met. My parents did not know this, but she had traveled with Móndyalítko, and she taught me many things. As a girl, your mother wasn't interested in her teachings, but I hope to teach you and Adrienne many things, too."

Anna was torn.

She loved her aunt, but their spirits and natures

were different, and even then, Anna was not certain of Siobhan's black-and-white view of the world and of the need for swift justice.

Still, she couldn't forget the feeling of power that flowed through her that night in the forest.

One afternoon, Aunt Siobhan was in the girls' room, showing them how to make a satchel from lavender, and their mother walked in. When she saw them sitting on the floor with the lavender, she stopped.

"What are you doing?" Her voice was strained.

Adrienne held up her satchel. "Auntie says that if we put these under our pillows, they'll cut off bad dreams."

Like lightning, Mother grabbed the satchel from her hand and then turned on Siobhan. "You will *not* teach my children any of that filthy nonsense. I thought you'd given all that up years . . ." She trailed off and took a step back. "Siobhan, you didn't have anything to do with all that timber dying?"

"Of course I did," Siobhan answered. "What did you think happened?"

"Out," Mother said. "I want to talk to you."

Both women left. Anna and Adrienne stared at each other, uncertain what to think.

After that, their mother spent more time with them each day. She and Siobhan seemed to make up, as they were close sisters, but Siobhan was no longer the only adult in their lives, and she never again taught Anna to cast more spells.

The summer Anna turned eleven, the manor was abuzz with talk of the yearly gathering of the princes in Kéonsk. The gathering was intended for the most powerful men of the land to discuss matters of state, but their wives came as well, and a good many social events were planned.

Other nobles were invited, and Anna's parents often attended.

Before his marriage, Anna's father had never been part of such gatherings, but now he was closely connected to the house of Hilaron and behaved as if such invitations were his due. He, Anna's mother, and Siobhan packed for numerous dinners and dances that would take place at and around Castle Kéonsk.

They would be gone three weeks, and the children were left under the care of the family's housekeeper and under the protection of the manor guards.

Although Anna knew she would miss her mother and aunt, their absence provided an opportunity for more freedom.

By this point, Landon was thirteen. He'd outgrown his childhood ailments and had graduated from a pony to a horse. The children used this time of less supervision to go riding almost every day. The land of their estate was heavily forested, with a large rock quarry in the northern quarter.

Their father was careful about harvesting timber, and as opposed to clearing the land for crops—as was so often done—he had stumps removed and he replanted trees. It would be years before they were large enough to be of use, but this was how his father had run the business and it had proven successful.

The rock quarry was also an interesting playground with many places to hide.

Three weeks passed swiftly.

However, when their parents and Aunt Siobhan returned, Anna felt a shift in the world. Her aunt had changed. She barely welcomed Anna with a distracted kiss and showed no intention of regaling the children with stories of her adventures in Kéonsk. Instead, she paced the manor restlessly and spent much of her time listening for hoofbeats out in the courtyard. Whenever she would hear anyone approaching the manor, she would run out to see if it was a messenger.

At dinner, she ignored her food, and sometimes drank too much wine.

"What is wrong with Auntie?" Anna finally asked her mother.

"She's besotted," her mother answered, and would say no more.

A week following their return, hoofbeats sounded in the courtyard and as Siobhan was running, a messenger came to the door. She snatched the note from his hand, and when she saw the front of it, she gasped and tore it open.

Upon reading its contents, she leaned back against the wall for support and looked to Anna's mother.

"He's coming," she breathed. "He's coming here."

Anna pieced together what had happened. During the visit to Kéonsk, Siobhan had met a man.

That evening, Anna went out to the stables after dinner. She knew her parents preferred she remain inside after dark, but one of her father's spaniels had given birth to five puppies and Anna wanted to bring the mother a bowl of milk and see how she fared with her new pups. Time passed quickly, and by the time she slipped back into the manor, she realized it was late enough that she might be scolded if she was seen.

Upon entering the house, she heard her parents speaking in the dining room, and something in their voices made her pause. They sounded tense, and their words came quickly.

Anna's parents never expressed love for each other, but neither did they argue. They were partners in all things.

Going to one side of the archway to the dining room, Anna listened.

"Are you certain your expressions of concern aren't due to his station?" her father asked, sounding bitter. "Does it trouble you that you married a timber and stone merchant, and your sister may marry the brother of a prince?"

"No, it isn't that," Mother answered, not sounding remotely offended by his accusation. "It is her . . . passion toward him. You know well that she's given to extremes, but even for her this seems excessive, almost an obsession. Such excess of feeling does not bode well for a marriage."

Peering around the corner, Anna could see her father by the hearth. He shrugged. "At her age, I find the whole affair ridiculous."

That surprised Anna. Did her father consider Siobhan to be old? Although she was nearly thirty, she still looked young and beautiful.

"Hardly ridiculous," Mother answered, "Malcolm Yegor is over thirty, and he's never been married, either. I simply wish Siobhan would show some reserve."

Anna withdrew, for fear of being spotted, but that night when she crawled into bed with Adrienne, her mind was full. What kind of man could have such an effect on Aunt Siobhan?

Six days later, she found out, and nothing could have prepared her.

The family all awaited their expected visitor in the courtyard as he rode in. Aunt Siobhan had not been able to eat or sit all that day.

When Lord Malcolm of the house of Yegor swung off his horse and landed on the ground, Anna could only stare. He was tall with broad shoulders and tan skin. His face was young, but his hair was already turning silver. It suited him. He wore it longer than most men Anna knew and it curled back behind his ears.

His open smile was like magic as he took in the sight of the family.

"Siobhan," he said, "you are lovely as ever."

She ran to him. Anna had never seen a woman run to a man. Her face shone with a fire Anna had never seen before, either.

"Malcolm."

The one whispered word was filled with raw love.

Malcolm looked over at the rest of the family. "Henri. Roweena. So good to see you. Thank you for the kind welcome." His eyes moved to Landon, Anna, and Adrienne. "And who do we have here? Siobhan told me of children, but the lot of you look nearly grown." He flashed another smile. "Let us go in. My backside is sore from riding all day."

Adrienne smiled back at him. His manner was so easy and open.

Anna and Landon didn't smile. Again, they took after Father's side, but Anna felt a rush of affection. Malcolm was like a force of nature who brought laughter along with him.

Dinner was an enjoyable affair that night.

Malcolm teased Siobhan, Anna, and Adrienne in equal measure, and he told comic stories of his journey there, such as when he was served the worst meal he'd ever tried to eat at a tavern along the way and attempted to choke the food down out of politeness.

Anna couldn't remember her family ever laughing so much at the dinner table.

All through the meal, Siobhan watched him with hungry eyes, as if she couldn't drink in the sight of him enough.

The next day, Malcolm went out riding with the children. Anna never forgot that day. He was almost like one of them. They wandered the quarry and talked of small things. In the forest, he showed them a number of spiders' webs and told them all about the different spiders. In the pond, he found a gelatinous sack of frogs' eggs first and then some hatched tadpoles, and he told them of the life process of frogs. He knew a good deal about nature and the land.

In all her life, Anna's father had never once spent a day like this with his children.

Unfortunately, when they returned to the manor,

Aunt Siobhan rushed to meet them in the foyer. She looked unhinged.

"Where have you been?" she cried at Malcolm.

Anna was stunned at the panic in her voice.

But Malcolm swept Siobhan into his arms, looking down into her face. He almost appeared pleased by her wild anxiety to see him.

"What is wrong?" he asked.

"You were gone all day," she cried. "I didn't know where."

"I was out with the children. Forgive me. I should have told you."

The two of them began to exchange soft words, and on instinct, Anna drew her brother and sister away.

Her father would have been mortified should their mother have ever made such a scene, but apparently Malcolm wasn't troubled. He appeared drawn to Siobhan's need for his company.

At dinner, things had returned to normal, and once again, the manor was filled with laughter.

The next day, when the children and Malcolm went out riding, Aunt Siobhan came with them. It did strike Anna as somewhat odd that Malcolm had no interest in talking about business or politics with her father as most grown men had always done before. Malcolm preferred less serious company.

Before Anna knew it, wedding preparations had begun.

A magistrate came from Kéonsk. Malcolm and Siobhan were married in the rose garden behind the manor. A celebration followed, and Anna always remembered this as the happiest of days. Aunt Siobhan's face glowed from morning to night.

The next day brought sorrow, though, as Siobhan began packing and Anna realized her aunt was leaving them for good.

Though Anna was known for her reserved nature, she could not help weeping, and her aunt rushed to her.

"Don't cry, my girl. We will see each other."

"Where will you go? How far?"

"A good distance, I fear. Malcolm's older brother is the prince of Yegor, and Malcolm was given a vassalage in the south. We will live in his keep and oversee those lands."

"I don't want you to leave."

Siobhan held her close. "It's time you learned this is the fate of women. Men stay in their homes, at least first sons. Women marry and leave. That is the way of things."

Anna drew back and wiped her eyes. "What do you mean? I'll never leave here."

"You will. Landon will inherit the estate. Someday, you and Adrienne will both marry and be taken away, as your mother was taken from her home, and now I am taken from my second home here."

This was a revelation to Anna, and she didn't like it. The thought made her stomach go tight. She loved the land of the Janvier estate and had no wish to ever leave.

But Aunt Siobhan joyfully rode out of the courtyard the next day, leaving Anna feeling abandoned. Why did things have to change? With the departure of Malcolm and Siobhan, some of the life went out of the house.

Anna had no choice but to accept this change.

The following year, another shift occurred, only this one brought her happiness.

The summer she turned twelve, a man, a boy, and a few guards rode into the courtyard, and as Anna walked outside with her father and brother, she realized the visitors were expected.

Her father's expression was cautious, and she wondered what was happening.

The man in the lead was well dressed, in a dark blue tunic and polished boots. He dismounted and took Father's hand in a friendly manner.

"Janvier," he said. "So good to finally meet you. I do apologize for not coming sooner."

The boy dismounted next. He looked to be about Landon's age, only taller with a solid build and red-brown hair.

"My son, Tobin," the man said, motioning to the boy.

Within a few moments of listening to the man and her father talk, Anna began to understand the situation. Apparently, these were their neighbors on the east side of the property. The man's name was Phillip Bonnay, and his own elderly father had recently died, leaving him to inherit.

As opposed to timber, their lands had been given over to vineyards, and they grew miles and miles of grapes. The elderly father had never seen fit to make friends with his neighbors and had ordered no unnecessary contact. But Philip Bonnay felt differently, and now that he was in charge, he'd come to visit.

Or this was how Anna interpreted the meeting.

Within moments, she could see her father relaxing

as he, too, began to see the situation for what it was, simply a friendly visit. Given the nature of their neighbors to the west, no wonder he had fostered some trepidation at first.

"Come in and have some wine," he said.

The boy, Tobin, looked to Anna and Landon. "Could we ride around the land for a while? I'd like to see the quarry."

Landon had never had a male friend his own age, and he was eager to agree.

"Let me run and get Adrienne," Anna said. "She'll be angry if we leave her behind."

And so, while the men sipped wine and talked in the house, all four of the children rode to the rock quarry. Within the first hour, Tobin had become a natural fourth in the trio of siblings. He had some things in common with their new uncle, Malcolm. He was quick to laugh and smile, and he put other people at ease. Unlike Malcolm, he didn't appear to need the esteem of others. He was himself, and he let people take him or leave him as he was.

Anna, Adrienne, and Landon all found his company most welcome.

He and his father spent the night—as the ride back to their own estate took half a day—but this was the first of many visits from Tobin. Anna's father was glad for Landon to have a male friend, and so Tobin was often invited to come and stay as long as he liked.

The children took lessons from their mother in the morning, mainly writing, arithmetic, and languages. Tobin joined them and appeared to enjoy himself. He was possessed of great imagination, and when they all went riding in the afternoons, he began to make up games for them to play such as "knights against villains." Anna and Landon nearly always played the knights, and Adrienne and Tobin played the villains. As Anna was not the type to think up such games herself, she came to value Tobin more and more.

He helped her to miss Aunt Siobhan less.

In addition to proving a fine playmate, Tobin was also a good listener. Anna rarely shared her fears or feelings, but one day, when they found themselves walking alone in the courtyard, she told him what Aunt Siobhan had shared about "girls," and how they must marry and leave home one day.

"I don't want to leave here," she confessed, "and go to some strange place with the man I marry."

He listened and then said, "I may have to leave my home, too. My older brother will inherit the vineyards."

Anna stopped walking. "You have an older brother? You never said."

"You never asked." He sighed. "He's a good brother. His name is Edward, and he's nearly twenty, so he has little interest in me. He's not like our father when it comes to visiting. He rarely leaves the estate. But he'll inherit our home, and I don't know what I'll do."

In that moment, life seemed very unfair to Anna, that only the first son of any family had the right and privilege to remain in his home once he grew up.

At the end of that summer, a letter from Aunt Siobhan arrived, and Anna's mother smiled upon reading it.

"She's given birth to a healthy girl named Jenelle.

Mother and baby are doing well. We must send them some gifts."

"A girl?" Father said without much interest. "Hopefully, she still has time to give him a boy."

For the next year, Anna tried to push aside her fears of being married off and sent away when she came of age, and she tried to enjoy her life as it was. Tobin's entire family was invited for the winter celebration and feasting, and Anna met his mother and older brother. She liked his mother, who was plump and sweet-tempered. His older brother, Edward, reminded her a good deal of her father, serious and interested mainly in his business and family economics. The two of them got on well.

Anna knitted Tobin a black wool scarf, and he gave her a new pair of leather riding gloves.

The following summer, the world took another shift, this one much darker. It began slowly at first.

Mother began hesitating before opening any letters from Aunt Siobhan, and then she began taking them off in private before reading them. Anna had a sense something was wrong but did not dare to ask.

Near the end of that summer, Anna's mother came to her.

"Your aunt is having some . . . difficulties and has asked me to come south for a visit. Your father has agreed, but I think it best that you accompany me. You've always had a calming effect on Siobhan, and your mere presence might make things more evenly tempered."

Anna was surprised on several levels. Did she have

a calming effect on her aunt? She hadn't realized. More, she'd never in her life been off the Janvier estate. The borders of her father's lands were the extent of her world.

Several days later, she and her mother and a retinue of guards rode south. Though Anna couldn't help feeling some fear at first, the journey itself proved enjoyable. She'd never had her mother's full attention. They spent the nights at inns along the way, slept in the same bed, and whispered to each other.

Mother told the story of how she had met and been courted by Anna's father. Anna marveled that she'd never heard this story before. Away from home, Mother was more relaxed and open. Anna found herself wishing they'd taken a journey like this before.

When they reached the southern region of Droevinka, the sun shone more and the fields around them stretched as far as the eye could see. Anna had never seen so many fields of wheat or orchards of apples.

Finally, they arrived at a well-maintained, one-towered keep.

"This is your aunt's home," Mother said.

A single solid stone wall with a gatehouse surrounded the keep, but the portcullis was open, and the small contingent was expected.

Anna found herself looking forward to seeing her aunt and Uncle Malcolm and the new baby.

The moment they entered the keep, her excitement vanished.

Siobhan was just inside the main doors, alone, waiting for them. The change in her was startling.

Her hair hung down her back, unwashed and uncombed. There were lines in her face, and her dress looked as if she'd slept in it. Her eyes shone with a manic light.

She rushed to Anna's mother and grabbed her arm. "You've come!" she cried. "Here. Come in here."

She pulled Anna's mother along and without knowing what she should do, Anna followed them down a passage into a small side room, where Siobhan closed the door.

"He is unfaithful!" she hissed, sounding half-mad. "Unfaithful."

Anna's mother flinched and glanced at Anna. Apparently, the presence of Siobhan's niece did not have the desired effect. Nothing had been tempered.

"And he only lies with the lowest of women," Siobhan rushed on, "servants and maids and village girls . . . always girls, never women, rutting with them shamelessly in some back room or outside in the trees."

"Siobhan!" Mother gasped, glancing again at Anna.

"He doesn't come to me anymore!" Aunt Siobhan babbled on as if her sister had not spoken. "Not to me! I beg him. I weep for him. I've dismissed all the pretty servants, sent them packing, and I hire only ugly pock-marked women, but it does no good. He finds someone! He always finds someone but me."

Anna stood frozen. She knew little of what took place between men and women. She only knew that she pitied her aunt and was also embarrassed for her. Siobhan seemed so small, so diminished.

Where was the woman of power who sat over a

cauldron, looked up at the sky, and called down revenge upon her enemies?

Was this the result of love? If so, Anna wanted nothing to do with it.

Giving up on attempting to reason with Siobhan, Anna's mother instead turned to offering comfort, but this had little effect.

Dinner that night was an equally uncomfortable affair. When Malcolm walked into the dining hall, he smiled and welcomed his guests warmly as if there were nothing amiss.

"My girl," he said to Anna, taking her hands. "You've grown taller and more lovely. How are your sister and brother? How is your father?"

His behavior struck Anna as bizarre considering the state of Aunt Siobhan. Was he not concerned?

At the table, Siobhan sat with him, hanging on his every word, and he appeared utterly unaware that his wife had not dressed for dinner or combed her hair and watched him with a mix of hunger, love, and hatred.

There was only one instant when she thought his obtuse manner might be a facade.

As dessert was served, Anna asked, "May I see Jenelle tonight? I should so like to see her this evening."

Aunt Siobhan frowned. "Jenelle?"

"Yes, the baby."

It hit Anna that Siobhan hadn't recognized her own daughter's name. A look of panic crossed Malcolm's face, and then it was gone.

He smiled. "Of course, my dear. I'll take you up myself. She'll be in her crib by now, but you can see her."

Rising, he motioned her follow, and they went up to the nursery.

Jenelle was just a year old, and a sweet, chubby baby with reddish hair. Anna loved her right away. Malcolm looked down at the child curiously, as if he'd not seen her in some time. They didn't stay long that night, but Anna returned the next morning.

She came to realize Jenelle had been left in the care of servants and nannies, and for the duration of this visit, Anna was determined the child should be loved by someone from her family.

Also, as guilty as she felt about this, she couldn't help wishing to avoid Siobhan. Several days later, she sat on the floor of the nursery, helping Jenelle to stack a set of painted wooden blocks.

A shadow passed over them, and Anna looked up to see Siobhan in the doorway.

"Come in, Aunt. We were playing with some blocks. Jenelle is a lovely child."

Siobhan barely seemed to see the baby.

"The worst thing is that he won't admit to anything," she whispered, her eyes drifting. "He can almost be caught in the act, and he denies everything. It's almost as if he believes his own innocence even after he's left the bed of some slut. He'll never admit to anything. Never."

Anna sighed. "If he has done so much intentional wrong, what have you done to punish him?"

Wasn't this what Anna had been taught as a child? That intentional wrongs must be met with swift justice?

For the first time, Siobhan's eyes cleared, and she

focused on Anna. "That is my heartbreak," she whispered. "I cannot punish him. I cannot."

And then Anna understood. Not only were her aunt's mental and physical deterioration due to her obsession with her husband, but her love for him was so strong she couldn't punish him for his infidelities.

It was killing her.

After a week, Anna was not sorry when the visit came to an end, but upon leaving the keep, she worried for Jenelle.

The journey home was less intimate, as Anna's mother was deeply concerned for her sister. The problem was that Anna's mother believed all problems could be solved by self-control and that Siobhan would be fine if she simply cleaned herself up, stopped worrying about Malcolm's affairs with a few village girls, and focused her attention on the proper running of the household.

She viewed Siobhan's grief as weakness.

Anna knew her aunt to feel things deeply. Siobhan could no longer stop loving Malcolm obsessively than she could stop breathing.

This left Anna and her mother with little to discuss.

Upon arriving home, though, Anna found Landon, Adrienne, and Tobin all waiting for her at the manor. She was so glad to see them and begged to go back out and walk on the land right away. She wanted to wash away the visit to Yegor.

Years passed.

Anna's life was peaceful and happy for the most part, broken only by infrequent visits from Siobhan and Malcolm. They never brought Jenelle.

Siobhan slowly seemed to descend further into madness, and Malcolm staunchly pretended that everything was well, but his polish and laughter had long since ceased to charm Anna.

For some reason, he refused to acknowledge reality.

Every time they left, Anna fought guilt over the relief of watching them go. She had once loved her aunt so much.

The summer Anna turned eighteen her parents invited her to join them in their visit to Kéonsk to the gathering of the princes and nobles. Landon would be going as well.

"You've grown into a fine young woman," her father said, catching her off guard. "It's time you met other . . . people of your own class."

He means other men, she thought.

Terror filled her at the thought of being handed off to some strange nobleman, and she begged to be allowed to remain at home for one more year.

"I'll go next year," she said. "I promise."

Both her parents were baffled by why she would prefer to remain at home when she could be dancing and eating fine food at banquets in the company of princes and nobles, but they didn't force her.

As they were packing to leave, Anna heard hoofbeats outside in the courtyard, and she went to see who it was.

Tobin came riding up and jumped off his horse at the sight of her. His expression was concerned, almost distraught, and she'd never seen him like this before.

"What's wrong?" she asked, hurrying to meet him. "If your father ill?"

"My father?" He shook his head. "No, I just heard about the gathering and that your family was preparing to leave. I heard . . . I heard they were taking you this year."

"No, I've begged off. I would rather stay at home."

His expression shifted, as if she'd given him good news. "You're not going?"

"No."

Why would it bother him if she went to the Kéonsk gathering?

"Come and walk with me," he said.

They headed around the back of the house, toward the rose gardens, and to her surprise, he reached out and took her hand, holding it as they walked. His red-brown hair hung down past his collar and in the sunlight, his eyes were a shade of dark green.

"You won't be lonely while they're gone," he said. "I'll come as often as I can."

That night, in bed, Anna found herself thinking on three weeks of Tobin's company with no other companions except for Adrienne. She remembered the feel of her hand in his, and her palm tingled.

Soon, Anna came to understand her aunt a little better. What she came to feel for Tobin was not an obsessive love, but it was strong. He came to the manor one morning, and they slipped off without telling Adrienne, riding all the way to the eastern border of the Janvier estate. He showed her his family's vineyards. The neat rows of grapevines stretched for miles.

Standing beneath an aspen tree, he leaned down and touched his mouth to hers. When she kissed him back, he pressed harder, and she felt her heart jump. She loved his face and his smile and the way he got her to talk of things that mattered—things she would tell no one else.

"I love you," he said simply. "I always have. Will you marry me?"

"I would marry no one else."

The problem was that for him to ask for her hand, he'd need a profession or some way to prove he could support a family. She didn't like the idea of him joining the military, as did so many second sons.

They kept their engagement a secret for a year.

The following summer, as Anna's family began preparing for the gathering at Kéonsk, fear washed through her. They would insist she go this year. They would insist she dance with young noblemen and put herself on display for proposals.

She didn't know what to do.

Then a miracle happened. Tobin came racing up to the manor and when she went to greet him, he drew her off alone into the stables.

"I have news," he said, holding both her hands. "I told my father and brother about us. I was desperate for help, and they have been kind. There is a cottage . . . a large cottage with six bedrooms, down at the southern end of our estate. No one has lived there in years. It sits on four large fields of white grape vines that have fallen into a state of neglect, as white wine has been out of fashion. But it's coming back into demand. Father says he'll give us the cottage and those vineyards, and my brother was glad to agree. He'll inherit the rest of the estate."

He gripped her hands more tightly. "Don't you see, Anna? We will have a home and a good living."

She did see. Even more, she wouldn't have to leave these lands she loved. She and Tobin could build a life together here. She kissed him. Her heart was bursting.

"I'll go and talk to your father," he said, rushing off.

That was the part that concerned her. What would her parents say?

After Tobin left, they called her to them.

Her father's face was not angry, but nor was it happy. She couldn't tell what he thought.

At first he seemed lost for words, and then he asked, "Anna, is this what you want?"

She exhaled. He had asked the right question. "Yes, Father. I want it so much."

He exchanged a long look with her mother, who appeared equally at a loss. "Then if your mother has no objections," he said, "I don't. I'd hoped for much greater things for you, but the Bonnays are a good family, and I couldn't think more highly of Tobin. He's managed to take part of the estate from his brother, and I think he has good prospects."

This was not exactly the case. Tobin had been given part of estate, but such things didn't matter.

"Mother?" she asked.

"If this is what you wish, I am of the same mind as your father."

Father nodded. "You can use your dowry to refurbish the cottage."

With joy, Anna ran to Adrienne and told her the news. Adrienne was glad and hugged her fiercely. "I knew," she said. "I knew you'd end up with Tobin. He's a good man, and he has always loved you."

Had Adrienne known this before Anna?

They planned the wedding for early autumn, as Tobin and Anna would need time to make some improvements in the cottage before winter set in.

By late summer, the manor was such a buzz of activity that Anna almost forgot about a pending visit from Aunt Siobhan and Uncle Malcolm.

When they arrived, Anna hoped that discussion of the pending wedding might help fend off some of her aunt's more painful behavior, but Siobhan had no interest in the wedding. She had no interest in anything other than her husband's affairs.

Once again, they didn't bring Jenelle. The poor child must be seven years old.

Thankfully, Siobhan seemed to be paying more attention to her appearance, and she wore a crushed velvet gown with her hair properly styled up on her head. But her face was lined with bitterness, and every time she got Anna alone, the conversation was the same.

"He spurns me for maids and village girls," she would whisper. "He has not come to my bed in years. I put potions in his drinks. I cast spells. Nothing works, and I cannot live much longer without his touch."

"Oh, Auntie, can you not leave him?" Anna said. "Can you not take Jenelle and come back here to live with Mother?"

"Leave him? No, I cannot live without him." Her eyes drifted again. "If only he would admit his guilt just once. He lives in lies. All these years, no matter how flagrant he's been, he claims innocence as if he's never strayed even once."

Anna gave up. There was no way to help her aunt.

That afternoon, Malcolm came to her and asked her to go riding. She didn't wish to go, but also didn't see how she could refuse. They saddled up and rode toward the quarry at a walk.

"I made the worst mistake of my life in marrying your aunt," he said. "I was so drawn to her love for me, for her passion, but I was a fool. I should have married a woman with dignity, someone more reasoned with self-control, like you."

Anna stopped her horse. It was wrong of him to be saying these things to her. It was inappropriate. "Forgive me, Uncle. I've forgotten that I promised to help Mother plan the menu for dinner."

"Of course," he said smoothly, and accompanied her back to the stable.

Dinner that night was the usual strained affair with Siobhan staring at Malcolm, and Malcolm chatting away lightly as if nothing was wrong. Anna counted the days until their visit would be over.

The next afternoon, however, she vowed to try to distract her aunt. They had tea together in the dining room, and then Anna said, "Auntie, come out to the rose gardens with me and help me choose the best blooms to decorate the table. You have such an eye for roses."

For once, Siobhan seemed to reflect at least a shadow

of her former self and nodded. In years past, no one could create table arrangements like Aunt Siobhan. The two women walked out into the passage and then down through the servants' quarters.

"I think a mix of white and pink," Anna said. "Or do you think yellow?"

A door opened up ahead and she was not paying much attention until she saw Cora, a young maid, perhaps seventeen, whom her mother had recently hired.

"Cora, what are you doing here at this time of . . . ?"

The girl's hair was down and her dress was partially undone. At the sight of Anna and Siobhan, she clutched the front of her dress, turned, and fled down the hall, vanishing into another room.

Anna was perplexed, but Siobhan shot forward, shoving the first door back open and looking inside wildly.

Anna drew a sharp breath as she followed her aunt's gaze. Malcolm stood there buttoning the front of his shirt.

"Here?" Siobhan whispered. "In my sister's home?"

Malcolm gave her a warm smile. "Lost a button," he said, holding up the bottom of his shirt. "Came here for help." He turned the smile to Anna. "Nice girl, that Cora. Sewed a new one on for me."

For a second, he was so calm and friendly and sincere that Anna could almost believe he'd lost a button and come looking for help. Then she remembered Cora's hair and undone dress.

How could he stand there and smile as if he were speaking the truth?

"Unfaithful," Siobhan sobbed, tears of hate and rage

and love in her eyes. She tore out a handful of hair. "For once tell the truth! For once don't hide behind your lies."

"My dear, calm down. I lost a button. That is all."

"In my sister's home," Siobhan whispered. "This . . . this is too much."

Turning, she ran down the other direction, down the passage, back toward the stairs leading up to the second floor.

Anna studied Malcolm a moment longer and he said no more. Then Anna continued onward, going out to the rose gardens for air. She wished Tobin were here, but it was now late summer, and he was home helping his father and brother to check the progress of the grapes in the fields.

That night, she wondered how she'd be able to make it through dinner. Everyone began gathering in the dining room at the expected hour, but Siobhan didn't appear. More time ticked past.

Finally, Anna said, "Perhaps we should check on her? Mother, will you come with me?"

She didn't wish to go alone.

"Of course."

Anna and her mother went upstairs. Siobhan and Malcolm were always in separate guest rooms now. Anna's mother went to the door of Siobhan's room and knocked.

"Sister? Are you well?"

There was no answer. After a brief hesitation, Anna's mother opened the door and gasped. Then she cried out, "No!"

Anna ran forward and looked at the scene inside the room.

There was so much red.

Siobhan lay on the bed with both wrists slashed open. Blood had saturated the comforter and mattress.

Slowly, Anna walked past her mother into the room. Siobhan was dead, her eyes open, and a scrawled note lay on the pillow above her head.

My love was unfaithful. Ever unfaithful.

Perhaps this was the only way she could think to punish him.

They buried Siobhan in the rose garden, and everyone agreed to say she caught a fever and died quickly.

Anna agreed to keep to this lie if only to protect Jenelle from ever learning the truth.

Malcolm left right after the burial.

When Tobin learned of Siobhan's death, he left his father's fields and came riding to the manor. Only then did Anna allow herself to weep. She told him the truth.

"Oh, Anna," he said, holding her. "I'm so sorry."

After crying until she had no tears left, she somehow felt a little more like herself. She hadn't been able to eat, but Tobin got her to drink some tea with milk.

He was a good man.

He had to go home the next day. For grape growers, late summer and early fall were busy.

The days passed, and each one got a little easier, but Anna would never forget the sight of her aunt on that bed, dead by her own hand, brought to such depths by obsessive love. To Anna, love seemed to be either the most healing emotion in the world or the most destructive.

Thankfully, her love was one of light, and she'd never allow it to become destructive.

Every day, she put fresh roses on her aunt's grave.

In early autumn, several weeks before the wedding, a maid came to her room while she was dressing for dinner.

"I'm sorry to disturb you, miss, but your parents want to see you in your father's study."

Anna's father had taken a small room on the main floor as his private chambers with a desk and all his papers. He rarely allowed anyone in there. From what she understood, most men didn't like anyone else inside their studies.

Puzzled, she went downstairs and found both her parents standing behind his desk. She knew them well enough to see that beneath their calm veneers they were both excited.

"What's happened?" she asked.

"Sit down, my dear," her father said.

He never called her his dear. She sat.

"I think you know that Malcolm's brother, Kristoff, the prince of Yegor, is ten years his senior?" he began.

She nodded and tried not to wince. It hurt to be speaking of Malcolm.

"Did you also know that Kristoff has no heir and his wife is long past childbearing?" he asked.

She didn't, but what did that matter to them now?

"Kristoff's health is failing, and he's not expected to live much longer," her father continued. "Do you understand what that means?"

"Yes, of course. When he dies, Malcolm will be

named prince of Yegor." This conversation was uncomfortable, and she couldn't help adding, "What does that have to do with us now?"

"Malcolm has asked for your hand," her father answered.

For a moment, Anna didn't think she'd heard correctly.

But her mother clasped her hands to her breast. "My dear, you will be princess of Yegor."

Anna felt the floor shift beneath her feet. "I cannot marry Malcolm. I'm engaged to Tobin. The wedding has been planned. He's begun repairs on the cottage."

Her father waved one hand. "That is nothing. Tobin is a boy of no rank. His father will understand, and there will be no retribution." He smiled. She wasn't sure she'd ever seen him smile. "You will be princess of Yegor. Do you know what that will mean for our family?"

"And his treatment of Aunt Siobhan doesn't concern you?"

"Your aunt was mad," he answered. "I'm sorry to say it, but she was. I never saw any fault on Malcolm's part."

Though Anna somehow managed to remain composed, her face must have shown a hint of the shock and nausea she felt inside. Her mother said quickly, "I can see you are nearly overcome, my darling. And who wouldn't be? Go up to your room, and I'll be up directly."

Anna fled. Instead of going to her own room, she ran to Adrienne's.

Her sister was nearly ready to go down for dinner,

but she whirled from the mirror when she saw Anna's reflection. "What's wrong?"

"Mother and Father want me to marry Uncle Malcolm. He's asked for my hand." She had trouble breathing as she choked out the words.

"What?"

Their mother appeared in the doorway, looking in.

Adrienne turned on her. "You can't be serious? He's our uncle! Twenty years older than her."

"There is no blood connection between them."

"He is a seducer of women."

Their mother looked at her as if she were simple. "Yes, and that is his only vice. He does not gamble. He does not drink to excess, and he never once laid a hand on my sister in anger no matter how she provoked him. For a nobleman, his virtues are almost beyond compare." She exhaled. "Do you truly think mine is the only bed your father has visited over the years? It's time you both grew up."

"You want me to marry Uncle Malcolm?" Anna asked.

"Stop calling him that. He's no longer your uncle."

"But you want me to marry him?"

"I want for you to be the princess of Yegor and to enjoy all that goes with such a title. You have no idea. When you're older, you will thank me."

Anna looked at the floor. She couldn't fight both her parents. She didn't know how.

Two days later, a message was sent to Tobin's father, breaking the engagement. That same afternoon, Anna and her parents left the manor with a retinue of guards, traveling to Yegor.

Anna wasn't even allowed to tell Tobin good-bye.

She didn't speak much along the journey. She tried not to let herself think.

They arrived at the keep in the evening, and it looked much the same as when she'd visited the place as a girl. Malcolm might soon be prince of Yegor, but for now, he was his brother's vassal. He met them in the courtyard and kissed her hand when she dismounted.

"I will make you happy," he said.

He did not smile or tease her or make jokes, and for that, she was grateful. They entered the keep, and he announced dinner would be served as soon as they'd had time to wash and change from the journey.

"A magistrate will be here tomorrow to conduct the ceremony. It will be a quiet affair."

Anna said little at dinner and flushed with embarrassment when her father asked Malcolm about his brother's health. She was confused when Jenelle did not join them. The Janvier children had all left the nursery and joined the dining table by the age of six.

"Where's Jenelle?" she asked toward the end of the meal.

Malcolm shook his head. "I don't know. With her nanny, I expect."

After the meal, Anna asked directions from a maid, went upstairs, and found the girl. She was alone on the floor of a room, playing with a doll.

"Jenelle?"

The child looked up but didn't speak.

"I'm Anna."

"You will marry my father?" Jenelle asked.

Anna went in and sat on the floor. "Yes, tomorrow."

"Do I have to call you Mother?"

"No, not if you don't wish. Call me Anna if you like. Did you know I am your cousin? Your mother was my mother's sister."

Again, the child didn't answer, and Anna reached out. "May I see your doll? She's lovely."

She played with Jenelle for an hour and then put the child to bed herself.

The next afternoon, after breakfast, a magistrate arrived at the keep, and a short ceremony was conducted in the dining hall. Anna's parents acted as witnesses, and she insisted that Jenelle be allowed to attend.

The six of them had dinner afterward—the magistrate being the only outside guest.

Anna tried not to think of the wedding she'd planned with Tobin . . . of the flowers and cake and musicians.

That night, several serving women led her to a large chamber with a four-poster bed. She was undressed and a white nightgown was slipped over her head. The women left.

A short while later, Malcolm came in.

Again, thankfully, he didn't try to make light of this or pretend all was well and that they were a normal, happy bride and groom on their wedding night.

"I can't imagine what you think of me," he said. "But I am beyond grateful that you have agreed to be my lady."

She never knew what to think of the words that came from his mouth. At forty, he was still alarmingly handsome—or most women would find him handsome. Coming to her, he leaned down and kissed her on the mouth.

She didn't feel the spark she felt with Tobin, but neither was she as repulsed as she'd expected.

He led her to bed, and she endured what followed with as much grace as she could draw from inside herself. If he was disappointed, he didn't show it. Perhaps he'd not expected much of a response.

"Trust me," he whispered. "I swear I will make you happy."

Her parents left for home the next day, and Anna began her life as a married woman.

Over the years, Siobhan had let the household of the keep fall into a sorry state, but this proved to be a lifeline for Anna. There was much to be done, and if her mother had taught her anything, it was the proper running of a household.

This kept her almost too busy to think on other matters in those early days.

She interviewed and hired more servants. The overworked, understaffed cook was a woman named Helen, and Anna employed her counsel when it came to hiring more kitchen help. As a result, she won Helen's undying loyalty.

Throughout all this, Anna kept Jenelle with her,

sometimes asking her thoughts on certain matters. The girl began to open up slightly from the interaction and attention, and she was soon Anna's shadow by choice.

Rooms were cleaned.

Tapestries were beaten.

The lauder was inventoried and restocked.

None of this was lost on Malcolm, who often offered silent expressions of gratitude. Anna made certain Jenelle joined them for dinner every night, and he never objected.

As time passed, she came to realize that he worked hard, too. As vassal for his brother, he was in charge of a large number of villages and crops and fields. The people who tilled and planted the fields kept half the crops for themselves and paid the other half to Malcolm. He saw the further sale of such crops and kept a portion for himself and sent another to his brother.

But he never overtaxed his people, and he worked with them actively, solving problems when need be and always listening when they came to him. He knew an astonishing amount about weather patterns and pollination and how to prevent diseases on apple trees or wheat fields. Anna couldn't help remembering that first day with him out on the Janvier estate, long ago, when he'd shown her the tadpoles and explained their journey from eggs to frogs. He had made a study of the natural world.

His people respected him. They sought to please him.

"You're a good vassal lord," Anna said to him one night. "A good leader."

He was taken aback by her praise, as if he'd never

heard it before. Perhaps he hadn't. Aunt Siobhan had been mad for him, but had she ever cared for how he spent his daily life? He was accustomed to being admired for his charm, but he knew better than to try to use it on Anna. Should she be surprised that he possessed actual virtues?

She began to wonder if she'd seen Malcolm only through the filter of her aunt's eyes.

Later, she learned that he could be quite hard when he felt himself crossed.

He heard a report from the commander of his guard that one village had been hiding grain and shorting him on their taxes. His eyes went dark, and as opposed to sending someone else, he had three wagons prepared. He rode at the head of them himself.

That night, he came home with those wagons filled with grain.

"What did you do?" Anna asked.

His eyes were still dark. "I sorted it out."

There were many sides to Malcolm.

Though he was always kind to her, six months into their marriage, she noticed him sometimes glancing at her stomach, and she realized he was waiting for a child. Her mind was still too focused on all she'd lost in the past to care too much, but just over a year into the marriage, she began to feel sick in the morning, and she missed her courses.

"I am with child," she told him.

Overjoyed, he moved to embrace her and then stopped. They rarely touched unless committing the act of marriage in bed.

Instead, he said, "Be careful and do not wear yourself out. Have new dresses made if you need them."

In her earlier life, Anna had never cared much about clothes, but she knew he liked her to look the part of his lady, so she was more particular now, dressing mainly in velvet and silk. As opposed to ordering new gowns, though, she simply had some of her own let out as her stomach grew.

Pregnancy agreed with her. After the initial morning sickness, not only was she well, but she was astonished by the love she felt for the growing child inside her. The months passed swiftly.

Her pains began one morning, and the midwife was sent for.

By evening, she was in agony, exhausted and soaked with sweat, and the baby seemed no closer to coming.

"What's wrong?" she asked the midwife weakly.

"Nothing. It is a first child, and they take longer."

But the woman's voice held a hint of fear. No midwife wanted to fail in the delivery of a noble child, and Anna knew something was wrong.

Though she'd managed to remain quiet all day, after darkness fell, the pain was so great that she couldn't help crying out, and she heard the bedroom door crash open.

"My lord!" the midwife cried. "You cannot be in here!"

"Get out of my way," Malcolm ordered.

The next Anna knew, he was at her side, gripping her hand. "Anna."

"You must leave, my lord," the midwife insisted. "Men are not allowed!"

"Why hasn't the child come? Why is she in so much pain?" he demanded.

"I don't know. The baby isn't breech, but your lady has small hips. She cannot seem to push it out."

Malcolm remained in a chair by Anna's head all night, whispering comfort and begging her to stay strong and not to leave him.

Shortly before dawn, somehow, she made a final push and the child was finally born.

She heard it cry.

"It's a healthy boy, my lord," said the midwife.

Malcolm still hovered by Anna's head. "Hand him to me and see to your lady. Make sure she is properly tended."

He remained in the room during the expelling of the afterbirth and the other unpleasant realities of childbirth. He never flinched, and he showed far more concern for her than he showed to the fact that he had a son.

Anna slept much of the day.

Only when he came to see her later did he kiss her forehead and say, "Thank you for giving me a son. If you don't mind, I'd like to name him Lysander, after my father."

Things were different between them after that. On some level, Anna knew Malcolm loved her.

Another year passed, and she began to feel some measure of happiness and peace. She had Jenelle and Lysander to love and a husband she'd grown to respect. If he ever cavorted with any maids or village girls, there was never a single sign of it, not even gossip among the servants or guards.

There were entire days when she no longer thought on the past or on all that she had lost.

Then one day, a letter arrived from Adrienne. The two sisters wrote often, and Anna appreciated the connection to her family's home. Feeling pleased, she took the letter to her room to read it in private while sitting at her vanity.

> *My Dear Sister,*
>
> *I have news of an odd nature, and I wanted to write to you as soon as possible, as I could not bear the thought of you hearing it from someone else.*
>
> *Though I never told you, Tobin took the breaking of the engagement very hard. He moved out of his father's house into the cottage, and he began living there by himself, working his own vineyards.*
>
> *Out of pity and worry, I began to visit him there.*

Anna stopped reading as a knot built in her stomach. She looked at the wall across her room for a moment and then forced her eyes back to the letter.

> *He and I were always friends, and I sometimes helped him with the vines.*
>
> *This past summer, Mother and Father forced me to go to Kéonsk, to the gathering of nobles, and I've never been so miserable in my life. Such a bore. So many false smiles and vapid conversations. I couldn't wait to get home.*

A week ago, down at the cottage, Tobin and I decided we would marry. Father and Mother have agreed. He will never love me as he loves you, and I know that. I do this because I care for Tobin, and I much prefer the prospect of a life with him than with any of our parents' prospects for me.

Please don't hate me. You always have my love. Try to take comfort in the thought that I will be living in a small cottage and growing white grapes for my living, while you will be the princess of Yegor.

With love,
Adrienne

Anna stared down at the letter as the contents slowly sank in. Adrienne would marry Tobin, and she would live in the cottage adjacent to their beloved family lands.

Folding the letter, Anna considered burning it, but then put it away in the drawer of her vanity. She didn't blame or hate her sister. How could she? Adrienne only sought the same life that Anna had herself.

That night at dinner, Malcolm looked at her in concern. "Are you all right?"

She managed a smile. "I am fine."

Malcolm's brother lived longer than expected. He even outlived his wife.

But the year Lysander turned three and Jenelle

turned thirteen, word arrived that the prince of Yegor was dead, and that Malcolm was the heir.

The family left their home in the keep, and they rode to Castle Yegor.

The following year was as busy as the first one of Anna's marriage. The household of the castle and the management of the lands had been badly neglected, and Anna almost felt as if she was starting over. Malcolm was just as busy riding out to villages to meet their leaders and assure them they could come to him with any problems.

In the middle of this, they were also expected to travel to Kéonsk for Malcolm to be officially named the prince of Yegor in a ceremony. While he was a social creature in some ways, and he needed the admiration of others, he'd never enjoyed the company of his noble peers, and he had no interest in long discussions of politics or matters of state. He preferred to be riding his own lands, interacting with the common people there, or being at home with his family.

Much fuss was made over Anna during this visit to Kéonsk. She was called "beautiful" and "a fine lady," and she could see that Malcolm was proud of her.

Both her parents came to the coronation ceremony, and her mother beamed.

"You see, my darling. I knew this would happen. You are the princess of Yegor."

Anna glanced away.

Thankfully, Malcolm kept this visit as brief as possible, and then they went home and got back to work. He hired new guards and began to put the barracks in order.

That first spring, Anna was told of an unusual tradition stretching back for generations. Apparently, each spring, caravans of the Móndyalítko people would roll into the vast meadow below the castle and remain there all summer. Their help was welcome with the berry and apple harvests.

When the Móndyalítko began to arrive, she and Malcolm walked down together for a visit. They were warmly welcomed, and although Anna had heard stories of these people all her life, this was her first meeting, and she found the visit enjoyable. Their colorful clothing and compact homes and way of life intrigued her.

Only one thing gave her pause.

As she was speaking with a little boy tending his family's chickens, she looked over to see Malcolm staring at something. Following his gaze, she saw a strikingly pretty girl of about seventeen in a bright red skirt and a low-cut white peasant blouse. The girl was small and slender with black hair.

Malcolm seemed almost locked in place as he watched the girl. Then he noticed Anna watching him, and he looked away. The moment passed.

Not long after, the harvesting of the strawberries began.

It was then that she noticed a change in Malcolm. He was distracted and sometimes could not be found when he was needed. She would have accounted this to him simply being so busy overseeing the harvest, but it was often his own men who couldn't find him.

When she asked him about this, he'd smile and make some plausible excuse for where he'd been. But his easy and casual answers reminded her of . . . something, though she couldn't remember what.

One especially fine day, she decided to leave Lysander with his nanny and take a walk through the blossoming apple orchard. She thought the orchards the most beautiful of the fields in this part of Yegor.

As she walked, admiring the white blossoms all around her, a noise caught her attention, and she looked to her left. At first she saw nothing, but as she peered around the side of a large old tree, she saw two people on the ground, a short distance down the row.

She went still.

Malcolm was half-naked with his pants undone, and he was on top of a Móndyalítko girl, thrusting himself inside her. The girl moaned in pleasure and arched her back. It was the same girl he'd been watching in the encampment.

Anyone could have come upon them out here.

Anna withdrew and walked back to the castle.

Going to her room, she sank down in front of the mirror, taking in the sight of her long face and white-blond hair.

What should she do?

It was then she remembered how he'd reacted when Aunt Siobhan had accused him of infidelity, how he'd always offered the same sort of flippant excuses he'd been giving lately about his absences. She remembered the discord this had caused between them.

If she told him what she'd seen today, he'd most likely say the girl had tripped and he'd fallen on top her, and then he'd tell Anna not to be ridiculous. She didn't think she could stand that. More, she understood him better than Siobhan ever had, and she knew he needed to be admired and he hated to be embarrassed.

Should Anna cause such a scene between them, it might well ruin the harmony of their family and their household. And what possible good would it do to accuse him?

Was she jealous?

No.

Perhaps her mother was right, and for a nobleman, Malcolm was as good as they came.

Anna said nothing. She greeted him that night for dinner and asked about his day.

The summer passed and in the autumn the Móndyalítko left, and everything returned to normal.

Their only worry regarded Lysander, as it seemed he'd inherited his uncle Landon's childhood penchant for sometimes losing his breath and gasping for air. Anna hoped he would grow out of it.

It troubled her that she'd not conceived another child, but Malcolm didn't seem to mind.

The following summer, she was somewhat disconcerted to hear whispers among the servants about Malcolm's new "camp girl," and she realized he was repeating his behavior from the year before—only with a different girl.

Again, she feigned ignorance, knowing this to be her best and only option. Openly acknowledging such behavior on the part of her husband was beneath her dignity.

She was the princess of Yegor, and her son would be the next prince of Yegor.

Another year slipped past.

Though Jenelle's heath was strong, Anna began to worry about the girl's state of mind. She was restless and had grown short-tempered with some of the servants.

"Is something wrong?" Anna asked her.

"Nothing besides the fact that we're holed up here in this castle like hermits, and we never go anywhere and no one ever comes to visit. Isn't being a prince supposed to mean something? Father behaves exactly as he did as a vassal."

The girl sounded so discontented, and Anna realized she should have seen this sooner. It was true that most princes entertained a near-constant flow of guests, with nobles and merchants visiting on extended stays. They also traveled to Kéonsk and Enêmûsk several times a year for meetings with the other princes to discuss matters of state. These meetings weren't mandatory, but most men of power wished for a voice in such matters.

Malcolm did not. He cared for his lands and his home and his family and the people who lived under his rule, and those were the extent of his interests.

"How will I ever meet anyone?" Jenelle pressed. "How will I find a husband and get out of here?"

How ironic that Jenelle's only wish was to leave home as soon as possible. At her age, Anna had only wanted to stay.

"You're too young to be thinking of husbands," Anna said. "But I will try to speak to your father about entertaining more guests here."

She did try, but little happened in that regard.

Time flowed on. Every summer Malcolm had a flagrant affair with a different girl from the meadow encampment, and he grew more careless and blatant each year to the point of bringing them up to the castle. It grew harder for Anna to pretend she knew nothing.

When Jenelle turned eighteen, Anna knew it was time for the girl to be introduced into society, and in the spring, she asked Malcolm for permission to take Jenelle to Enêmûsk for a visit. This was the home city of the Äntes, and a good many nobles made their homes there.

To her surprise, Malcolm agreed readily, saying he would arrange the guard contingent himself. "Go and enjoy yourselves," he said. "You both deserve a change of scene."

When Jenelle heard, she was overjoyed, hugging Anna fiercely. "Thank you so much."

Preparations began. Such a trip took planning and Anna wrote several letters to announce their upcoming arrival: The princess of Yegor and her stepdaughter were making a journey to Enêmûsk.

Grand Prince Rodêk's secretary wrote back, inviting them to stay at the castle. Jenelle could barely contain herself. Anna had new gowns made for them both, and she even began looking forward to the upcoming visit.

This was tarnished one afternoon as she walked toward the open front doors of the castle and overheard two guards standing outside.

"The girl he's picked this year is a nasty piece of

work," one man said. "But he's hot for her. Yesterday, he just left us to take her off into the woods as if he couldn't wait to get at her. I've never seen him like this."

The other man murmured in agreement.

Anna drew back before one of them realized she was there. No wonder Malcolm had agreed to let her go for a month. He wanted to enjoy time with his newest camp girl. Still, perhaps that was best.

Clearly, he needed something from these girls—something she couldn't give him. In the beginning, she'd believed this was physical passion, but now she thought it might be something else. Perhaps he sought lost youth? Perhaps he needed more admiration than she was capable of giving?

Whatever it was, again, if this was his only vice, she was determined to overlook it. At the end of summer, the girl would be gone, and next year, he'd choose another.

A few days before the journey, in the evening after dinner, Anna was alone in her room, going over the list of what still needed to be packed, when a soft knock sounded on her door.

"Yes?"

The door opened, and Helen, the cook, peered in. "May I enter, my lady?"

"Of course. Is something amiss in the kitchens?" Looking over, she saw Helen's face. The aging woman was distraught and trembling. "Helen, please come in. Are you unwell?"

She'd brought Helen with her from the keep and named her head cook here.

Slowly, Helen came in and closed the door. She held a torn piece of paper in her hand. "My lady, I would never trouble you or cause you pain, but you are in danger."

"Danger?"

As she came closer, Helen's distress only seemed to grow. "Yesterday, a letter came for me here. I don't get many letters, but my nephew is coming through Yegor, and he asked if I could put him up in the servants' quarters. I can manage that, and I wanted to write back to tell him." Her eyes dropped. "But I didn't have any paper. The only place I could think to look was the prince's study."

"Oh, Helen, you know no one is allowed in there."

"I know, my lady, and I wasn't trying to steal. I didn't think he'd miss a single slip of paper, and I wanted so much to answer my nephew."

"Were you caught? Are you in trouble?"

Helen lifted her eyes again. "No, my lady. But I found something in one of the drawers, a draft of a letter."

Anna shook her head. "I don't understand. Did you take a letter from Prince Malcolm's office?"

She could hardly believe it. She'd have trusted Helen with the entire treasury.

"It's a draft," Helen said, holding it out, "but it's addressed to Grand Prince Rodêk. It's a request for a marriage annulment."

Anna went cold and took the letter.

The handwriting was Malcolm's, but it was messy and slanted. Several words had been crossed out and rewritten. There were spots of red wine splattered across the top.

But the letter was a request for an annulment of his marriage to Anna on the grounds that she'd not provided him a healthy heir and that as he had first been married to her aunt, the family bond was too close. He wished to marry a younger woman who could give him sons. Malcolm promised that in return for this favor, he would back whomever Rodêk chose in the upcoming election.

Anna looked up. "Have you any proof that a final draft was written, sealed, and sent?"

Helen's right hand clenched into a fist. "This morning, that camp girl, Lilah, came to the kitchens to boss us around. She said she'd soon be the mistress here, and we'd better lick her boots. After seeing that piece of paper, I believe her."

Lilah.

Gripping the stained letter, Anna managed to say, "Please go, Helen. Leave me."

"My lady . . . ?"

"Go."

Still trembling, Helen turned and hurried for the door.

Once alone, Anna sat in stillness, letting the ramifications of the last few moments sink in. Malcolm was going to annul their marriage, make his own son illegitimate, and marry a Móndyalítko girl.

She would never have believed it had she not seen the words written in Malcolm's hand.

He would make his own son a bastard.

He would discard her like last night's refuse.

She thought on her husband smiling at her that morning at breakfast. Her mind flowed back to the night Lysander was born, when Malcolm had burst into the room and stayed with her all night.

And now he would thoughtlessly throw all that away as if she and Lysander were nothing.

Aunt Siobhan was right.

Malcolm was unfaithful. Ever unfaithful.

For the first time in her memory, anger rose inside Anna. As a young woman, she'd given up the man she loved, the home she loved, and the life she wanted because Malcolm had asked for her hand.

She'd married him and served as his lady and borne him a son and risen above his infidelities.

Opening the drawer of her vanity, she drew out the old letter from Adrienne and read the last paragraph.

> *Please don't hate me. You always have my love. Try to take comfort in the thought that I will be living in a small cottage and growing white grapes for my living, while you will be the princess of Yegor.*

Anna looked at herself in the mirror.

The princess of Yegor.

Anger continued to rise until it turned to rage. She felt the spirit of Siobhan beside her. Her aunt had loved Malcolm too much to punish him, but Anna suffered from no such affliction.

Intentional crimes must be punished; these were the teachings of Aunt Siobhan. That night, so long ago, on the edge of her father's lands was burned into her mind as if the events had happened yesterday.

Rising, Anna stored both letters in her vanity and

then left the room. She went downstairs, straight to the kitchens. Helen wasn't there, only a few girls scrubbing the last of the pots.

"Leave," Anna ordered. "You can finish those later."

The girls scurried off.

Alone, Anna looked around until she found an iron hook with a stand, used for cooking over an open fire. Then she found a flask, poured water into it, and tightened the stopper. She found a large cast-iron pot with a handle, a sharp knife, a flint, and some thin-cut firewood used for the stove.

Finally, she took up a canvas bag and put all that she'd gathered inside it.

She left the castle. It was a spring night and not yet fully dark. A few guards glanced her way, but she often took a short walk in the early evening.

Leaving the courtyard, she walked to the berry fields first, breaking off leaves and dropping them in the sack. Then she went to the apple orchards, moving through the trees until she was deep inside them and out of sight of anyone else. She cut several snippets of branches.

There, she built a fire and hung the large pot on the hook and sat cross-legged before her makeshift cauldron. Unstoppering the flask of water, she poured it in.

"Aunt Siobhan, be with me," she whispered. "Lend me your strength."

The water in the cauldron boiled, and she looked up at the sky.

"Hear my cry!" she called.

Then she looked into the cauldron, and tore at the hem of her gown, ripping off a piece of fabric.

"For the one who was wronged," she said, dropping the piece into the water.

Picking up the knife, she slashed her hand open, letting blood run into the water.

"Life force from the one who seeks justice," she said.

Then she picked up the bits of branches from the trees and leaves from the strawberry plants and dropped them in.

Closing her eyes, she whispered, "A curse upon the crops and fields; only those that bring in wealth; death and dust upon the spoils, but nothing else will be touched."

With her eyes still closed, she raised her head again.

"Hear my cry! Feel my strength!"

She chanted.

A curse upon the crops and fields.
Only those that bring in wealth.
Death and dust upon the spoils.
But nothing else will be touched.

She focused, channeling her aunt's strength along with her own and letting it flow into the earth.

The apple trees beside her began to change color, fading and dying. The white blossoms withered and fell to the ground. The earth grew dry.

This began to spread, and she stood up, watching it as it moved through the trees. It would probably be morning before anyone else saw the damage.

She would say nothing of any of this for now. She would not confront Malcolm until he confronted her with the news that she was no longer the princess of Yegor and her son was a bastard.

Until then, she would hold her head high and carry on with dignity.

Malcolm might indeed get his annulment. He might marry his camp girl. But those two betrayers would have nothing to celebrate.

They would inherit a kingdom of dust.

CHAPTER SIXTEEN

Amelie broke contact and pulled away, gasping for breath.

Sitting on the floor, facing her, Anna asked, "Did you see all that?"

Unable to speak yet, Amelie nodded.

"See what?" Malcolm demanded, shoving again at Jaromir.

This time, Jaromir let him go. Jenelle and Céline both stood to one side, watching in silence.

Rising from the floor and smoothing her gown, Anna turned calmly to her husband. "I am the one who laid the curse."

For a long moment, no one spoke.

"That's impossible," Malcolm returned. "How would you know how to do such a thing?"

"Siobhan showed me. Long ago."

At that, rage passed across his face, and he started forward toward his wife. Jaromir moved to cut him off again.

"How could you do this?" Malcolm shouted at Anna. "To your son? To the villages?"

For the first time, her calm expression wavered. "I didn't think about the villages, and I had no idea what this would do to Lysander. I only wanted to leave you and your new wife with nothing."

Malcolm stopped. "New wife? What are you talking about?"

This was too much for Amelie, and she found her voice. "Don't lie or play the innocent. She saw a draft of the letter. She knows what you've done."

His face shifted to complete confusion. "What letter?"

"For the sake of the gods," Anna said. "Will you be honest for once in your life? I have a draft of the letter you sent to Prince Rodêk requesting an annulment. You would make a bastard of your own son! That girl you plan to marry has been down in the kitchens ordering our servants about as if she's already mistress here."

Malcolm stumbled to one side and then steadied himself. "The letter," he whispered. Some kind of realization seemed to dawn, followed by a flash of horror. "You laid this curse on our lands?" he asked Anna as if he still needed convincing.

"What would you have done in her place?" Amelie asked.

"It isn't the same," he answered.

"It's exactly the same!" she shouted back. She had no pity for him.

His eyes were on his wife. "I had those people in the meadow imprisoned. A man was killed, and you said nothing."

Anna's back was straight. "That was none of my

doing. You ordered those events." She pointed to Amelie. "Were it not for her forcing this from me, I would have waited until the day you and your bride-to-be, Lilah, came to tell me and my son to leave this castle. Then I'd have told you."

When she spoke the name Lilah, he winced, and Amelie thought on her reading of Anna's past, of how Malcolm couldn't stand to face up to his own infidelities, how the truth embarrassed him.

Anna knowing the name of his current mistress seemed to cut him. It was as if she'd poured all his sins out on the floor to be seen.

After running a hand over his face, he looked at Jaromir. "Let me pass," he said quietly. His anger was gone, and Jaromir stepped aside.

Malcolm walked to his wife.

"Anna, listen to me. You cannot think I would cast you off. Or disinherit our son. You are the crowning jewel of my life, and every day I marvel that you stand at my side. You are the lady of my house and the princess of Ycgor."

Again, her calm expression wavered. "But what of the letter?"

He winced again and then began biting off words as if they pained him. "It was a game. You had gone to bed, and I had . . . I had Lilah come up to the castle. We were in my study so no one would disturb us, and we began drinking wine, too much wine. She wanted proof of my love, and somehow we began writing a letter together. I was drunk and our first attempt was a mess. We laughed and drank more wine and rewrote it. I used my seal and promised to send it off. Of course later, I burned it, but I forgot about the draft, and it must have been put away with my other papers."

"You never sent any letter?" Anna asked, incredulous. "But what about the girl? She believes you did. She thinks you will marry her. Why would you let her go on and on believing such a thing?"

He closed his eyes. "I told you. It was a game. It pleased her to believe and . . ."

"And you fed upon her admiration and excitement?" Anna finished.

"So what did you think would happen at the end of the summer?" Amelie asked Malcolm. "That you could give Rupert a pouch of money and Lilah would just go quietly?"

Céline and Jenelle had been watching this exchange in silence. Jenelle appeared stricken.

But Céline spoke in a clear voice. "None of this matters. All that matters is reversing the curse."

Anna put one hand to her mouth. "It can't be reversed. If it could, I would have already. I would have reversed it the moment my son fell ill."

Jaromir's jaw twitched. "There has to be a way. If we can't reverse it, people will die of hunger this winter. The economy of this region will fail."

"Do you think I've not realized that?" Anna asked, her voice breaking. "If I could, I would undo what I have done, but I don't know how."

Céline turned and began walking for the archway. "Then come with me. If anyone knows how, it will be someone down in that meadow."

* * *

Céline stood inside the white wagon, back near the bunks, shortly after Helga had collected a small gathering of women. The wagon was crowded, but everyone had enough room to sit or stand.

The group consisted of Helga, Alondra, Céline, Amelie, Sinead, Anna, and a thin woman in a threadbare dress from the line of Klempá named Isadora.

Anna showed no hesitation in explaining exactly what she had done, including the details of the spell she'd used.

To their credit, none of the women judged or chastised her. They simply listened.

"Why did you cast it?" Sinead asked.

"I believed my husband was going to put me aside and make our son illegitimate so that he could marry a girl from this encampment. I decided to leave them with nothing."

None of the women showed surprise.

Sinead nodded and looked to Isadora. "Can it be reversed?"

Helga stood near Céline and leaned closer. "Isadora is a skilled kettle witch. Her grandmother trained her."

"No," Isadora answered. "It was a call for justified revenge. She flowed her own strength into the earth and called on the strength of her dead kin from the sky. It cannot be undone."

Could this be true?

So far, Céline and Amelie had never failed in solving a crisis once they were set to the task. Had they come all this way and then found the person responsible, only to fail?

"There must be something we can do," Amelie insisted, clearly thinking along the same lines as Céline. "Now that we know what was done and how it was done, we can't just give up."

Sinead looked to Isadora, and Céline couldn't help noting their stark differences. Though both women were Móndyalítko and about the same age, Sinead was tall and lovely with glowing skin, wearing a fine sapphire blue gown. Isadora's face was pinched and thin. Her hair was brittle, and her faded dress was coming apart at the seams.

"Isadora, is there anything that can be done?" Sinead asked. Her voice held deep respect.

The other woman was quiet for a while and then said, "We could cast the restoration blessing, but you must know the . . ." She trailed off.

Anna's head swiveled back and forth between them. "What? What is it we must know?"

Céline stood rooted in expectation. What was Isadora suggesting? Helga frowned and Alondra glanced away in discomfort.

Sinead spoke directly to Anna. "In generations past, in desperate times, our people would sometimes take money to cast restoration spells on land that had been played out. The land would be restored to its former health."

Amelie stepped forward. "Well, let's do that. Why hasn't anyone suggested it before?"

"Because we did not know what we were dealing with here, and because there is a price," Isadora answered. "To cast this, our people join hands on the dead lands and they provide a conduit, but one of us must function as a single anchor, and it is his or her life force that restores what had been damaged."

Céline's body went stiff. "Does this person die?"

"No, but years of life are taken, and the process is painful."

"Then that idea is out of the question," Céline said, "and we'll think of something else."

"I'll do it," Sinead said quietly. "The land must be healed, and there is no other way."

"Not you," Anna said. "I'll be the anchor. No matter what the price, I'll pay it. This is on my head."

Sinead studied her face. "All right. If that is your choice, my lady, I'll go and gather the people."

Céline wanted to speak up and argue, but she didn't. Something told her to be silent.

Amelie had never taken part in anything like this.

In a surprisingly short time, every person in the Móndyalítko encampment had gathered in the nearest strawberry field.

Anna stood a good ways into the field with Isadora on one side and Sinead on the other. They joined hands, and then Isadora and Sinead took a step back. Helga grasped Sinead's hand and Alondra held Isadora's, but they, too, took a step back, so that the five women formed a V shape.

"My girls," Helga said.

Céline took her hand and Amelie took Alondra's.

Marcus took Céline's other hand, and Jaromir took Amelie's.

Without being told what to do, half the Móndyalítko came to Marcus's side and the other half went to

Jaromir's, and they joined hands to create a large V with Anna as the front point.

There was no cauldron and no fire.

There was only the dead land and the formation of the people.

Prince Malcolm was not there, and that was probably a good thing. Amelie had no idea what Anna was risking, but she had no doubt Malcolm would have stopped his wife.

Isadora looked up at the sky, and Amelie wavered in unease, wondering what was about to happen.

Céline grasped Helga's hand on one side and Marcus's on the other and bit the inside of her mouth to keep silent. She wanted to grab Lady Anna and stop this, but she kept hearing Sinead's voice.

The land must be healed, and there is no other way.

If this was not done, and it was not successful, many, many more people would suffer.

"Clear your head and focus on helping us," Helga said quietly. "We need you."

Céline nodded.

"It's time," Helga whispered.

Isadora spoke in a strong voice. "Marcus and Leif, call to the sky."

Before Céline could even think, Marcus threw his head back and howled. A similar sound came from down the line. The dual howls were clear and loud, rising upward like a song.

A few moments later, both men stopped in unison and the last ring of the howls faded away.

Isadora's voice carried out for all to hear.

*By the blood of the people and the strength of the
    old bonds*
By the shifters and the Mist-Torn
*By the love of the world and the sound of rolling
    wheels*
*By the songs and the stories and the fires in the
    night*
By the ancestors among us, inside us
And the ancestors yet to be born
Let our strength flow through the dust and decay
Rekindling lost life
Let our anchor be the guide
For life and health and harvest once more

Raising her own face to the sky, she cried, "Now!"

In unison, the voices of all the Móndyalítko in both lines rang out, repeating Isadora's chant. Céline found herself chanting in perfect rhythm . . . and then she felt a tingling in her palms and feet.

Warmth passed through her from Marcus's side to Helga's. Within moments, it increased from warmth to heat.

The chant began again, louder this time, and her voice called out of its own accord.

Then she heard a gasping over the top voices, and she looked to the point of the V.

Anna's white-blond held streaks of gray, and lines appeared in her face. She was in pain.

Céline instinctively moved toward her, but Helga gripped down tightly in warning and, somehow, Céline held her place, not breaking the chant.

The earth began turning a rich dark brown, and the

strawberry plants turned green. Blossoms grew and changed to red berries before her eyes. The green began to spread.

Anna dropped to her knees.

"Enough!" Isadora called.

The people fell silent.

Helga let go, and Céline ran to Anna, dropping down beside her. "My lady!"

Anna's eyes were looking ahead, though, as the green continued to spread at a faster pace, moving through the raspberry fields, the blueberry fields, and to the orchards. White blossoms burst from among green leaves as the trees returned to health.

The land was restoring itself as if the curse had never been.

Anna's face and hair and hands were altered. She appeared to have aged twenty years in a matter of moments.

But when she turned to look to Isadora, her eyes were filled with peace. "Thank you."

CHAPTER SEVENTEEN

After that, things seemed to move swiftly.

When Prince Malcolm saw what Anna had done to herself, he was too stricken to notice the crops had been healed. Still, Céline believed he would recover.

Men like him normally did.

Hopefully, he'd now be more aware of how his actions affected others.

The Móndyalítko held a somewhat subdued celebration in the meadow that night, with venison stew and music, but no one forgot the past days of tragedy and that even though Anna herself had placed the curse, she'd sacrificed much to make amends.

Céline and Amelie ate dinner with Sinead, Terrell, and the pack of unruly male cousins. Céline enjoyed herself.

The following morning, Jaromir vanished after breakfast and then came striding from the tree line. He wore his armor, tabard, and sword.

Clearly, he saw no further reason to play the Móndyalítko husband.

"Our work here is over," he said. "It's time to leave."

Setting down a mug of tea, Marcus asked, "Already?"

Céline had known this was coming, and she wanted to go home, but that didn't make leaving any easier on Marcus, and it didn't make saying good-bye to those here any easier, either.

Helga had been crouched by the fire. "I need to go talk to Alondra."

"Of course," Jaromir answered.

"And we need to talk to Sinead," Céline added.

Amelie flashed her a look of alarm. She hated any kind of emotional good-bye. Reaching out, Céline took her hand. "We must."

She was about to start down the row of wagons when she saw Sinead walking toward them. Perhaps their aunt had known this was coming, too.

Sinead stopped an arm's length away. "Can I not convince you to stay? You would be loved, cherished among your family."

"We can't stay," Céline answered with regret for causing disappointment. "Our home is in Sèone now."

Sinead's face was sad. "I knew you would say that, but I had to try. I know you feel torn between worlds, and I hope you're not sorry you came."

Céline cast her gaze at the line of the wagons and the people busy making breakfast. "Never. We'll never be sorry we came."

Seven days later, Amelie sat up on the wagon's bench beside Jaromir, and in the distance, she could see Castle Sèone.

They were almost home.

On the journey from Yegor, she and Jaromir had

spent every night together in the white wagon. Céline had slept in the blue wagon with Helga, and Marcus had slept outside.

It seemed that whatever had happened between Céline and Marcus, Céline had ended it upon leaving the meadow.

Amelie had no such wish. Whatever was happening between her and Jaromir, she didn't want it to end.

And yet . . . though she'd dreaded him pushing her into a conversation about the nature of their relationship, now that they were going back to their normal lives, over the past few days, she'd expected him to say *something*.

He hadn't, and the castle was in sight.

Though it was the most difficult thing she'd ever done, she reached inside herself and asked, "Jaromir . . . what happens when we get home?"

"What do you mean?"

She wanted to hit him. Was he doing this on purpose? "What do you think I mean, with us?"

"Anything you like."

That was hardly helpful. "Now what do you mean?" she asked.

He shrugged. "It means I'll do anything you like. I'll marry you if you want."

She clenched her fists. "Well, that's a proposal every girl wants to hear . . . and no, I don't want to get married."

He pulled up the horses and looked down at her. "You seem to think you're the only one who's floundering here. This is all as new to me as it is to you, and I have no idea what you want."

Could that be true? Was he as lost as her?

"Even if you don't want to get married," he went on, "will you still move into my apartments at the castle?"

"And what would I do all day?"

"Do? What do you do at home?"

"Work in the gardens, help Céline make medicines, do the shopping, do readings for money, help Céline with her patients. I'm busy all the time. What would I do up at the castle if I was living with you? Mend your shirts?"

He was quiet for a while. "I never thought about that. Of course you like to be occupied." He paused. "I can't come and live with you at the shop. My job is in the castle."

"I know."

He started the horses again. "We'll have to work this out as we go. You can come to me sometimes, and I can come to you. But I don't want it to end."

"I don't want it to end, either."

He dropped one hand over hers. "Well, all right, then."

When the wagons reached the first wall surrounding Sèone, Céline was up on the bench of the blue wagon beside Marcus. Dusk wasn't far off.

She knew he'd been hurt on the first night of the journey home when she began sleeping inside with Helga, but he never said a word, and Céline had spent the days with him up here.

They spoke little, but they didn't need to.

As they reached the first gate, the white wagon stopped ahead of them. Jaromir jumped to the ground and began striding toward it. Amelie wasn't far behind.

"What's wrong now?" Céline asked Marcus.

"I don't know."

They both climbed down.

Helga opened the back door of the white wagon. "What's going on?"

As Jaromir reached Marcus, he said, "Do we go on up, or do you want to go home now? I do need to make a report to Prince Anton, but will your family want the wagons back as soon as possible?"

Céline then understood. They'd borrowed the wagons and horses—and Marcus—from the Marentõrs.

Marcus glanced at Céline and then back to Jaromir. "I should probably get home as soon as possible."

"That's what I thought," Jaromir said. "I left my horse out on the homestead with your family. We can drive the wagons out now, and I'll ride back." He looked down to Amelie. "You want to come? You can ride home behind me."

She nodded.

This meant Céline and Helga were at the end of their journey. Céline spoke quickly to Jaromir. "Take your time. I'll go up and report to Prince Anton myself, at least let him know we're back and what happened."

"Good," Jaromir said. "I'll see him as soon as I get back."

"Helga," Céline called. "Will you get Oliver? We'll need to walk ourselves up from here."

Marcus stood rigid by the front of the blue wagon, and thankfully, Amelie and Jaromir had the sense to head over to pretend to assist Helga.

Céline moved closer to Marcus. "I don't know how to thank you for all you've done."

"You don't need to thank me."

"Yes, I do."

In her mind, in her memories, she knew him so well, and yet he was almost a stranger now. She'd never wanted to hurt him.

"Will you come out to the homestead sometime?" he asked. "Mercedes and Mariah would like to see you."

"Yes," she rushed to answer, and she meant it. "I'm sure Jaromir would ride out with me. I'll come to see you soon. And you are always welcome in our shop. You don't need to send word. Come anytime." She reached for his hand. "You are ever my friend, Marcus."

His body was still stiff, but he nodded. "I'll come to visit."

She gripped down on his fingers.

After walking up through the village, Céline stopped at the apothecary's shop only long enough to deposit Oliver—who was overjoyed to be home—and change into her lavender wool gown. She washed her face and brushed her hair, and then she and Helga continued on to the castle.

When they reached the entryway, Helga stopped her. "I'm going to go up to my room. The prince won't want to see me anyway. But I wanted to tell you . . . I wanted to say . . ."

"You don't have to tell me anything. I know."

"You stood by me when I asked. I won't forget."

On impulse, Céline leaned over and kissed her cheek. Then she turned swiftly and walked toward the great hall. At this time of day, Anton would be about to have dinner.

As she came through the archway, she saw him near

the hearth, crouched down, feeding bits of meat to a few of the spaniels who seemed to live in here. He wore a sleeveless burgundy tunic over black pants. As always, his brown hair was tucked back behind his ears. Guards and servants and a few nobles milled around before the meal was served.

At the sight of her, Anton rose. "Céline."

He closed the distance rapidly. "You're back. Are you all right? You're well? Where's Jaromir?"

She smiled at the rush of questions. He was normally so reserved. This wasn't like him. "I'm well. Jaromir and Amelie are bringing the wagons back to the Marentŏrs. They'll be home later tonight."

"You were successful?"

In brief, she filled him in on what had occurred, but as with most men of his station, the main thing he wanted to hear was that the southeast crops had been restored and the economy in that region was safe.

He hadn't wanted them to go in the first place, but he seemed pleased to hear of their success.

"Still," he said, "it's been almost three weeks, and I will admit it's been a long three weeks. I would prefer never to do without Jaromir for so long . . . or to be without you, ever again."

From him, this was quite an admission, and Céline drank in the sight of his face. "I would prefer that, too."

"Stay and have dinner with me."

He held out his arm, and she took it. They walked toward the head table where a few nobles and merchants waited. Céline had never dined with Anton without Amelie and Jaromir being present as well, and Anton had never before offered his arm.

Everyone watched them cross the hall, and she knew it looked as if they were . . . together. For once, he didn't seem to care.

As she sat beside him, he poured her a goblet of wine.

Although she had no memories or feelings that she'd done this many times before, here, in this life, she was sitting exactly where she was meant to be.

ALSO AVAILABLE FROM
NATIONAL BESTSELLING AUTHOR

Barb Hendee

WITCHES IN RED
A Novel of the Mist-Torn Witches

Far to the north, the men of an isolated silver mining community are turning into vicious "beasts" that slaughter anyone in sight. The mines belong to the noble family of Prince Anton—ruler of Castle Sèone and Céline and Amelie's patron—and Anton's tyrannical father has ordered his son to solve the mystery as a test of his leadership. He has no choice but to send the witches into the perilous north to use their abilities to discover the cause of the transformations. Given how much they owe the prince, the sisters have no choice but to go.

Together with the overprotective Lieutenant Jaromir, Célene and Amelie enter the dark world of a far-off mining camp tainted by fear, mistrust, and enslavement. Now the two must draw upon strength and cunning they never thought they possessed not only to solve the mystery, but to survive....

Barb Hendee

THE MIST-TORN WITCHES

In a small village, orphaned sisters Céline and Amelie
Fawe patch together a living selling herbal medicines and
pretending to read people's futures. Forced to flee a
warlord prince, the sisters agree to use their "skills" as
seers to solve a series of bizarre deaths involving pretty
young girls, in exchange for the protection of the
warlord's brother, Prince Anton. But as the sisters
navigate a dark and mysterious world, they soon discover
they have far more power than they had ever envisioned...

Also in the series:

"Hendee gift... her characters
some of

Available

fac